CHESTER STUBBS

CHESTER STUBBS

Craig Miles Miller

20 01

FIRST EDITION
Published March 2001

Dustjacket painting and title page by
Joe Servello.

ISBN 0-939767-36-8

Dennis McMillan Publications
11431 E. Gunsmith Dr. Tucson, AZ 85749
(520)-760-8642 dennismcmillan@aol.com
http://www.dennismcmillan.com

To Sue

Remember to love yourself.

–Søren Kierkegaard

CHESTER STUBBS

PART ONE

Whiskey, Cigarettes, and Kidney Punches

CHAPTER ONE

We was both drunk as a couple of bowling balls when she took me on up to her apartment. There weren't any lights on inside as she led me on to her room, a little square of a room where some street light squeezed on through the window blinds. She went and got undressed and I could see now she was a big woman, bigger'n I'd made her out to be in the bar. Not near big as me, though.

She lay down upon her bed then, waiting for me like some circus animal lying in its straw. I ain't been to the circus in a long while, so I went ahead and began to take my own damned clothes off.

"Why'd you have to hit him so hard?" she then asked. She hadn't said anything about it on the drive over, just kept her pink hand on my leg–and other places–telling me where to turn and such. But here I was, near naked and in her room, and now she wanted to talk about it.

"He swung at me first."

I'd met her at Bobby D's, on Pensacola Beach, and we'd sat there, chatting it up, me drinking coldbeer and her something with vodka in it, until way past last call. Then we'd gone out to the gravel lot and this wild-looking guy comes over and

1

starts yapping at her. Then he yaps at me, saying I was a sonofabitch. Which I didn't argue none. But when he took a shot at me, well, it kind'a got my interest up.

"But you hurt him," she said.

I'd only hit him the once, in the gut, and he doubled over like a nightcrawler on a fish hook. Threw up on his shoes. Then we went and left.

"Well, who the hell was he, someone important? Like the teevee weatherman or something?"

"My husband," she said, matter-a-fact like. "We're separated."

I got naked. Got down upon her and gave her a kiss, tasting liquor and cigarette smoke. Kind'a stubbed my dick around until it fell into the right place, as cozy in there as a pig-in-a-blanket.

"Least I was charitable enough not to hit him in the face," I told her. And she didn't say nothing more, so we commenced to hump it and just general slop around there, the mattress squeaking like a mockingbird with a sore throat.

Only there weren't really much fun in it.

When we was done I lied on top of her, catching my own bad breath, and I could feel her breathing slowing down, slower, until I was right positive she done fell asleep.

And sure enough, she was snoring.

So I clambered on off her and stood there, looking down at that woman in her own bed, a big sleeping pork chop of a woman. Nothing like my ex, Marleen. No one was like Marleen. Not that that was any of this here woman's fault. But the hell if I could recall her name. The hell if I could think why we'd wanted to cling to each other so.

So I went out, naked, looking for the bathroom.

It was at the end of the hall—where I flipped on the overhead light, about blinding me—an itty-bitty room with a shower stall no bigger than for a billy goat. There was a pink toilet and sink and a tall mirror above that. I closed the door behind me. I went and took a hard piss then washed my dick in the sink, standing up and using lots of bar soap—just like I'd been taught to do back when I was in the Navy. And as I was rinsing off, I couldn't help but to look at myself in the mirror. Look at all of me. And I didn't look good.

I mean, I was still the same old red-headed Chester Stubbs, was still the same six-six, two-hunnerd seventy—some pound bastard I'd always been. But I didn't feel so big right then. Hunkered in front of the mirror, dick in my own hand like some ape in the Gulf Breeze Zoo, I knew there was something wrong inside me. More than just all that cheap coldbeer. Like I had sandspurs in my gut or something. Cement in my veins. I was all prickly and frozen everywheres.

I tried to come out of it, splashed cold water on my face. Put my hands on my head and rubbed the red fuzz of it. But I couldn't stop looking at myself, knowing I was only a man living from bad haircut to bad haircut, about as useful as a Canadian coin.

Eventually I went back down the skinny hallway to her room, found my clothes on the floor and dressed. She was lying face down on the sheet now. I knew she was gonna feel bad, in the night, when she woke up and no one was there.

But I weren't the cuddling type. Anyways, maybe seeing me in the daylight, she'd just as soon have breakfast all by herself.

I sat in the car with the windows down, listening to the whirring and clicking of the air conditioners, feeling about dizzy as a cat in a dryer. Had no good idea where I was. No east from west or Bay from Gulf. But I started it up and drove, just to get moving some, figuring I could pick out downtown

Pensacola, maybe catch a smell of the bay, and get on back home from there.

But that bathroom mirror feeling come back over me. That rusted-blood, bee-stung innards feeling. So I pulled into a Junior Mart, all lit in yellers and greens, and tried to stretch out in my front seat best I could. Wanted to sleep it away. Told myself just to stay put, like a lizard on a screen door, and it'd all be okay—even if my mashed-potato brain refused to believe it

I woke up to hard sunlight and car doors slamming, folks stopping in for their coffees and sweet rolls, their regular morning shit. So I unfolded myself from the car, rubbing the crust from my eyes, and went into the Junior Mart.

Bought me some coldbeer.

And when I finally come on back to the house her car was there. Marleen's car. It sat like a little brown mushroom in the drive, under the big pecan tree that spread out over the roofs, mine and the old couple's next door. Had the trunk up, looking like she was loading the rest of her shit in there, just like she said she was gonna. One'a these days, she'd said. And I guess today was the one

I parked in the street and got out. Went up to her car and closed the trunk. Hard. That's when I saw the Alabama plates. She'd told me she was moving up to Montgomery, was gonna leave Pensacola, get away from me. Told me she had her a night nurse job. I didn't see how she could do it, but I reckon she saw how. I mean, I knew she wasn't living on Hancock Street no more. I'd tried her number over a dozen times the last month, had driven by that many times too, but now I knew she'd gone to Bama for real.

That license plate about broke my heart.

Then I heard the front door open, saw her backing out backwards with a load of boxes stacked high as her pretty head. She turned and kind'a stumbled down the step, walking like a duck, peeking around the side once or twice but not seeing me yet. Didn't even see my car. I let her come on down, stayed to her blind side, let her come right at me.

I grabbed the top box.

"Ain't you going the wrong way, Marleen?"

I held the box, light as a feather it was. Must'a had her extra underwear in it or something.

"Chester," she said, not delighted at all. "I thought you'd be at work."

I was in the Navy Reserve. But I'd quit. My last day was less'n a week ago. And here I was—no job, hungover, breakfast of coldbeer in my car, the stink of a fuck-and-go night probably still upon me—getting to see Marleen again.

"Not today," I said.

"I came to get the last of my things, finally." Then she saw that the trunk was done closed. "Put the box in the back seat. Please."

It weren't a nice please.

I set it on top of the car.

She got a mite huffy and put her other two boxes down and opened the car door herself. She slid them boxes in there, paying no mind to me, moving kind'a fast. When she stood up she looked me in the eye, them green eyes drilling into mine. I stared at her for a bit, the eyes, the brown hair and freckles, her tiny face bones. I wanted to melt, even in the shade of that pecan tree.

"Come on, Marleen. I need you back home, you gotta come back home. I told you that."

"We're divorced. It's over. Can't you get that through your thick skull?"

I kept standing there, trying not to believe a word. I didn't care if we was divorced for a year now, didn't care if she had gone and moved up to Montgomery. Didn't even care that it'd been all my fault. I needed her back and I told her so again.

She was mad for sure now.

"What you need is a life, Chester Stubbs!"

Marleen slammed the back door, went round to the driver's side, reached in the open window for her purse. She rummaged around there for a bit, just like I'd seen her do often and again over the years, and come out with a pen and a tiny pad of paper. She wrote on it.

"Here's my address," she said, holding out the little torn sheet. "I've packed most of my belongings, in the house. Mail them to me. Understand?"

I didn't say anything, but I took the torn paper.

She opened the door and got in, then she climbed back out again. But it wasn't like she'd changed her mind or nothing. Because she was fingering a couple keys off her damn chain.

"And here's the keys to your house!"

She threw them at my feet, because I wouldn't take them.

I stood there under the pecan and watched her back up, the motor whining. She wheeled it quick into the street, almost hitting my old Dodge Super Bee with her little Honda, then off she went, not even pausing for the stop sign at the end of the block.

I bent down and picked up the keys. Added them to the piece of paper. I looked back where her car had turned, onto the highway, trying to see if even her dust was still there.

"Our house," I said.

I went and got my beer, took it to the front step. Was gonna open me one, but there was my old neighbor lady peeping out the window at me. Her gnarled stump of a face looking for gossip.

I bugged my eyes out at her, then went on inside.

I saw her stuff there on the floor. More boxes and a milk crate with books and magazines, some clothes covered with plastic, folded once over. I nudged all that shit with my foot to a dark corner, behind the easy chair, where I wouldn't have to look at it.

In the kitchen I cracked a can of coldbeer and put the rest in the fridge. I sat at the table and drank, tried to figure a few things out. But I'd never been much good at that. So I got up and went to the sink, where I kept me a bottle of George Dickle whiskey in the cupboard underneath. Poured me a glass, took a sip, stood there and looked out the window at the scramble of a back yard.

I drank the glass down and reckoned it was about as good as I was gonna feel all day.

CHAPTER TWO

That afternoon, my last paycheck from the Reserve showed up in the mail. I drove down to the bank and cashed it. The whole of it. I folded the green in half and stuck it into the pocket of my cut-off jeans. I didn't own no wallet anymore. Just kept my license and money all scrunched up back there. Then I drove on over to Crow's house.

Crow was out in his driveway, or at least his legs was. I could see those big black negro legs of his, about dark as the midnight, sticking out from under the car he was working on.

Crow liked to fix cars. He made a lot of side-money that way and was probably the best shade tree mechanic in all of goddamn North Florida. Or at least in Pensacola. Crow's a strong sonofabitch like me. He used to box, which was how we met. He's got some Cherokee in him, or so I was told, and I believe his Mama named him Crow due to that Indian in him. Either that or it was some kind'a joke on the old Jim Crow Laws. I couldn't say for sure, and I wasn't gonna be the one to ask him. He's from Louisiana, the delta. Creole country, I reckon. I been to Louisiana a number of times and I always figured it to be like the California of the South. Only, it ain't where all the nuts move to, it's where they come from. Born and bred.

I was born in Jackson, Mississippi. But I moved to Montgomery, Alabama early on and consider that my home town. It was my Daddy that was from Florida. The panhandle. Vernon, Florida, north of Panama City. My Mama was from Jackson.

Anyways, Crow was my friend, about the only who'd put up with me anymore. We was both in the Navy and we both was heavyweights. Though I got a few inches on him in height and reach, he's still as wide. A big bulldozer of a fighter. Crow's the only man who ever knocked me down in the ring.

I boxed Crow when we was both stationed here in Pensacola. Later we both went and bought homes and we been here ever since. I boxed a lot of folks–military folks–around here and up in Milton, but most all of them have moved on. I fought some Marines, heavyweights, on a aircraft carrier when I was doing my sea duty, though not a one of them ever knocked me down. I do believe I had more fights in the bars and out in the field than I ever did in the ring. But I was about the only white heavyweight around–at least down thisaway–and with my red hair and freckles and being from

Alabama, well, that always attracted me some attention. Being the only white boy never meant much to me, but it did to some. You'd be surprised how much it meant to some. And the truth is, that even though there's only the two of you in the ring, you end up fighting a whole lot of other people's goddamn fights for them. Whether you like it or not, or even try to think of it or not, you're carrying all that shit on your back when you climb them ropes. Dumbfucks or officers, it don't matter. They think they're in there with you. I reckon that's one of the reasons Crow didn't turn pro. Didn't even train for the Olympics, though he was invited. He quit not long after I did. I believe he could have made it too, in the boxing world. Crow was that good.

But I got to give him credit for being a smart man. A whole pile smarter than me. It seems he's known what he's wanted from the start and how to go about getting it.

I didn't know want I wanted anymore, not since Marleen left anyways. And other than having her and getting out of the Navy, maybe I never knew. I was always just fumbling around with whatever was handy.

I'd brought my pack of coldbeers. So when I parked in the street, I took the beer with me and walked up to his drive where his black legs was still sticking out from under that car. I unhooked a can and rolled it on underneath. The can rattled over the grit and I heard him grunt to get it.

"Chester," he said without looking, still under that machine. "What the hell are you doing over here?"

"This is Flag Day," I told him. "We are all supposed to celebrate."

He drug himself out into the daylight, his body all soaked with sweat and grease. He sat up, looked around like he was expecting to see some Old Glorys floating in the neighborhood, then opened the goddamn beer. He stared at me while he drank it on down, thirsty.

"Flag Day," he said, when he'd come up for air. "Nobody goes drinking because it's Flag Day."

I gave him a shrug.

"Then we'll have a few out of lack of interest."

He eyed me.

"A few?"

"A few and maybe a few more," I said.

He looked the other way, touching his sweaty head.

"Well, let me get it past Della. She won't like it, but hey, if it's Flag Day then it's Flag Day. A man can't help it if it's a holiday."

He wiped his hands and arms off with a rag and went on to the house.

Crow didn't get drunk much anymore. Della saw to that. He may be a heavyweight, but that woman had a hold on him. I guess maybe me and Marleen weren't too different. Della's good—for Crow at least. She don't care a whole lot for me.

Crow came on back out. He was still sweaty but he had a clean shirt. We walked down to my car, ready for whatever come our way. When I drove back past the house, I looked. There was Della standing at the screen door, a hard scowl on her face and her eyes piercing through the sunlight. All of it just for me.

I drove from Pensacola across the Bay bridge to Gulf Breeze, us finishing up the beer as we passed Gulf Breeze High—home of the Fighting Seashells or some damn thing like that. The school sat empty and square, it being summer and all. Unless there was some kids stuck in summer school. I'd done that time, myself.

"You ready for Dirty Joe's?" I said.

"The beach?"

I gave him a sidelong glance.

"You just want to get all fucked-up," he said, "and then pick a fight."

"I won't fight. I promise. I just want to drink where I don't have to wear shoes."

Crow shook his sweaty head as we looped past the big Pensacola Beach sign with its blue-green sailfish grinning like a long gone drunk. And before you knew it we was at the toll booth on the bridge. It always angered me some, them wanting us all to pay a toll to get onto that spit of land, like it was extra special. Angered me time and time again.

But I took four quarters from my ash tray, plunked them on down into the crappy toll machine, and drove us across the bridge and into the coming mystery of the day.

I parked in Dirty Joe's lot, which was across the street from the beach, across from some condos and a motel and all that shit.

Inside, Crow and I bellied on up and I bought rounds of coldbeer and Dickle. The place was dark and cool as the shade of a oak tree, quiet enough to hear the bartender fart. The concrete floors was all damp and grainy from people tracking in sand and seawater all day. A couple of women was shooting pool, wearing bathing suits, showing off their little parakeet behinds. Other than that, there was nothing going on. All the active folks in the world was out having fun in the sun, I guessed, leaving me and Crow to waste away in the dark.

After a bit, Crow took a break and watched me. I was buying all the drinks.

"You're trying to set a record, ain't you," he said.

"Let's just drink the goddamn whiskey and coldbeer. Okay? I don't need no running commentary."

"Please man, stay nice and calm. You got trouble? Tell me about it. Or go home and ram your head into a wall. Don't just get shit-faced and mean."

"Today's about my first day of honest unemployment," I told him. "Reckon I'm bored."

"Unemployment? What about the Reserve?"

"I done quit. For good and ever."

"So that's what we're doing? Pissing your money away because you ain't got a job? Now that's real smart, Chester."

I turned to him. I could feel my red freckled frying-pan of a face begin to heat, my back hairs bristling up like a hog's.

"There ain't nothing wrong with throwing money away. Ain't no harm in getting drunk. Hell, everyone's wasting what they got one way or another. . . . I'm just fitting in with the crowd."

I ordered us up some more after that speech.

The Dickle was going down easy, scary, but I needed it. It was about all that was holding me together. Since the divorce—hell, even before we was divorced—drink was my major pre-occupation. That's what Marleen called it, my preoccupation. Sure, it played hell on my innards, but that was a small price to pay for not feeling like some damn jigsaw puzzle everyday.

"All this, it really ain't going to solve anything, Chester. To-morrow you'll still be with no job, only you'll be broke and hungover, too."

"The hell, Crow. You don't fucking know. Being unemployed and being broke ain't nothing."

"Well, then, what is it? You might as well tell me now while you're still halfway sober, otherwise when you tell it to me drunk you'll be crying and shit and I'll probably laugh."

I studied my empty bar glass. I rubbed my hands on top of my head. I didn't want to tell him about seeing Marleen this morning. About how it'd got me all riled up in the heart. Then again, pride was something I done gave up long ago. I could tell him a little.

"It's Marleen," I went and said. "I still love Marleen. . . ." I looked over at him and he didn't say nothing.

Crow kept a flat face and looked straight ahead into the smudged mirror behind the bar. Then he began to snicker. He let loose with a laugh. He was goddamn laughing. The jackass.

"I'm sorry, Chester, but you are dreaming now. Marleen? She ain't never gonna take you back, son. Too smart to do that. She ain't gonna dial your number."

I felt my jaw thicken up. I stared at his sonofabitch face in the glass, his big black face getting all gooey as he tried not to laugh no more. Crow knew Marleen good. She and me and Crow and Della was good friends. I never did have a lot of friends and Marleen and I never got around much, but Crow and Della was the best of them. Crow was my one pal in Pensacola and here he was laughing in the face of my personal grief.

"Is that how you treat a man who just confided in you? Goddamn laugh your ass off?"

"I'm sorry, man. But there's plenty of other women out there, Chester. If anyone ought to know, you should... Don't be torturing yourself over what you lost, even if it was someone as good as Marleen."

"I'm talking about love here, Crow. Love! Not a goddamned computer match-up or something. I don't want some piece-of-ass to hand me beers, turn the teevee channels and spank the kids. This is love."

"You don't know shit about love, Chester."

"I don't know shit about love? What in God's dick do you mean by that? You want to see what I know about? I'll show you what I know about, you sonofabitch!"

I was popping out of my bar stool, gathering my fists, standing up so fast my head banged into the hanging lamp. The yellow light swung around above me as I yelled, not sure what I was even saying. What folks there was in the bar was staring at me, like I was a crazy man. And maybe I was. Maybe just crazy enough to take a whack at Crow.

"Hey, okay. Settle down, man. Settle down."

Crow put his hands on my shoulders. Easy. Got me to sit back down. He reached up and stopped the lamp from swinging.

Still, I had a hard time calming myself.

The George Dickle was right where it ought to be, galloping along in my blood, and my temper had done exposed itself like a broken bone. But what kept me steaming was that Crow just didn't know. He didn't know even half the shit I'd gone through with women and things, he didn't know what Marleen meant to me. He pretty much knew why we'd divorced, because I was cheating on her so, but he didn't know nothing about how that divorce had sent everything else flying, too, how it gave me nothing but air to grab. How can a man pull himself up with nothing to grab onto?

"Now you cool down, Chester Stubbs," Crow kept it up. "It's only four in the afternoon and already you're acting like lard in a frying pan. I'm sorry I laughed. I'm sorry."

"Shit, Crow," I said, sitting still, thinking maybe I should just drink beer. "And it ain't all Marleen, you know. Things are breaking up inside . . . I got to get me a life."

I didn't tell him that Marleen'd said that, just today. But I knew I had to get straight, ought to quit all this here drinking and bumbling around. Had to stop going in circles like a fucking pony ride.

"Maybe I just gotta get myself somewhere, where I got some hope in the world."

And having Marleen back would do it, I figured.

"Amen to that," Crow said, not snickering no more. "And you can do it if you'll try. But for now, you just cool your jets. Give it some time, Chester."

"Shit," I said.

Crow stayed with me for another hour, then he caught a cab home. He was about drunk, though you couldn't see it but in his eyes. Della would see it in his eyes, though, and that'd be one more mark against me. She wouldn't want this big ol' white boy—ex-husband, ex-Navy man, ex-boxing opponent, ex-everything—coming around her house no more.

So I sat there and drank alone. The bar emptied out pretty good, a doldrums lull between the day folks and the night folks. But I liked that time in bars, between crowds, quiet, when there ain't nothing but you and the shift of sunlight and the tick of clocks and the spill of alcohol. There were no sun-bunnies or tourists or bikers. There was only me and the new bartender starting his shift.

An uneasy calm settled inside me for a spell. A welcome calm. But slowly it done left me, like a high tide receding back from the mouth of a river. And my river was a bad one, water chock full of cottonmouths, snappers and alligator gar.

I got to feeling so low that I drank a tall double Dickle on ice, quick-off, for cure. Drinking like that is like holding a aspirin on a achy tooth, knowing that it's bad for you but wanting anything to ease the pain. And the Dickle did the trick. Shook my illness just like the drug that it was. But I knew it weren't gonna last. I was rolling downhill, now. I was a downhill ball, a big black leadweight full of piss and broken glass. I recognized it in me as sure as I could recognized my own broke nose. But I couldn't stop it. Hell no. I didn't even want to stop it.

"Hey you," I called and the new bartender came trotting on over.

He was a young kid. A little kitten of a man wearing some tee-shirt with the name of some university on it. Probably the place he flunked out of or made the mistake of graduating from.

"Hey you," I said again, even though he was right there, ready to serve me, eager as a truckload of fucking beavers.

"Yeah?"

"Tell me, you ever been divorced?"

He held up a second, looking me over now.

"I've never even married," he said.

"Well, you got a girlfriend then? Maybe a boyfriend?"

He stepped back a bit, knowing I was trouble. I'll give him that. He sensed it like a bird knows there's a cat in the weeds.

"A girlfriend," the kid came back. "In Tallahassee."

"Pour me another beer and tell me what she's like."

"What?"

I took out my money, slapping a fifty on the bar top.

"Pour me a coldbeer and a double Dickle on the rocks and tell me what you do . . . I mean, do you ever screw out on the beach? Ever in a grocery store? Or on the garage roof? Tell me, kid, you ever fuck on top of a garage under a full moon drunk to hell on tequila? Ever done that?"

"No."

"Well I have. I goddamn have," I said, wild-like, looking down as he slid more liquor under my nose.

I stared straight at him while weaving in my chair. I already knew I was a asshole, but this kid was gonna find out too. But all I really wanted was to tell it, tell this pissant bartender about the stupidity that'd done ruined me. Just spit it all out on him about Marleen and that night on top of my own goddamn car port with Trisha-Lee. That was all. It wasn't like I was gonna hit the kid. But I couldn't stop myself from trying to scare him some.

He must've sensed different, though. I know he had to seen that I was just boiling in my seat, seen my red hair as nothing less'n the fuzz of lava, my dry eyes cracked open and the sweat beading up on my under-lip. He seen enough, anyways, because he shied away from me then. I saw him go over and pick up the telephone by the register, him trying to be casual about it all, but being about as discreet as a dead skunk in a telephone booth.

I knew who he was calling. And it sure as hell weren't his little ditty in Tallahassee.

Drunk though I was, even I could see it was my cue to leave. It was obvious that my public side was done for the day.

"Well, thanks a lot," I said, smiling. "See you have a nice day now."

I drained down my full glass of beer, left the whiskey, put him a ten dollar bill for his troubles. Then I stumbled away, out into the low sunshine.

I drove my Super Bee slow, across both bridges. I headed on home to Warrington—my little one-bedroom house—where if you could spit across Bayou Grande, it'd hit the Naval Air Station.

And when I got home, I sat on the couch and kept up the drinking, not bothering to turn on no lights. Hell, darkness went good with whiskey. So I didn't do nothing except refill my jelly glass now and then and mope in the muggy shadows of my living room.

When the time came to lie my fat head down to sleep, it wouldn't come. All I could do was lie there, alone, in bed, my naked body sogging the sheets with sweat, my mind racing around like a cockroach caught in a mayonnaise jar. My brain kept hopping from one thought to the next, one worry to the next, all of them sad and lonely and chock full of Marleen.

Memories of Marleen naked. Of Marleen sleeping. Marleen in the sunlight, on the beach, washing dishes, petting a goddamn dog. Any little recollection of Marleen that ever existed played out in my mind, and her voice too, soft words she had spoke from over the years coming into me like a ghost radio. And the yells too, when she found me out. All coming in like a station I couldn't change.

Marleen, I knew, was up in Montgomery. But we'd met here, in P-cola at the hospital, when I was laid up with broke ribs after Crow beat me in that boxing match. We ended up dating some after I got out and before long we tied the noose. Marleen was no fool. She'd had a rough past herself, had been in detention school at one time. So she was no stranger to my type. I guess she figured she could calm me down some.

And she did.

Only it didn't last.

I got out of bed and sat in the living room again. My windows was open to the summer night where the cicadas was sawing in the trees. Their buzzing cut me, the damn crackle of it. Cicadas singing good as chainsaws. I had no recourse but to open another bottle.

It's a terrible thing when a man can't sleep. Makes him wallow around in the wrong parts of his mind. Especially when there's a bottle of George Dickle involved. I was stuck there in the night-heat and insect noise, thinking over wrong moves, sour love and things done frittered away. All the shit I'd scooted into the dark corners of my brain.

I was dying for to sleep. Wanted nothing more than to lie down and get my head to shut up. But sleep wasn't gonna be mine—just like the dream of me getting my life all sorted out, nice and calm like, wasn't gonna be mine. And I guessed it was always gonna be like that, about hopeless, at least until I did some damn thing about it.

Come sunrise, birds'd took over the noise of the cicadas. But it was too late. I had come to a decision. My mind was all monkey-greased with Dickle and no-sleep and I'd decided that I should take me a drive.

A drive to Montgomery.

CHAPTER THREE

I took off in the rising heat of morning, up Highway Twenty-Nine. In sleepy Flomaton I bought me a six of coldbeer for company. Bought a melon to eat from a roadside stand. I already had me about half a bottle of the whiskey. I broke open the fresh melon and ate it like a damn caveman, letting the juice and guts of it spill all over. From the State Line I slid off on the smaller, country roads to avoid any chance of the law—at least any law that gave a shit—spinning through towns with names like Burnt Corn and Skinnerton, Old Texas and Letohatchee. I sped on down roads that the southern tourist offices like to call Scenic Trails of The Deep South, done in with Civil War history and dappled with shade. Shit like that. Though all it meant was some crook in county politics done took the money they was supposed to fix the road with and used it to put him up some chippy down in Gulf Shores.

Anyway, I wound my way through south Bama, stopping once or twice to piss in the weeds, my old green Dodge Super Bee rattling and clanking but still about as trustworthy as anything I ever owned. More trusty than myself, I'd say. Crow hated my car. But it suited me just fine, right down to the hole rusted out in the floorboard, near beneath the break pedal. That hole was big enough to squeeze a empty beer can through, providing you stomped on it good. Beer can'll go right on down like a hot boiled peanut, leaving no evidence at all for the Highway Patrol to sniff at. So, there I was driving sixty, slamming beer and stabbing at the Dickle, so drunk I was sober, stamping them empties through my floorboard and hearing them tinkle off into the kudzu as I spun northward.

And it felt damn good.

Here I was hauling it through the Dixie countryside, old familiar countryside, the wind washing through my car, me drinking and thinking that I was doing something right, that now I was a man of action, about to rendezvous and conquer. Marleen would be mine once again. I could see it in my mind as I beat it on up to ol' Montgomery.

The city hadn't changed all too much.

Guess it was too damn poor to change. Probably always will be.

Not like Birmingham, understand. Birmingham was a big blob of a modern town now. Like a little Hotlanta. But even though Montgomery was the State capital and all, it was just too far down in the sleepy-side of Alabam' to ever get a fire under its ass.

I drove on past all the outside shit of the city, the strips of gas stations and Burger Kings and all that. I went right on by, smack through the center of my hometown, going slow past the white apartments across from the Greyhound Station, the same apartments where I used to live with my Mama when I was a boy. I could even spy my old room. I went on by the Whitehouse of the Confederacy and other little landmarks of my own upbringing, till I got to the north of town where things had done gone and changed, where all the new duplexes and complexes and mini-malls was lined up like stringers of dead catfish along the street.

Marleen lived in one of them complexes.

It was one of them fancy ones, ones that look nice and got themselves swimming pools and grass-sloped ponds and weight rooms and saunas and lighted tennis courts. The kind that cost a butt and a dick to live in because they look so nice, though they ain't made of nothing but plywood, paint and bad cement. The kind'll get blowed down by the first hurricane winds to come their way.

I'd writ down her address on a bigger piece of paper, so I found her building, parked my wreck and unloaded myself out the door. I stood there a bit, sweaty and numb, feeling a mite hazy all of a sudden. It was then I realized I was only dressed in my cut-off jeans, and that them cut-offs had a big hole in the tail end. I didn't have no shirt or shoes. I didn't wear underwear anymore. . . . But what the hell. Marleen knew what I was like. She'd seen my ugly ass many times. So I headed right on in the door.

What with the alcohol, insomnia and my sureness that Marleen was gonna comply with my dirty wishes, well, I got

21

a big hard-on as I stomped down the apartment hall, looking at all the gold numbers on the oily doors.

I had a lot of big ideas floating around in my brain when I knocked on Marleen's.

I had to knock pretty hard, for about two minutes, before she answered. She must'a peeped through the peep-hole, because I heard her give a loud breath and I could tell she weren't too pleased just by the way she undid the safety chain. But I had a picture of her in my mind—a sweet and sexy picture of her which didn't include much talking or clothing—and as the door swung open, I was ready to commit any foolish act that come to me.

And there she stood, looking at me, just her pretty half-awake face staring up at me outta a big bathrobe. Before she said a thing, before she could even sigh or cuss or wide-open them green eyes of hers and affix me with her stare, I jumped in, slammed the door, and grabbed her and undid that robe.

She was all naked under there and I got on my knees and run my swollen hands all over her as she backed up. She kept backing up and I kept following her on my knees, my calloused palms trying to grip her all over, me nobbling after her like some crazy blue crab until she was in the kitchen and then up against the stove.

"Marleen," I went. "Marleen, I'm on a two-day drunk. I ain't slept and I got a hard-on that just won't quit. I love you, Baby. You gotta know I fucking love you, Marleen."

I got a hold of the hem of her robe then, one hand gripping, pulling her low, and I tried to free my dick from my shorts. But the zipper was rusty or something. I couldn't get it done one-handed and on my damn knees like that. That's when she squirmed on out from the robe. She just twisted and left it like a invisible woman, leaving but a banana peel of terrycloth. I still had one hand stuck in my shorts and the other one dropped straight to the linoleum, clutching the empty cloth, and my face fell full weight into the oven door. It whumped and clanged but didn't hurt none. I got back up to my knees, turned myself around, and went after her again.

That was when she slapped me.

My beautiful Marleen went and smacked me full across my cheek, hard enough to wake Jefferson Davis from his grave, wherever that may be. I took it and stopped and kind of sat down on my haunches.

"What in the hell do you think you're doing?" she finally got to yell, full naked in front of me, wobbling with her anger.

But I weren't done.

I got on my knees again and lunged for her, for the vanilla of her thighs, not ready to listen at all to what she had to say. But she didn't have no more to say. She went and socked me again, this time with a closed fist.

She pulled back and caught me on my jaw, hard as she could.

I fell backwards and bit my own tongue when my head clunked hard on the floor. I sprawled out, my eyes wide open, my whole body smarting.

"Chester Stubbs!" I heard her yell.

She continued to yell but I didn't hear her no more. I stayed on the kitchen floor and everything got real dreamy and happy like. The room kind'a blurred up and took a creamy shine to it and I closed my sore, bloodshot eyeballs, closed them up tight seeing only orange and orange and I didn't hear nothing, didn't smell nothing, didn't even taste no tin of the blood in my mouth. But I know I smiled, smiled big as I drifted away.

Asleep at last.

CHAPTER FOUR

When I woke up it was raining. It was either dawn or dusk. I was sober and hungover and on the kitchen floor as it rained hard outta black summer skies. At first I thought I was in Pensacola and that them rain clouds was sweeping in from the Gulf. But then, between the lightning flashes and lumps of thunder, I noticed that the open windows was Marleen's windows, and the air smelled like land, not sea. It didn't smell like no Florida rain.

I was full awake but did not rise. Didn't think that I could. Not with the weight I felt on me, like a big cast iron cannonball perched on my chest. I felt a hunnerd percent terrible. My heart felt like it was two miles long, two fucking miles of diseased and broken red muscle pumping only a black sadness—all of it due to my own self.

I thought I was heartbroke before. But now I didn't even have a name for the terrible pity that had me anchored to that kitchen floor.

I knew Marleen wouldn't of moved me to a couch or the bed even if she could've. I've committed plenty of foolish acts in my days and never felt especially ashamed over them, but this was beyond all them others. My shame was a year late and a million dollars short. My only luck was she didn't call the police or something.

I tried to move. Tried to sit up, to roll over, to wiggle my goddamn ape of a big toe. But I couldn't. I knew I should get up and be gone, as lickety-split as I could, but any forward movement was gonna have to wait a spell.

24

I closed my eyes again, hoping I could drift back to slumberland, back to where I wouldn't feel so sober and stupid, wouldn't feel the pain. But the heft of my heart and the flow of shame was in my blood, running along my whole big body, splashing in there like the sad slash of the rain out the window.

After a while, the thunder and lightning moved off, leaving a steady drizzling full of the Alabama smells of red earth and hickory trees and asphalt. But there was something else I smelled, something else.

Coffee.

The weather kept passing out Marleen's windows, moving on further, on toward Auburn, on to Georgia. Thinking of it moving like that, of them clouds blowing all that considerable distance, and smelling the strong coffee between gusts of fresh wind, well then, I began to think that maybe I could do it. At least I could get off the damn floor.

I pulled myself up, shaky as a litter of pups. I leaned against the stove, taking in the dark apartment, still trying to figure if it was getting light or going dark. I made my way over to the counter where the pot of coffee steamed. It was hot and thick with chicory—I could tell by the smell and look of it when I poured me a cup. Marleen was the one that got me to drink it that way. She always drank it that way. Called it motor oil. Only she put a lot of sugar in hers. I never cared much for sugar. And there was a note too. I looked it over, at the small, neat handwriting. Marleen's writing.

I didn't dare read it yet. Didn't want to. All I wanted was to drink the hot coffee.

I figured it must be evening time, what with the low light and the storm flying way back to the east now. Plus, I was mighty hungry, though my gut was having a hard enough time with the coffee. Needed to piss too, so I hitched myself up to the sink and let it go. On down the drain. Ran a little water after it. I figured Marleen had gone on off to work, that I'd slept on through the afternoon. Goddamn I felt terrible. Felt like I needed more sleep, like I should soak my head in a tank of spring water for a hour and then drink it. Terrible, tired and thirsty. Felt guilty as shit, too.

I held up that note again. Guessed I might as well get it over with:

> CHESTER:
> Drink this pot of coffee. Turn off the warmer.
> Get the hell out.
>
> M.

I sat on down at her table and didn't let it bother me much. It was a damn nice note, really, considering and all. Anyway, I was having a hard enough time just sitting and drinking and breathing.

When I got up for another cup of black coffee, I heard me a sound. At first I thought maybe it was just a new pain pounding in my dull head, but I heard it again and it come from the other room. I looked out into the grayness of her little living room. The storm was long gone, the rain had even stopped, and I noticed that the day was growing, not shrinking. Some turtle doves was beginning to hoot out there in the wet trees. That's when I saw there was someone on the couch.

I poured a extra cup of coffee, putting in a little sugar.

"I'm sorry I had to slug you one, Chester. But you deserved it, you sonofabitch."

We was both awake and sitting on her green sofa—she on the one side, me far on the other. She sat there cradling her cup with them strong little hands of hers, her pretty legs tucked up under her like a quiet cat, like she always sat back home in Pensacola when we was married. And I had to look at her face, puffed from sleep, beautiful sleep, her eyes that sharp green I ain't never seen nowhere else. And I had to sit from the far reaches of her couch and look at her and know I was a fool and know I'd never have her back again.

"I know I deserved it, Marleen. You did right."

"After I hit you and you didn't get up, I thought maybe you were hurt, but I checked your pulse and remembered you'd said you'd been drinking, so I knew you were just your usual self."

I could tell she was still mad, not near as mad as when I attacked her. She wasn't even as mad as when she wrote that note. But she was far from happy, and she knew I knew it.

"You slept near eighteen hours, Chester Stubbs. . . . What the hell is going on with you?"

"I don't sleep so good anymore. That's all."

"Well, you can't come on up here to Montgomery and sleep on my kitchen floor every time you got insomnia."

"Hell, Marleen. It's more than that. I don't know how to tell you. . . ."

"Oh, you know how to tell me all right, only I don't want to listen. I'm not part of you anymore, Chester. None. And you are not part of me. I told you that just two days ago."

Except for that morning, we hadn't seen a hair of each other in about six months. But for her to say there weren't nothing between us, well, that just weren't true. If it was the truth, then I might as well put my heart out on a stick for the buzzards to eat. And she must've saw something, saw how what she'd done said hurt more than her punching me, but still, I didn't care for the pity in her face. It made me feel worse.

"C'mon, now," she said to me. "What we had will always be there, Chester. But it's what we had, not what we have. You got to accept it. I wasn't the one. . . ."

"I know whose fault it is. . . . But I'm serious as hell about you, Marleen. Why don't you come on back to Pensacola? Let's us start all over again. I'm changed. I am all changed over."

She gave me a hard look. She wanted to laugh at the idea of her returning to me, of her coming on back to Warrington and sharing my spongy bed again, my life again. She was gonna laugh at the idea of me being changed and all.

But she held it back.

"This is what you changed into? Some half-naked drunk who doesn't sleep too good?"

I made the mistake of looking at myself. I went and looked down at my shirtless, shoeless, ratty-assed self. I was all tarnished with dried sweat and spilled beer. My fly was wide open. I had a watermelon seed stuck in my navel. I could feel welts on my tongue from where I bit it. I was full of two-day-old whiskey and bad food. I was crusty-eyed, ham-bellied and gooshy-headed.

I looked back up at her, sad-eyed, but she didn't budge.

"You're a mess, Chester. Can't you see that? You are a mess of a man and we are divorced. Those are two cold facts. You'll never change the second fact and you don't look to be making any progress on the other."

I knew I was pig-headed. Stupid as a blind mule. And I have paid dearly for it. But even so, when she was still in Pensacola I could sometimes worm my way back into her arms and we'd get it on like crazy in the bedroom or the living room sofa or those couple of times out at the National Seashore at Navarre Beach, out on a blanket under the stars with the black waves slopping in and in. . . . I reckon that had scared her a bit, the fact that we could still get together, that she could near hate me and still want to sleep with me. Maybe. I guess maybe she saw what I told her: that we two belonged together. Which was why she took on off for Montgomery. Put some distance between us. Got away from her big mistake.

She's a smart one, Marleen is. And it ain't too becoming of her to be attracted to a ass like me.

"You'll never change, Chester. You've got a whole lot of learning to do. A lot of growing—inside," she said. "You're already too big on the outside as it is."

She untucked her brown legs and stood up. She began to pace around a bit, like she had something big to say.

"Anyway, I met this man. . . ."

This man, she said, let it hang there like moss in a tree.

"He was doing residency up in Tuscaloosa, then he came down here to work. We've been seeing each other and. . . . He's from up north, really."

"Up north? Like Tennessee?"

"More like New Haven."

"New Haven?"

"Connecticut."

I almost didn't know what she was talking about.

"Anyway, Chester, you understand. I believe he may want to marry me. It's a ways off, maybe, but he's planning on moving back up there, to New England, as a G.P."

I finished my coffee, though it'd gone half cold.

"What's a G.P.? A Goddamned Prick?"

She gave me a burning look.

"You're making it up," I said.

"It's true. He's real sweet on me. He's going to take over his Grandaddy's practice up there. . . ."

"He's a goddamn Yankee?"

"He's got two young boys."

"He's divorced?"

"So are we, Chester."

"Yeah, but we're divorced from each other."

She shook her head and sat back down on the couch, a little closer now.

"And he. . . ."

"And he's got a fucking load of money," I said.

That stopped her, cold enough, but she got that hard look in her eyes.

"Love ain't enough to support everything, Chester. Look where it got me last time. I don't need any more Good Ol' Boys."

"I ain't no Good Ol' Boy," I said under my breath, not looking at her. "Ain't never been that."

She leaned over and put a hand on my raw shoulder.

I don't know exactly how we come to it, but I know I moved slow as a box turtle across that couch and got hold of her. Maybe I let a tear come to my eye, or maybe had me a face of such unashamed pity that she let me hold her, let me open her robe and put my head on in there, resting on her naked white breast while she rubbed my broad back, nice and easy, rubbed and rubbed as I kept my eyes closed, my face buried and held her.

Then she slid down and I lay on her. I was on top of her, her robe all open, my cut-offs slung to my ankles, our bodies scrunched together on that couch. "Just a minute," she went and said and got out from underneath, went to the kitchen drawer and come back with a condom. A damn rubber. A thing we ain't ever used between us before. But I didn't say no, wasn't gonna say no, and it was something just the way she tore open the little pouch and put the damn thing on me, like something sexy, like all part of the plan, so that we was back together on the couch with no hitch, back to lying skin

30

on skin, us moving good and even, familiar as sleep. We rolled together like a ocean. Marleen and I again.

She had her mouth and full lips to my ear, her sweet blossom breath, saying to me: "This is it. The last. Here's your first lesson, Chester: this is the very last of it."

Then it was over and we was quiet. Rested and silent.

And though I had her in my arms, I didn't feel good at all. Because this time I believed her.

She sent me packing for Florida before noon. There wasn't nothing more I could tell her. Wasn't anything for her to tell me. I drove home on the lousy Interstate, not needing to steer no better than a zombie, everything seeming too far off to be important. Drove on to Atmore and took the small roads past pines and a few faded cotton fields, then into the traffic of Pensacola.

When I got there, I closed myself in my house. I didn't even think of drinking or eating or showering. I sat in my teevee chair without the teevee on and did nothing. Hell, I hadn't even remembered to take Marleen's boxes up with me.

I'd have to look me up a job. And more than that—getting me some kind of goddamn job or other—I reckon there was bigger things I ought to attend to.

But I couldn't remember what Crow had told me at the bar, when I told him I wanted Marleen back, when I wanted to get myself changed over to normal. I barely even recollected what Marleen had said, about learning and growing . . . my first lesson.

The hell.

I reckon I had a whole boatload of lessons ahead of me, just lying-in-wait.

CHAPTER FIVE

The damn phone rang.

"Hello?"

"So, how are you?"

It was Marleen. Her honeysuckle voice long distance.

"I answered the phone, didn't I?"

"I was worried a little. That's all. I wanted to make sure you were alive."

She was worried. I liked that. She must of been thinking about poor ol' me since I'd left, since I'd seen her, touched her, since we did the tango on her green couch. Though it'd been three days past.

"What the hell do you care," I said. "You're off to Yankee-land with some quack when you ought to be back with me."

"Listen, Chester. This is only a call out of concern. I just wanted to make sure you weren't dead."

"I ain't dead. You can tell by how persistent I am."

"Persistence is not a charm, Chester."

The phone call went downhill from there. And it wasn't long before her voice was gone and I was alone again with nothing but bad feelings and time on my hands.

And that's how the summer went on, downhill. Marleen never did call again, though I heard tell she asked about me from Crow and Della. Either way it didn't do me any good. I still believed she meant it when she'd done told me it was the last, but sometimes I thought she was hoping I'd try again. So I sat with a mind full of confusion as the hot months steamed along.

If nothing else, that confusion helped me hang on. I mean, it gave me something to grab onto, even if it was only bullheaded sadness. I needed it because I stayed jobless, broke and miserable. I borrowed money from Crow, read the paper, watched the old lady next door go about her yard chores. I started smoking again, even though I couldn't afford it much. Seemed to make my days go faster, gave my hands and mouth something to do. I'd smoked since I was a kid then quit when I'd trained for boxing for real. Picked it back up again after I quit boxing but Marleen'd got me to quit—she being a nurse and all. But here I was alone and hopeless, so the cigarettes kept my body occupied a bit.

But my mind stayed mainly busy with Marleen and ol' Doctor Yank from Conettycut.

It wasn't till hurricane season was about over that I got me a job. Crow got it for me. He worked at C. C. Cotton Food Distributors, a warehouse up off Old Palafox and Olive Road, past the I-10. I was ready to work by then and I sure needed it. Once again, Crow proved himself to be the only sonofabitch looking out for me. Even better than I looked out for myself.

Work kept my mind numbed-up and gave me money to boot. All I had to do was drive a forklift all boring day long, loading up pallets of canned ketchup and mustard and salty vegetables, or blocks of frozen meat or potatoes—teevee dinner kinds of foods—then load them pallets onto trucks bound for the Naval Base or Ft. Walton or Mobile or Pascagoula and a few points north. It was easy as it was stupid. About the only career my goddamn Navy experience'd proved good for.

All those early years I'd spent loading cargo on ships and Navy planes I thought I was protecting the American Way, and here I was only paving the way for a eight dollar a hour job.

33

But I reckon it suited me fine enough.

I hadn't drunk much since the march to Montgomery. I'd even steered clear of women and fighting. When I begun work, I had a time trying to get along with the other folks at the warehouse. I didn't have no arguments or nothing, it was just that I hadn't dealt with nobody but myself for quite a spell, so it took a while to get used to knowing other people. And they was maybe a bit afraid of me, due to my size and consternation and all, so the ice didn't break anytime soon.

It was like a month after my first day—a Friday, paycheck day—and me and Crow and some of them other guys went downtown, that's when I kind'a felt like I was fitting in. When we all went down to Traveler Smith's.

Traveler Smith's was a popular bar, for downtown anyways. It was a big place with a bunch of airplane and World War Two crap hanging all over its junky walls. Smith, the man himself, ran the joint. He had been in the RAF or some bullshit like that, so that's why his place was all decked out in fly-boy memorabilia. And though Pensacola is plumb surrounded by water, it's a Naval Air Station, and it's like the town's always looking up to the skies for recognition more than anything else.

So anyways, we went to Traveler Smith's that night and I was buying rounds of beer for all the other guys, about six of us, all of us boys settling in for another nice night along the Redneck Riviera. And drinking the beer and talking, I got to feeling like one of them, a regular worker. Life in a damn beer commercial. But slowly they all began to filter on out, heading on back to their homes and wives, their dogs and house trailers. Crow left too. Near soon I was all alone, sitting up at the bar with a bad hankering for George Dickle whiskey.

My feelings for Marleen was still throbbing, low, somewhere in my heart. Nothing like last summer, but it was still there, waiting like a buzzard on a tree limb sniffing the air for something rotten.

So I went ahead and ordered up a double Dickle on ice. Then had me another.

I kept up the glasses of coldbeer and had the barman refill the highball glass for a third try. The bar was crowding up some, it being a Friday night. So I sat and just sort of soaked up the lousy atmosphere, like some goddamn lizard taking sun on its back. I sat glassy-eyed and dumb and damn near happy, just waiting to see if something was gonna fall my way.

And it did.

That's the nice thing about drinking heavy in bars: either something does happen or you get so goddamn shitfaced you're sure something did.

But something did happen that night.

I was considering leaving, maybe going out to P-cola Beach to finish my drunk, or maybe just going on home, when this here tall, straight-blonde-haired gal sat down next to me.

"Are you from here?" she asked.

She had a foreign accent. Real foreign.

"I live in Warrington," I said and she looked confused, like she was going over a world map in her head thinking Warrington was some chickenbone country in Asia or something.

"Pensacola," I helped her out. "Right here."

"Oh," she laughed. A deep one. "I'm from Bremen."

I looked at her like she'd just done looked at me.

"Germany. Bremen, Germany."

Now I had no fucking idea where that town was. I mean I knew Germany was across the Atlantic Ocean, jumbled in there with the rest of them jigsaw countries where if'n you drove a hundred miles you needed a new language, but other

than that it might as well of been the goddamn capital of
North Dakota.

But I smiled for her and nodded my head and went and
bought her a drink. Bought her the same as I was drinking.

"George Dickle," I said when she stared at the whiskey.

"Is this anything like a Rob Roy?"

"I ain't interested in your old boyfriends," I said.

She done laughed.

So we sat and talked while commencing to drink ourselves
drunk.

Her name was Eva. She was over here bumming around
the States, she said. She said she'd been working as a cook on
a boat, some rich pecker's yacht. She'd gotten on down in the
Caribbean. She said the owner was a drunk, a loudmouth, a
lecher and a asshole. I said most rich people are and that's
how they got to be rich. She said that by the time that ol'
yacht landed in Fort Lauderdale, the owner was so pissed he
done fired the captain and crew. She told me that she took off
with the captain, headed for New Orleans, but by the time
she got this far, to P-cola, she found out that the captain was
a drunk, a loudmouth, a lecher, and a asshole. I said that
most of them are and that's how they got to be captain.

She'd spent some time in a town called Grayton Beach
before coming back on to Pensacola. Now she'd been in P-
cola for a damn year, waiting tables somewheres, had her a
visa, and was looking for something new to happen.

But if she was thinking about hooking up with me, well, she
weren't about to improve her batting average any.

We traded some looks and then she reached out and began
to feel my big arm.

"You play sports?" she asked.

The way she was kneading my biceps, I knew she wasn't
exactly wanting a game of baseball or nothing.

"I used to box some," I said.

That seemed to interest her.

"That's how you got that pretty nose."

"Sure," I said. "I fought a plastic surgeon once, and he prettied it up real good."

A pretty nose. Believe it or not, it'd been said before.

It weren't all that unusual for women to come up to me, in bars anyways. When I was boxing, whether they knew I was a fighter or not, women used to buy me drinks all the time. And even now, though I'm a ugly cuss—and I am, I know I am, big and ugly—I'm just far big enough and ugly enough to make me interesting. Ugly enough to be handsome, is how a few women put it. I'm interesting on the outside, I figure. They sure as hell couldn't be attracted to what was on the inside of me.

She was a good-looking gal, like I said. She was tall with all that straight blonde hair. She wasn't a real beauty or nothing, but she didn't wear a lot of makeup or push-up bra and shit, which was good by me, and she was young and looked a mite supple. Had her a nice chest. That alone impressed me plenty enough. Just thinking about her breasts in my hands, maybe all slippered up with some peanut oil or something, was a pleasant distraction. My mind has always wandered off to the simple things in life: a pair of tits, whiskey on ice, punching a man in the nose.

Things like that.

Anyways, if she was out for experiences, I aimed to show her a few.

"Hey," I said, "you want to make two-hunnerd thousand bucks?"

"Bucks?"

"Money. Dollars. Two-hunnerd grand."

"You win the lottery or something?" she asked, showing me the white teeth in her smile, talking with that gutty accent which I was becoming a mite fond of.

"Nope. But maybe you can."

"Okay, how am I going to make it?"

I told her about the standing bet ol' Traveler Smith had. It was a bet with anybody in the world that if they could catch him wearing a matching pair of socks, that is say two white socks or black socks or a pair of damn argyles on his little white feet, if'n anyone ever caught him wearing them then he'd shell out two-hunnerd grand. I reckon it was more a gimmick than anything else, but it was a real bet. Folks tried it on him every-other day.

"Just a pair of socks?" she asked. "All that bucks if he's wearing the same socks?"

"That's right," I said. "Go on over and ask him to show you. He'll be happy to have you ask."

She got on up and I watched her long legs as she went on over to Smith. He was standing by the bar, talking to some tourists and getting his picture taken. He was that kind a guy.

She looked back at me for a second, smirking, and then got his attention. It didn't take much to get it. He was that kind a guy too.

Now, like I said, the socks was a true bet. If a man calls him on it, Smith will lift up his pant leg to show the guy he was wrong. Then they'll chuckle, maybe buy another goddamn drink and that'll be that. But if a woman, especially a tall looker like Eva, if a woman asks the man to see his socks, well ol' Traveler Smith will open his pants at the belt-line and have them peer on down his baggy pant leg to see his socks. And for all I knew, the man didn't wear no underwear, just like me. Then again, I don't wear no socks either.

38

So after she done looked back at me, she went ahead and asked and he went ahead and pulled out his pants at the waist and she went ahead and looked. Most of them look, strangely enough. Guess they don't think not to.

Now, like I said, I didn't know if Smith went around wearing no underwear like I did, but that Eva girl got a big Howdy-Doody face on her. She didn't scream but she put her hand up to her pretty mouth and took a gulp of air and come running on back to me.

She grabbed me by my freckled arm.

"Let's get out of here. That man is a preevert."

We went to her place.

She lived in old town Pensacola, close to the Seville Square. Had herself a upstairs apartment in a big house. Old town was a nice enough neighborhood, but it was ancient-like. They had cockroaches living in them homes that were older than me, some been around since the pirates used to sail Pensacola Bay.

We sat in her room in the near-dark, no lights on except what came in from her windows. It was a one-bedroom place–she went and called it a studio–with a tiny kitchen and a second door that led to a bathroom that was smaller than me lying down. We sat on the floor in the front room, on top of this big hard cushion thing that didn't have no legs. It was the only seat she had in the place, except for a huge bed. Expensive looking thing, the bed was. Like some big ol' osprey nest sitting there in the corner, full of coverings and pillows and shit. She didn't have a lot, but what she had looked mighty fancy. I was surprised. I mean, she talked like she was some boxcar left to idle here in P-cola, waiting for the train to come take her on down the track to some other dead-end. All her things was kind'a old and particular and smelled like someone else's money. None of it looked like it come out of any Wall-Mart I'd ever done seen.

"You look pretty settled in for being a foreigner," I told her.

We were both drunk as high school janitors and she was happy I'd taken notice.

"These are my things," she went and told me. "My father shipped them to me when I decided to stay here for now. My father runs an import-export. A very rich man. He likes that I travel so much."

"Sure he does," I said. "He's probably smiling right now."

She began to talk about her trips all over the world: the Carib', Mexico, over in India and the old Soviet Union. This woman was about ten years younger than me and she'd been about everywhere, hopping the globe like it was some kind'a ride at fucking Disney World.

She went on to tell me where each knickknack and wall-hanging and piece of furniture come from. She went on and on about this scrubbly-looking rug by her bed, one that'd come from some hardluck country or other where if they had toilet paper and toothpaste they'd make a salad.

It didn't bother me much, really. I sat there and listened and even asked a few questions, but all I was waiting for was to run my beaten hands on her flesh and get her all skinny-naked so we could screw like oiled weasels on that big French bed of hers.

"And this," she said, holding up a long, clear liquor bottle "this comes from Spain, from the island of Ibeza. It's only made there. You can't buy it just anywhere."

"There might be a good reason for it," I said.

There wasn't no markings on the bottle, just a cork holding back the insides which was thick and piss-yellow. And among that damn liquid was twigs and stems with thorns, briar patch shit. It looked to me to be a pile of sticker weeds in a bottle of cane-liquor left out in the sun too long. It sure weren't no George Dickle.

She done handed me the bottle and I held it up to the window-light, looking in at all them thorny sticks and all.

"Go ahead," she said, didn't even offer me a glass.

I smelled it first, like a stray cat trying to smell out the anti-freeze in its milk. But it smelled more like dog. It smelled – not that I ever come to honestly smell it, understand – but it smelled what I kind'a thought was like a dog in heat. Kind of she-hound stinky. Maybe like bad sex.

But the way I'd been lately, bad sex was a far sight better than none.

So I took me a drink.

And it weren't half bad. It was thick–syrupy, you know– but it left a clean long burn down to your belly and you could feel its punch.

"Ain't too bad," I said and she seemed real pleased that I liked it.

"Oh yes. It has absinth. You can't get that in the States. Most Americans do not like it. Oh yes."

Well it made me real happy that she was happy and kind of set a hard-on up in my jeans and I was about ready to jump her German bones when this here cat comes flopping into the room. A big ol' hairy cat. And she goes for this cat, get's excited and calls it some cheese-ball name, like talking to a baby or something, and just plain interrupts the ideas I did have.

"Ohhh little Shoobecker," or some shit like that she said.

And this cat is ugly. This fucking cat is huge and furry and all puffed out like a walking and breathing lintball. I mean, cats is all right I suppose, but they don't do a whole lot if you ask me. A dog'll go hunting at least. Maybe a dog'd jump in and try to save a man drowning in a river, but a cat'd sit on

41

shore and watch, like it was taking notes or something. Probably would throw you a rock if it could. Just can't trust a cat. But she sure liked this one and she began to talk it up like all her other things.

"Feel his fur," she said. "I brush him one-hundred times a day. I got him in Mobile, Alabama for only fifty dollars. He is a pure-bred."

"Well ain't that sweet," I told her. "But I'm a pure-bred myself. Let me show you." And I started to take off my clothes.

She put the cat aside.

She took off her own clothes.

Now the night was getting interesting.

We was nothing but peeled onions, sitting there on that mattress-thing, about a arm's reach away from each other. But we wasn't quite ready for the slam-bang of her bed yet, as she was still passing that bottle between us. And so I decided that that was all right. Hell, I liked to drink.

But that shit hit hard. It did. And she knew it. Not that Eva couldn't drink, she was right up there with the best, but I got to noticing how she was taking little sips while I was taking down big chunks. And as good as I did felt, seeing her long body all naked and near and about ready for action, I was also getting a mite queasy from that Spanish liquor. But queasy'd never kept me from anything before, so I paid it no mind.

"Here, have another drink," she told me, then got up and curled up in her bed, waiting.

I smiled, watching her. Then I took that bottle, tipped her up and damn near drained it.

Should've seen the look on her face.

Whooo, but did that shit kick. It was fire water in my plumbing.

We was in bed, kissing and lapping and just general treating each other like deers at a salt-lick, when that fucking liquor started to attack me. I mean that crap burbled around in my stomach like two dozen out-of-season oysters and I knew I wasn't gonna hold it. I was lying on her and kissing the whole of her long body when I had to roll off.

Now, having to puke ain't so bad, and any Navy veteran has got a lot of experience to fall back on when it comes to it, so I figured as drunk as we both was, I could go ahead and get it out and then get back to the sex at hand. When you're drunk and you got your mind set, you'd be surprised at the things you can do. But what happened was, I rolled off her, best I could manage, and up-chucked off the side of her big bed—quiet-like, you know, just a muffled glug glug thing—but it so happened that right below me was that fancy cat. It was sleeping on that expensive rug of her's.

I hit that animal square. It looked like a feather duster dipped in a pot of seafood gumbo. Man. And the cat didn't care for it at all, it jumped up and commenced to scream around the room like it was on fire.

The commotion got Eva jumping up too.

She sat up fast and mean, her skin as white as canned turnips, and she began to yell at me. Meanwhile the kitty flew up into bed with us and began to shake vomit all over the place. It was a ugly mess.

She hit me on the chest, good and hard and full of malice. She slapped my face. She yelled in her natural born tongue, words that were probably as foul as any I ever knew. And it was loud too, because it woke some neighbor folk. They banged on the walls for us all to shut up and used language I understood just fine.

I felt bad, I did. I felt bad for her. But she knew I was a sonofabitch when she went to bed with me, and now I couldn't help but to laugh.

And I laughed hard and heavy. Damn it felt good. So I kept it up as she hit me all over, scratched me, screamed. She got madder because her hitting didn't hurt and the madder she got the harder I laughed. I could not help myself. Poor girl. I mean I saw her red face and her cat mewing around in bed all covered with puke and I couldn't stop it none.

But then she popped out of bed and began to pick up them doodads of her's and toss them at me. She had a bad pitch. Most of that shit hit the big wood bedboard behind me. But she was up and raging, still beautiful and naked, and I was humored so much I almost couldn't dodge the things she was flinging at me. Finally her aim improved and I got hit a few times. I knew I had to save my hide.

I scrambled right quick, not even bothering to try'n put on my clothes. I felt I should leave her some damn money or something, it could go to her pet-psychiatrist bill, maybe. But I didn't have no chance for that. I grabbed my wad of clothes and shoes and high-tailed it, drunk and laughing and naked, out and down the stairs and into the dark street.

I dove into my Super Bee and took off.

And there I was, driving down the late-night city streets, pea pod naked, listening to the radio as I headed for home.

Never did see ol' Eva again.

But Christ, did I sleep good that night.

CHAPTER SIX

In fact, I slept good lots of nights. That's how I figured I was gonna be okay. I mean, I knew there'd be some new punches to take, but at least I'd done healed up from the ones of summer. Maybe I'd got myself normal after all. That easy. Had my job, even if it was as boring as a possum at noon. I had my weekends when I could drink and round up a little adventure. And the ghost of Marleen was at rest, for a spell anyways. Can't say I was exactly fulfilled with it all, or nothing, but I lived pretty damn peaceably through them early fall months.

Then the first wind hit that calm, when this here manager come down from Dothan, Alabama. He visited once or twice a month to check in on how much money the ol' warehouse was making. The company was based in Dothan, though they'd shut down the warehouse there. Evidently this guy's job was to travel to the one here in Pensacola, then to the one up near Tuscaloosa and over to one they had in Iron City, Georgia. Now, I didn't give a shit about some white-collar boy coming around a few days out of the month and looking over the other white-collar boys' books, but he was one of them fellows who thinks he's got to mix with us common workers. Or maybe he was sniffing around for employee theft or drugs, or just plain laziness, that of which there was plenty.

We all obliged the man with our best behavior, though the truth was none of us could stand him much. Being from a town like Dothan made him naturally kind of a dipshit. And if that weren't enough, our man from Dothan fancied himself a expert on boxing too. Said he had been a Golden Gloves

45

champ in Alabama, light-heavyweight Novice Class, quite a few years back. The man had gone to seed worse than me, yet if he was inclined to believe himself a boxer, then I wasn't out to disprove it any. But when he got wind of me and Crow's past in the Navy, well, he became more than just a dipshit from Dothan.

Charlie was his name. Charlie Cotton. A nephew or something of the original company owner.

Charlie was the kind of guy who kept his white shirt sleeves rolled up, instead of wearing short-sleeves in the summer, and who wore his neckties way too short thinking it'd make him look taller, maybe. He was a guy who wanted to see me and Crow fight. He didn't care much for brawling—which was about all I was good for anymore. No, the man wanted a bout in a ring, with professional rules—all that Marcus of Queensbury shit that I learned in the amateurs when I was about twenty-two. Even better, when he found out Crow and I was friends and wasn't about to mix it up none, he wanted to fight one of us hisself.

It didn't take long before he suggested putting up some ropes in the goddamn parking lot so we could slip on some gloves and get a real match going. "Eight rounds of controlled mayhem", as he put it. . . . The asshole. . . . And all I wanted to do was get him in the walk-in freezer and club him with a frozen turkey leg or something. Crow just laughed it off. As I said, he was a smarter man than me. Always had been. He told me not to get riled up about Charlie Cotton.

But I've been told a lot of things like that. Telling me just don't do the trick.

If Charlie Cotton hadn't been the big-man manager, if he'd been just another employee like me, then he'd of been on intimate terms with his dentist right quick. But seeing as how he was in control of not only my lousy income, but also the job that kept me sane and away from drinking my heart out, I let his wisecracks and offers to fight slide on by me.

Till about December, that was.

It was maybe a week after Thanksgiving when he came down and goaded me into fighting him. That was like a Wednesday. By the next Friday he was back and had with him the material to jury-rig a ring out in the parking lot.

I was going to fight him because he went on to me with this long story about his Alabama boxing days and how he had always regretted giving it up to go into the exciting world of business accounting. I could see why he'd regretted it: years of being beat in the head and gut and getting fucked out of his pay would've probably improved him some. His looks included. I ain't saying Charlie Cotton was outright ugly, but I'd seen things wash up on the beach that'd have a better chance in a singles bar. It was mighty pitiful.

Anyways, I knew the one who'd really be doing the regretting would be me, if I didn't take the opportunity to bash his nappy head in. So, with just a few words from me, the match was on.

That Friday of the bout was a cold one, at least by north Florida standards. I'd done finished a hard days work while no doubt Cotton had been sitting around his room at the Holiday Inn eating raw eggs and vitamins. It was a misty cold, one of them slurpy winter sea-fogs in the air, which was fine by me. The fog kept it so people driving by couldn't quite make out the stupid shit that was about to happen. And to tell the truth, I wasn't really up to it. When I got out there and all, I didn't want to fight. For one thing, I wasn't pissed at Charlie Cotton no more.

I went up to him and suggested we call the whole works off. I mean, I was a good four inches taller than him and I knew my reach was as good as that. Cotton probably out-weighed

47

me by five or ten pounds—all of it Piggly Wiggly flab. He had him a flabbier mind too, because he refused my offer.

"Mr. Stubbs," Cotton said, always the polite sonofabitch. "Mr. Stubbs, I'm not going to let you back out, sir. I heard tell you were a good boxer—be it years ago—but now you are against Kid Cotton. So be prepared."

He smiled what I guess he thought was a mean smile. Something he picked up from the cable teevee.

Well, Kid Cotton was about to get swabbed. That little horseshit speech had managed to raise my hackles. Here was a full grown man—from Dothan no less—going around calling himself Kid Cotton. That right there was plenty enough reason to knock his jawbone clean to Jacksonville.

So the battle was on.

Only it weren't much of one.

He came out in a goddamn bathrobe and honest-to-God boxing trunks. Man had him some white legs, beefy and sad looking. He had provided seven pound gloves for us—pro gloves—and he had some pal of his in a white shirt and bow-tie who was gonna ref the match. We'd agreed to go only three rounds, but he wanted to go ten now. Seems he was caught up into his dream pretty damn heavy. He was upset that I was gonna box in my tee-shirt and jeans and tennis shoes, but I figured I'd put him out of his upsettedness soon enough.

Kid Cotton had him a ring man too. Some pal who stood with tape and water and a plug of Vaseline, like it was gonna be a big long match. We didn't have no headgear, though Cotton at least had a plastic mouthpiece. I was glad to see the mouthguard. I didn't need no other man's dental bills to worry about.

We stood out there in the near drizzle-cold, in opposite corners of the crappy ring, and I wondered how in the fuck I had gotten myself into the predicament. I maybe could lose my job if I busted him up. Crow sure knew better. He wasn't even showing up for the fight. But there was a crowd of the boys around and a group from management as well.

Most of those folks was just curious: it was a unusual way to finish out the work week. But there was some strange faces too. Serious faces all lined up behind his side of the ring. Cotton had done brought hisself a handful down from Dothan.

But I phased them all out right quick. Because the more I stared at Kid Cotton, him looking like some big Eskimo Pie in boxer shorts over there, the more I realized that he was the idgit responsible for my being in the ring. It made me mad. I was embarrassed. And if I was gonna lose my job, then he was gonna pay for it.

So I geared it up. I worked up a sweat and an attitude like I used to before a bout. Some of my Navy fights came flashing back at me, the bloody tangle of it, the hatred, the no mercy, and I was ready. I was looking forward to it.

Cotton had warmed up and had him a few fellows in his corner. They all asked if I was ready and I said yes and then someone conked a tinny bell and Cotton came prancing fast out into the ring.

I took a few steps and stood there. Flat-footed. Easy-target-looking. Doing nothing. Cotton swirled around me once. He wound his arm in a circle, show-boating and showing me his teeth wedged in the clear plastic of his guard. He did some little jig and his pal the ref told me to get in and mix it up.

Which was all the excuse I needed.

I took three more steps and Cotton came to me. He crouched low and bobbed his head, acting like he was really gonna box me. I didn't take none of it.

I stepped into him, one step and he was in my reach. I charged and threw three little right jabs. Three. He didn't

49

even take one swipe. By that time I dipped my hip and brought my left hook around sweet, low and hard. Bam. Dropped the fucker quick as a fly into a toad's mouth. He hit ass-first, then straighted out like a car-struck dog on the mat. And it was over. One connection and it was done. Cotton lay on the canvas, in the cold parking lot, and he could not get up. He was a little green in the gills, but not the stone-white color of a man in trouble, so I knew he'd recover. And purt'soon he kind of rolled up a bit, curling up to sit like a sponge collecting the salty mist of the day.

I left the ring.

No one said much. Someone untied my gloves and I walked straight to my car to go on home.

Crow was there, waiting for me inside my car, out of the foggy weather. He'd been watching us, from a distance.

He gave my shoulder a rub.

"You done it now, Chester," was all he said, then he got out.

I drove my car out the gate.

It'd probably been better if I'd done put the man in a coma, because when Monday come around I was demoted.

They didn't call it a demotion, but the boys in the brown ties right off told me I'd been switched from a fork lift driver to a pallet loader in the frozen foods department. Which meant I was to work in the backside of the warehouse, inside a fucking freezer stacking and unstacking cold shit all day long, having to wear a coat and gloves, never to see the blue sky.

It meant that I'd have to work for Marty Skipps, a supervisor who never lifted a finger unless it was to put it up his nose. It also meant I was to work with these two Vietnamese boys. Well, they wasn't really boys, was full-grown men. And truth be, for all I knew they wasn't even Vietnamese. Hell. Folks just said they was. They was brothers. Duck and Wayne, we all called them.

I didn't know what their real names was. Nobody did, I reckon, except themselves. They could speak American but didn't do it much. Didn't have much call to, I suppose. Like I said, everyone called one of them Duck—he was the older brother—and they called the other one Wayne. I didn't plan on naming them anything different. I did know that them wiry little men was from some worn-out place, somewhere where the government'd as soon string you up as give you a parking ticket. These guys was picked up in the middle of the ocean while trying to row their way to fucking California. Of course, if they'd ever of made it to California, they'd probably been tempted to row right on back. But they was sent to Pensacola somehow and was given jobs at the warehouse. And they was put to work in the back of the building, in the freezer, just like me.

They tried to talk to me a few times, at first, but I didn't pay them no mind. I just went around, told myself jokes and complained about Marty. Them boys laughed at me some, but soon enough they was back talking their gobbledygook to each other.

As far as ol' Marty went, besides scratching his ass, he was addicted to the Dr. Pepper machine in the employee's lounge and to a certain young thing named Linda-May in the dispatch office. There was plenty of nooks and crannies up around there for the two of them to disappear in. I always knew when he was about to visit Linda-May by the way he'd fiddle with his wedding ring. Had a right guilty twist to it. So anyways, Marty was never around much. Which left me and them Oriental fellows all alone most of the time.

I had no recourse but to go about my cold job each day, cursing to myself. Maybe I was teaching those two Asian boys a word or two, if'n they could even understand me.

CHAPTER SEVEN

"I told you not to fight that man, I told you," Crow said, more'n a few weeks after I'd been transferred to the frozen depths.

"Shit, Crow, I couldn't help it. The man got what he deserved. How was I to know he'd hold a grudge. . . . At least I didn't go and get sued."

"Chester, you were never one to look on the bright side of things, so don't go starting now."

We was over at his house, in the grassless backyard where he had two cars he was a working on. He did have him a garage, a broken-down one-car job that was apart from his house, with an entrance from the dirt alley that ran in back. Inside it was his tools and benches and an old wood-burning stove, so there wasn't much room but for the front end of a small-sized car. Sometimes he worked in the street but most often he worked in his yard, which was why it didn't have no grass.

There was a good many trees along the fence line, though. Pines mostly. A little scrub live-oak—or what I call sea oaks. They weren't nothing like the big acorn oaks that grow up in Alabama or nothing. But the sea oaks was sized good enough, with lots of twisting branches and them waxy leaves, kind'a like magnolias but not near as pretty. I liked them, though. The pines was tall enough to keep him some shade to work in, come late afternoon.

Anyway, I stayed close to the shed and talked to him while he made his side-money. I was near the open door, where the iron stove was burning some wood, because it was a cold one. It was a whole lot colder than the day I'd punched the stuffing out of Charlie Cotton. It was Friday, right after work. Crow's iron stove was putting out good heat with the smoke chimneyed out the front, so you could watch it get blowed through all them oak branches, making its way to the tall Pensacola sky.

"Don't tell me about bright sides," I told him after a bit. "I work like a dog, a cold popsicle dog, listening to that gook lingo all day. Shit. Sounds like a bunch of pots and pans falling out of my kitchen cupboard."

"Watch your mouth, man."

"What did I say?"

"You working with those men, so don't go calling them gooks."

"Shit. I didn't call them gooks. I said they spoke gook."

Crow didn't say anything for a while. He stayed stoney and then went down into the hood of that car he was working on. It was like he done disappeared from the world, the way he worked. He'd always told me that if he could afford more tools and equipment, if he could build himself a real garage instead of using the little Mason Jar of a shed he had, then he would be at it full time. He'd open himself up a business.

But it's hard to get ahead in this world. Money don't fall on you, it don't come knocking on your door. Debts, now they fall on you. Debts come knocking on any working man's door. So Crow had nothing but a dream in his head, far as I figured.

I was a lucky man to own my house. I probably never would've if it hadn't been for Marleen. Shit, just marrying her saved my ass. I mean, I got myself in the Navy because I didn't know what else to do. Then I got myself into boxing because the Navy didn't teach me any better than what I taught myself. And after both of them was over, it was Marleen that'd done shown me a way to live, done give me some direction. Something to give a shit for. She was the one that wanted the house and to put all that money into it. It was her family, up in Florence, that'd give us half the mortgage for a wedding gift–and man, was they pissed when she let me have the house, when she took nothing but the good car, most of her clothes and things and the money from the bank. But she was like that. She didn't care much about things, she just wanted a new start with nothing hanging to bring her back to where she'd already been.

But now she was gone. And I didn't have no one to keep me from falling on my ass anymore.

"You ready for a coldbeer or not?" I finally said to Crow, after the silence was too long.

He come up out of the engine for air, his black head sweating, real steam rising from his cropped hair. Even in the cold that man sweated. He looked at me. I was sitting on a turned-over tub now, halfway inside the shed, keeping my backside nice and warm. He shook his head no.

"C'mon, Crow. You've been at that car all day now. A man needs some recreation. A man can't call it a Friday if'n he don't have a hangover the next morning."

Crow shook his head again, only it was for some other reason.

"I want to finish up these valves, here."

"You work too much. Even when you're off work, you work... Ain't you salted away enough money by now?"

He stopped.

"No," he said. "I haven't told anyone except family, but Della and I are expecting."

I sat there, maybe cocked my head like a dog.

54

"Expecting what?"

He about laughed.

"A baby. Expecting a baby. Della's not even a month along."

I still sat there. A baby? What the hell was Crow gonna do with a baby?

"Hey," I finally said, even managing to stand up and shake his big paw. "A baby. That's something, I reckon."

He smiled, proud already, though it must'a been no bigger'n a wren's egg in Della's stomach.

"We ought to celebrate . . . with a beer," I said.

I could see he was gonna give in.

"Okay, Chester. I guess."

I smiled.

"I'll go on down to the Tom Thumb and get us a case."

"Don't bother," he said. "You said you'd be over, so I iced some down. It's in the house. Just go on up and ask Della."

"Maybe you'd better get it. . . . She ain't likely to even open the door for me."

"Come off it, man. You're a big boy. Just go on and ask her for that pail of beer. She'll let you have it."

"She'll let me have it, all right."

I would'a rather walked the ten blocks to the Tom Thumb than walked those few steps to his house. I mean, she was probably right there in the kitchen, maybe oiling her handgun or something. She did carry a gun—Crow had told me that— for self-defense. Had learned how to shoot it, too. Dead-Eye Della. I didn't want to be her first target. But then again, being pregnant and all, maybe her aim was off a tad.

I stood on the step in the damp air and knocked on the back door. It took a little while before the curtains swayed back and Della's clean face showed in the window. She looked at me kind'a awkward and then opened the door.

"Hey, Chester," she said.

"Hello, Della. . . . Crow said he has a pail of coldbeer. Wants me to bring it on out."

"Is he done with that motor yet?" she said and peered on past me, out to where Crow was clanging away with a monkey wrench.

"Close to done, I imagine."

I was still standing and she held the door close to her so as not to let much heat come out of the house.

"You want the whole bucket?" she asked.

"I reckon we do," I said and I smiled for her.

She looked at me to see if I was drunk yet. I guess she decided to give me the benefit of the doubt, because she stepped back and let me on inside.

I even remembered to wipe my feet.

Their house wasn't much bigger than mine. I hadn't been inside it for quite a while. Della and Marleen was friends because of me and Crow and we all used to hang out at one another's home once or twice a week. Back in the salad days, that was. I hadn't been back inside much. It made me feel lonely some. And also Della, she was always giving me the cold shoulder since the divorce.

"That bucket's right on the porch steps, right there past the fridge."

I knew where the side porch was and clomped on over to get the shiny metal pail, which was sitting on the second step. It was full of ice and bottles, but there weren't no handle. It'd been broken off somewheres.

"You heard from Marleen lately, Chester?"

At first I didn't think she was talking to me. I had my back turned, was admiring the green bottles of beer floating in the icy water of the tub, thinking how best to lift it with no handle. And I sure as hell didn't expect no conversation from Della, especially no talk about Marleen. Maybe Crow'd said something to her about the way she treated me like a hunk of cornmeal or something.

"Oh sure," I lied, "Marleen and I done talked a day or two ago. She's doing fine. Montgomery's treating her good."

Hell, I hadn't heard from Marleen. I didn't know shit about what was up with her.

"Montgomery?" Della said. "She's not back in Montgomery, is she?"

I stood up and turned around, the cold pail was in my arms but my mind was traveling far away from any thoughts of beer bottles floating in a fucking tin bucket.

"No. Not Montgomery," I said. "She gone off to, to, you know where. . . ."

"New Haven," she told me and she smiled a little. "I'm surprised at you, Chester Stubbs. Surprised. I thought Marleen's plans would send you crazy. She sent me a letter and told me all about it. Didn't say if you knew it all, or if it was some kind of secret. But you're okay? Did you get a photograph too?"

Some things begun to move around in my peanut mind about then.

I set the tub down, gently, to the linoleum of the kitchen floor.

"No. I didn't get no photograph," I told her, calm as I could fake it. "You mind if I took a gander at your'uns?"

She looked at me a little different. Maybe she figured that she'd made a mistake in even talking to me. But she went on into the other room and fetched that photo while I stayed in the kitchen, standing there like a damn totem-pole.

"This is it."

Della came back and handed me a simple snap-shot.

I held it up under the yellow kitchen lights to study it. There she was, Marleen. My Marleen standing in a yard full of white snow and bare Yankee trees, with some big house in the background. And there with a arm around her was some middle-aged, silver-haired, five-foot-nine doctor—a big grin on his face like he'd just wangled a ten-dollar whore down to five. And there was two kids too, boys holding footballs, maybe old as their teens, smiling with silver braces, enough wire in their mouths to fence off a hog pen. It was like some family picture. Like a goddamn postcard picture: snow, smiles, smoke coming out of the chimney. All that was missing was a damn dog and maybe a snowman in back.

"Well," I said, trembling a bit, "there's the lucky bastard." I handed it back quick. "Thanks, Della. Thanks a lot."

I started for the door.

"Hey, Chester. What about the beer?"

"Oh yeah. The beer."

I turned around and grappled the cold tub into the crook of one arm. I took it and walked fast, sloshing frozen water out over my bare skin, soaking my shirt, but not feeling it much. I took it out to the garage and set it down in the dust by Crow's wood stove. I handed a bottle to him. I opened one for myself and drained the fucker.

"I gotta go," I said to Crow, who was sitting by the fire, all greasy and content. "I gotta take off."

I had plumb forgot about Marleen's Yankee doctor as to that moment, in the kitchen with Della. No doubt I'd forgot it on purpose—placed it outta my mind like a lost cat you always hated anyways—but the painful knowing of it had come back to me mighty quick. And it hit me. The knowing that she was up there with someone, with that man and family in the photograph, it hit me and gave me a sore gut.

It hurt so much I knew that the rest of the day—if not my life—was gonna lie in ruin.

CHAPTER EIGHT

When I drove off from Crow's, I had a sudden inclination to drive all the way to Dothan, Alabama, find Charlie Cotton, and crush his skull like it was a honeydew melon. I felt that mean. Of course I didn't go and do it. But smacking his damn face was just the first of many ideas I come up with.

So I went on home and paced and thought about the Dickle whiskey that was under my sink. But I didn't drink. I had no burning desire to even look at it. Instead I just sat down, sat there on my crusty living room couch, feeling lower than low until I finally stretched out, pulled a old sheet over me, and fell asleep.

I'd might as well of been lying in a casket as been asleep, because I didn't dream or wake or even move my toes for about ten hours. I fell into some nowhere spot in my brain, leaving all my pain and troubles for the next day.

Saturday.

A blind drunk Saturday.

I smelled it coming as soon as I threw the sweaty sheets off my body. I woke up mean and thirsty and headed for the bottle before I even took a piss in the morning.

I took a long slash of George Dickle whiskey, let it gurgle and burn through my innards and then I took another. Fuck it felt good. It felt so good to have that half-full bottle in my hand, feel the glass on my goddamn lips, knowing how it'd all bubble up to my brain and make me meaner. It'd only make my pain clearer, sharp as a bull's horn. I mean, I knew the shit hurt me in the long run, hurt me plenty. But right then I had to hurt someone. And I was the only one handy at the moment.

I couldn't get that photograph out of my mind. I sat and drank and didn't eat and thought about the picture. I could feel myself boiling up, my blood rising and falling. Even though the day was dry and turned warmer–the sky clear as plate-glass, the winter sun cutting in strong–I thought how everything in me was like a big swollen river. A slow-moving deep river flooding the bottomland, plowing its way along, down and down but never getting its chance to empty into the sea.

Fuck did I feel terrible mean.

And the day ran along like that: festering, drunk, damn pointless.

When nightfall came, I went out for a second bottle. I also picked up a case of beer, a pack of Camels and some kind of mystery-meat sandwich. I ate the sandwich in the car and drank a beer. At home I drank only the beer and paced. I walked back and forth and began to talk to myself. I'd drink down the beer and throw the cans to the carpet, or on the sofa or set them down on the teevee or table or anywhere I happened to be when the can was empty. I littered my house up pretty goddamn good.

Then I started on the whiskey again.

I started it all over, what with the misery and disbelief and the swollen river shit. I should have been long gone. I mean, I'd hardly eaten and was drinking enough to sink a battleship, so I should'a been all wobbly and fuck-faced and quiet as a stack of firewood.

But I wasn't.

Instead, I felt evil. Fierce. I could feel the anger crawling in my skin like fire ants and I knew I was gonna have to do something about it.

That's when I decided I'd take a drive on over to Dack's Saloon.

Dack's was a motorcycle bar.

I drove my Super Bee on out, over Navy Bridge, and into the small and packed parking lot of Dack's. Mine was about the only car in a gaggle of cycles. The saloon was dark as midnight: the whole fucking joint was painted Harley-Davidson black, except for the graffiti and stains and other shit splotted on its walls.

I got out and stood under the eaves where a sign said BIKER ATTIRE ONLY. I smoked a cigarette in the dust of the lot, watched traffic, listened to the rock and roll seeping out of the saloon's black door. I was dressed in my jeans and a wrinkled old silk beach shirt, its ragged tail hanging out. Had me my tennis shoes and no socks. I was cold as I stood and smoked and thought things over a bit, but I didn't shiver. Never shivered. But I was still drunk. I was still mean. I was tired of just hurting on myself.

So I went on inside.

I got a few crazy eyes on me right off the bat, dressed as I was like some beach tourist who done washed up at high tide. Of course, my size and the red torch of my big head drew me a little attention. And with the general lack of grease and vomit upon me, I kind of stood out from the crowd. Though motorcycle rags was required, not a one, not even the bartender, said shit as I went on up to the bar and ordered my usual double Dickle.

61

It didn't take long for me to see why they weren't ready to bother with me. What that group was up to was pretty disgusting—even by my standards. I mean, they was drowning in beer and liquor, some I saw was even snorting cocaine off the pinball machines. But what the big hoo-haw was was this initiation of a new member. A woman. And they were giving her what they call a "Winer," as in a bottle a wine. In this case, cheap sweet Mad Dog wine.

I had heard tell of such things, but the sight of it was beyond even my own crummy imagination.

It was ugly.

What they had was this girl—in her early twenties I'd say—had her sitting up on the far end of the bar with her fucking pants off. Gone. Who knew where the hell they were. And her legs was spread wide open like she was expecting her gynecologist to make a bar call or something. She was gone drunk to the gills, too. Just a big sloppy grin on her face and her eyes shiny as searchlights. But I suppose that's the best way to go through a thing like that. Because these boys was saddled right up next to her with that bottle of sweetwine, and they was sticking that bottleneck up into her. I saw it clear. A thing like that kind of draws one's attention. They was taking that bottle and dipping it into the crazy girl's twat. They'd all yell and yelp and clap and then pass the bottle around amongst them, taking a smutty slash.

The hell.

The girl was getting mauled all the time too, groped and teased and hooted at and cursed by all these ape-headed fuckers. They say it's a free country, but I don't reckon any revolution was fought for the likes of that.

The sight of it sobered me up a bit. I thought to try'n stop it, but even if she wanted me to—which I'd bet she didn't—I wasn't gonna. It was damn disgusting, but I didn't come into Dack's to be no hero. I was there for my own self. So I drank up and ordered more, staying silent, thinking it was gonna be a peaceful evening unless I quit acting like a two-hunnerd and seventy pound lamb with a glass of whiskey in his snout. But my opportunity came quick enough.

One of the long-haired boys, a skinny one with enough tassels hanging from his coat he could'a passed for a piñata, he went and offered me a swipe from that bottle.

The clown had him a black eye-patch, like he could only see outta the half a brain he had, and he poked that bottle up towards me and gave me a crooked smile.

"Hey, man. Take a drink."

I looked down on him and affixed my eyes on to his one and only.

He knew what he was doing. He had his glazed eyeball confronting me and his rotten-toothed mouth all cracked open and teasing. He passed that sticky bottle under his own snotty nostrils and then tried to pass it under my broken nose.

My anger come pure and clean.

"Hey," I went and said. "I wouldn't touch that. Ever! Now get the fuck away from me or I'll change you from a cyclops to a damn no-clops!"

My little section of the bar fell silent. Sure, the jukebox was still blasting and folks was still yelling and others was complaining for the damn bottle back, but I'd got me some attention—even if I was only the sideshow.

The bartender had heard me and politely asked me to get the fuck out. Guess my behavior was a mite rude for them. But really it was beyond rude. I'd done made a challenge.

I knew it.

They knew it.

And I had found my trouble for the night.

The smarter one's began to whoop and yip like coyotes, knowing that they had some fresh meat. But I wasn't about to stick around. No sir. I splashed down my Dickle, right-quick, and threw a punch. Just one to get it all started.

I hit Mr. Eyepatch. Got him square in his one good eyeball, just like I said I would.

Then I made my dash for the back door. I pushed my way through, slapped open the grey fire door and sprinted out into the winter night. Though I was drunk, I moved clean and quick. I knew that only the ones who really wanted it would follow me. I just hoped there weren't too many of them. I didn't mind being out-numbered, but I wasn't on no fucking suicide mission.

I ran to my car, jumped in and had the key cranked before the first of those fuckers barreled out and around after me. There must'a been about a dozen of them that poured out of that black hole. I flat-footed the accelerator and my Super Bee pealed on out into the street, showering the crowd with pea gravel.

The chase was on.

I looked back to see, and best I could tell there was only about five bikes following me. That was fine and dandy. It meant that there'd be seven or eight of them, at best, if some was riding double-up. And they was roaring right up on my ass too, like a mad string of bumblebees, all brightlights and full of sting.

I drove on down the city side of Bayou Chico, knowing right where I was headed. I snapped through a red light and spun on past the Burlington Northern tracks, down to a stand of trees. I crowded my car between the skinny trunks along a chunky dirt road spotted with palmetta sprouts and sand puddles, on down to the water's edge where the pines shaded the bay, where the water was lying all quiet-like and unsuspecting.

I looped my car along the pines, so it faced the way I'd come in, and left it running. I got out and stood, hearing them noise their hogs single-file down the dirt, coming in after me.

I put my back to the water and they came on in with headlights blasting like they was shining for out-of-season deer. When they saw me standing there they kind of circled up and dismounted. There was only four cycles and five riders, five sonofabitches gathering in front of me like jury and judge.

"Dead fucking meat!"

That's about all they said other than some alley-cat noises, before the first of them commenced to try me.

The one to step in was a hairy bastard with a beer gut. He was the biggest of the boys, with enough Harley tattoos on his blobby arms to start a dealership. I reckoned at least one of these guys had a chain or a sap on them somewheres, let alone a gun. They all had knives, right there on their belts. But this guy came at me with only his black-gloved fists, raised up in the moonlight.

And I was ready. It was what I was wanting.

He rushed in with a smile damn drunker than mine and gave me the biggest right-hand swing he could manage. A stoned haymaker of a swing. I saw it from six miles away. I took one step and let him reel on past me. Then I clubbed him one behind the ear, using lots of knuckle.

That sonofabitch hit the sand. Hard. I turned and kicked him one in the kidney, knowing he wasn't gonna get up without help.

These boys didn't know shit about boxing, about position and defense. But they didn't have to. They just had to act like a pack of jackals to bring me down. But it looked like they was gonna try me one on one, that way the more timid of them could see what I was about.

The fat guy in the sand ought'a given them a hint.

Two others come on in. One of them was the shithead with the eye-patch. I guess he could still see after all. This time I sunk my fist into his stomach and then clobbered his head sideways with my elbow. Give him double-vision, so he could see straight and thank me for it later. It didn't look like it felt too good, though. But while I was playing eye doctor with the one, I opened myself up to the other biker and he slammed me pretty good in the face, hitting me where it could do no lasting harm. By the time I turned on him they was all coming at me. Rabid as the day is long.

I took my share of pain.

I know I socked one of them, some guy with long girl-blonde hair, socked him so good I felt his cheek bone go, dropping him half in the water like one of them walking catfish. I gave them motherfuckers some licks they'd never forget.

But in the end they got to me good. It was the body punches that did me in. The legs and the body is where fighting really counts. My legs had gone long ago and my gut wasn't much harder than a slab of Velveeta cheese. My face took it too, but the body punches was what made me fall.

I fell hard, my face in the sand, and they started to kick me with their blunt-nose biker boots. Them boys smelled blood then and aimed for my sides and organs, even kicking below the belt as they got the best of me. I curled up and got my hands over my head. After a few bleary minutes of that shit, I knew I'd had enough. I struggled around till one of them stepped in close enough to my hands and I grabbed his skinny leg. I grabbed him and yanked him like a dirty carpet. I grabbed him and scrambled over him right quick, with one motion. And then I was standing. I got up and stood on that fucker. Used his face for traction as I sprinted out and away from them.

I line-drived it to my Super Bee and took off with them still screaming, their voices carrying on out across the water of the bayou.

They'd let me go.

The fight was over and they wasn't gonna follow me. Both of us could claim victory in battle. Those toads could return to the saloon, boasting that they'd had a right nice night–they's romantics that way–and I got to go on my own merry way too, knowing I'd done taught myself the same old lesson all over again.

The only problem was I'd overdone it this time.

Because as I drove, blowing wet blood out of my nostrils and into my hand, I breathed a familiar pain with each heaving breath. It was the sharp spur of broken ribs. Still, I was gonna head home–broken rib bones or not–and have me a celebratory drink of Dickle in the confines of my kitchen. But then my innards got all gurgly, some shit got to wanting to come up my throat. I pulled over, opened the door and heaved. It hurt. Then I had to do it again. And when I looked at it puddled down there on the asphalt in the street light, it was mighty bloody. I got to driving again but it got to where I couldn't hardly breath none at all. Along with chest pains, I couldn't get a decent gasp of air and the smart in my ribs was fast giving way to a new and more dangerous pain.

I had to grip the wheel hard. I had to concentrate on the drive. My brain wanted to shut it all off, wanted to send me down into a unforgiving nap.

So I never did make it on home to my bottle under the sink.

I drove myself on over to the emergency room instead.

CHAPTER NINE

Those Dack's Saloon boys had done fucked me up good. My little night out had got me some broken ribs and a punctured lung. My right knee was swollen like a rotten alligator pear. I looked to be laid up in the hospital for a spell. Shit.

I hadn't been in debt for months, so the hospital bills would take care of that. It felt good knowing I'd be in debt again. Damn good. Made me feel more American. Maybe I'd even lose my job.

There was nothing I could do about that. Nothing I could do about nothing, when it come down to it. About all I wanted to do was get out of the fucking hospital and get on with some serious kitchen drinking.

Marleen was still eating at me. I had tried to take the cure, but the fight hadn't gone and done it. She was there in my mind even when I thought she wasn't. Like some Mississippi River barge, pushing a load of trash to New Orleans where all you can see is the filth and crap piled high coming around a long bend, but not the tough little engine that propels the whole thing. Like that, she was that hateful little engine.

And I was the fucking junk.

I was in and out of it for the first few days, what with the I-Vees and the pain killer they was giving to me like candy. I don't recollect any visitors or any doctors for that matter. I did note the ugliness of the big night nurse, though.

It weren't until about the Thursday after that I had me a visitor I was aware of. One of the day nurses—who didn't

look too bad but was about as friendly as a teased crawfish—
she told me I had company coming. Right off I figured it was
Crow, seeing how it was six o'clock or so and he'd be off
work and would'a had him his supper by then. I wasn't looking
forward to seeing him, though. I didn't want his sympathy.
Even more, I didn't want him looking down on me in a damn
hospital bed, knowing how fucking stupid I was. I'd just as
soon no one come see me. No one.

But it weren't him.

Much to my surprise and general wonder, it was them two
Vietnamese guys from work who come into my hospital room.
It was Wayne and Duck.

I must not of looked too happy or something because they
kind'a shuffled on in and stood against the wall, holding their
baseball caps in their little hands and bobbing their black-
haired heads. That always irritated me some, the way they
nodded all the time. But the fact that they'd bothered to come
see me almost made me want to use my bedpan or something,
you know, entertain them for their trouble.

I was the one who had to break the silence.

"Hey, you two," I said. "Ya'll come to see if'n I was still
alive?"

They took it serious.

"Oh, we know you alive," one of them said. Half the time I
never could tell which. "We come. Maybe you feeling better?"

"Better? Better'n what?" I asked, irritated again. It weren't
their fault, though. "Ain't too likely I'll ever feel better'n I feel
right now," I said.

Now they took that as a joke. Hell, maybe it was. Maybe I
was.

"I'm all right, boys," I said, thinking that'd get rid of them.
"I'll be back stacking the frozen broccoli in no time. Stick a

69

live rat up Marty's ass for me and I'll be there before it finds its way out, okay?"

They laughed at that too. I was a regular king of comedy with them two.

They hung around for a few more minutes, saying this and that, being so polite and concerned it about killed me. I was damn glad when they went and left me alone and I could think about whiskey, cigarettes and the crawfish nurse again.

It was Friday when Crow come.

"Your face looks beat up as a rotten banana," he said first off.

I laid there in my hospital room bed and smiled a big fat mean one. I knew he'd come for a visit, knew he'd come and let me know what a goddamned loser I was.

"I don't give a God's dick," I told him. "I done cracked up the same ribs you broke on me. It feels good. Feels fucking wonderful, Crow. Had a lung down too. You ought'a try it yourself."

I shared a room with one other man—a old man who coughed all the time like he done swallowed a flock of starlings and was trying to get'm to come on back out. Me and him didn't talk none. Best I could tell, he took me for a nut. The sight of Crow had made him draw his curtains. Made him stop coughing too. Crow was his miracle cure.

But Crow sure weren't mine.

"I like my lungs the way they already are," Crow said. "How in the hell did you do it, anyway?"

"Didn't the doctor tell you?"

"Do I look like one of your family, Chester?"

"I ain't got no family," I said.

"We're all thankful for that," he said, then acted like he wanted to take it back. "But no one's told me what happened, not even you."

We looked at each other for a bit.

"I just made a neighborly visit to Dack's Saloon was all."

"You did, huh?"

He put a awful lot in that huh.

"Yeah, I did!"

"Della thought maybe it was her fault, maybe she told you something you wasn't supposed to know and you ran your ugly car. . . ."

"My ugly car is fine. It's my ugly self that hurts. . . . Anyway, it wasn't anything Della done. I just had me a few. . . ."

". . . too many," Crow said.

He got him the exact look on his face that I didn't want to see, at least not while I was laid up and couldn't take a goddamn swing at him.

I swallowed it. I didn't give a shit.

He went on and changed the subject and told me that my insurance with the company would pay a good deal of my bills. I guess he expected me to act like it was good news.

"Shit," I said, "I was hoping I could declare bankruptcy. Would've made me feel important somehow."

He didn't laugh.

"You're gonna get two weeks disability pay, Chester. You don't have any vacation time. So that's all. By looking at you, I'm guessing you'll need something more, so I'll see what I can do."

"Fuck it. It don't matter how long or short. All it means is I gotta go back to the fucking freezer and work with them floating boat-folks again. It ain't worth it."

He ignored me.

"Another thing, Chester. You know the company's got a program for substance abuse. They'll like pay for seventy-five percent of it if you want to enroll in a treatment center. You can do it out-patient like."

"Out patient?"

I sat up to look at him better. Got up too quick so that it pulled on my ribs and made me want to vomit. But I looked him square, at that big black chunk of a face of his, him staring right back. Both of us hard as rocks.

"Treatment?" I yelled, spitting it off my tongue. "Fucking treatment? If you think I'm gonna throw my ass into some Club Detox so I can sit around and hold hands and cry about what a lousy life I've led, you can just fuck-off, Crow."

He remained calm, at least his face did. But I saw something growing in his eyes that didn't look good.

"All I'm saying is you'd better do some drying out, son. Drinking is gonna kill you for sure. You're. . . ."

"Fuck-off."

He crinkled his big face.

"Chester."

"Did I say fuck-off? I'm sorry: fuck-off and get the hell out!"

He was mad. I was mad. Goddamn it, here I had to lie around all day with ugly nurses giving me pain killers and everything smelling like some bathroom deodorizer except when my old man roommate hocked up goobers on his food tray and I couldn't no way even get myself a decent drink or fuck or fight or smoke and here Crow came with all his damn news about money and insurance and goddamn alcohol treatment programs.

"Fuck! Off!" I said again.

"Fuck you too, man," he said before heading for the door. "You stay like this you won't even have a friend to bury you, you son of a bitch."

Then he was gone.

And I was glad he was gone. Glad it was done.

You come into this world all alone and it ain't ever any different as you go along. You're alone, no matter how you slice it. It ain't ever any different. So I guess I am a lucky one, because I like to be alone.

I fucking love alone.

I rang the crawfish nurse for more pain killers and then turned my attention to the goddamn teevee that was perched up on the wall. I had to turn the volume up because the old man behind the curtain had commenced to cough again, hacking up hairballs into his sheets.

What a fucking thing teevee is. God I hate teevee. God I hate hospitals. I hate Crow and Marleen and all the little shithouse jobs there are in the world.

PART TWO

Old Memories & Old Women

CHAPTER TEN

So I was hung up for a spell.

I got home from the hospital and I drank and smoked. I didn't care what the doctor said about it. I survived on grits and egg sandwiches, on beer and pain killers.

I was peaceful alone.

Only there weren't no peace. Though my breathing was a mite irregular and my ribs still felt like hot pokers now and then when I turned wrong, it was my mind that was killing me. And it wasn't Marleen no more—not that I was all past that craziness—but it was something new and just as trouble-some. Something I sure as hell didn't understand. Not that I ever understood much anyways, but it was a deep down fucked feeling no longer centered in my heart but now in my ugly brain. And damned if I could neither shut it off nor shoo it away.

So I lived with it.

Like I lived with my broken heart and my new found physical pain. I got by on drink and hate. And what's wrong with that? It's what drives a goodly portion of this world, I'd say.

Behind my back, Crow had gone and got my company insurance squared away. The hospital bills came on in like carpenter ants, but they all said they was pending on the insurance. I didn't even know I had no insurance. I didn't want no insurance. Fuck. What health did I have to care about? I'd quit the Navy before I could get a pension and any lasting Veterans benefits, far as I knew anyways. But Crow—and I knew it was Crow—had done set me up with the company plan, maybe pulling some strings since he'd been there so long. Too goddamn long.

It's not that I didn't want no man's charity, I just didn't want his.

Anyways, it got to where I'd file all bills and forms in the trash. Anything kind'a official-looking went straight in. They soaked up the grease and backwash-beer pretty good, there at the bottom of the can. I kept the junk mail. Even filled out a sweepstakes, ordering about six magazines I hated the look of. When the magazines came, they'd be pitched too. Phone bill went in the trash too. They disconnect pretty fast in Pensacola, but I didn't have to worry about harassing phone calls, thataway. And any collector coming to my door was making a big mistake, bad ribs or no.

But none did come.

Power bills I paid. I like my electricity. Keeps the coldbeer cold.

A few trips to the liquor store and the Junior Mart was enough exercise for me. And if my checks went bad, I'd buy me some cane alcohol on credit where I knew I could, up in Catamount. I could probably get a lot of things on credit. That's how things worked nowadays.

After two weeks I had things working just fine. My phone was cut. Hospital bills was filed in the trash. My air-conditioner was still broke. But it was winter anyways. In the summer I'd

75

sweat. Folks sweat all over the world. Yes everything was nice and fucking peaceful, except for that little dog of trouble gnawing at my Milkbone brain. But I was working on that, flushing it away with whiskey and no-thoughts.

In fact, I figured I was ready for the good life. That was, until the early morning when a ax come smashing through my bedroom window.

I was in my grainy bed, deep asleep in my pain-killer slumber, when there was a crash. And I mean a CRASH. Because I awoke to find my grey sheets covered with broken glass, along with the dull black of a ax-head lying on the pillow next to me.

There was even a few spots of blood where the slivers had cut me up some when I'd rolled from the noise. It was my bedroom window that was broken, my window shattered by that ax flying on through. I sat up to try and take it in, to survey the mess and gather what few thoughts I could. That's when I spied a face peering in, a old wrinkled face.

It was my neighbor, that old fossil of a woman, Mrs. Guffins. Cecilia, I think her name was, Cecilia Guffins.

I caught her eye and my own began to burn like hellfire.

"What in the goddamn. . . ."

She looked me over, like seeing that I was okay, like it was a apology or something.

"Could you kindly return my ax," she then said, calm as a stick of buttercream.

I was near naked and a bit bloody, and at a loss for crude words for the moment.

"You, you. . . . Crazy old woman. What are you doing? What the hell are you doing?"

I picked up the big ax from my pillow. It was heavy, the head of it black except for the worn silver of the blade. The handle was wood, shiny and brown from where a man's hands had held it.

"Mr. Stubbs, I do apologize. But I am trying to chop down this here pecan tree upon my property, and I need the ax to continue."

Now, this old woman must've been at least eighty or so, and she was telling me she was trying to fell that big old paper-shell pecan tree out my window.

"I am so sorry. I guess I didn't use it proper," she went, "and it slipped some on my back swing."

I knotted a sheet around my nakedness. I brushed the glass off my body, even brushed some fine dust outta my hair. Then I took the ax back up, got up, and looked at her from my broken window, cutting my feet some in the process.

She was dressed in a white jacket and pink pants. She had on some thin little gloves, like going-to-church-on-Sunday gloves. I about laughed. Then I looked her in her old wrinkled face, which was brown and about crusty, the edges of her mouth trembling a bit. But her blue eyes was like doldrums seas, just staring on back at me like she was waiting for a letter from the postman. I kept the sheet wrapped around me with one hand and held that ax up in my other, like the goddamn Statue of Liberty or something.

"Chopping down that big ol' tree? I'd say you was more like trying to kill me."

"Kill you?" she said, fixing me with them quiet blue eyes. "I'd say you're doing a fine job of that on your own, Mr. Stubbs."

I stood there looking as dumb as I'd looked in days. And that's saying something.

"Now please, sir, my ax?"

And I handed it on over. Right through the window it'd done blasted through.

"What you want to chop down that tree for?" I asked, calming, seeing it now as no more'n another weird day in my life. "It's been there a long time. Awful big for a old woman like yourself, ain't it?"

"Well," she said, "I'm not fixing to chop it in one day."

I took me a look at the tree. The big tan trunk of it had a few slashes in it, the white-green of live wood showing in its shadow. I shook my head. Then I looked at my shattered window again and at the glass on my carpet and sheets, and the little dabs of red blood on my arm. She'd done more damage to my window than to that tree. And then my anger rose up again. I didn't need any old folks terrorizing me and wrecking my house.

"Well, goddamnit! Why don't you have your old gizzard of a husband chop it down. Give him something to do with his damn time instead of digging holes in his yard."

The man was always out doing this and that, planting trees and bushes and taking them back out, mowing the lousy grass like he was giving the earth a haircut or something, always working in the heat with his sleeveless tee-shirts and no hat, looking like a fool. They had them a double yard, one that stretched back to the street behind us. Though he'd let the back property go near wild, he was always mighty busy in the other part. I hadn't seen him much, though, not in a long spell.

She blinked some.

"Jeffrey?"

"That's his name. . . . You better get ol' Jeffrey, so I don't go broke fixing my home, if you don't go and kill me first."

She let the heavy end of the ax fall to the ground, put her stare on it for a minute, leaned on it some, then looked back at me.

"I'm afraid Mr. Guffins passed away, Mr. Stubbs. Six months to the day."

"You mean he's dead?" I asked before I could stop.

"Yes. . . . He is."

Then I stopped. I felt damn stupid and pitiful. Looking at her leaning on that old ax, about lost to the world, I stopped being a mad ass.

"Well. . . . Ma'am. . . . I'd say you done enough for one morning."

She nodded her old blue-hair head.

"I'd say you are right."

She raised her face and looked over at that tree. Seeing her do it, I felt mighty bad for her. I never did know her or her husband much. The man came off as a sonofabitch—to speak ill of the dead—but they was a quiet couple. It looked like maybe she was gonna cry.

"You want a cup of coffee, Ma'am?" I asked.

"Coffee?"

"Come on over and we'll have a cup in my kitchen."

And so she did.

I washed myself up a bit, avoiding my face in the mirror, and threw on some unwashed jeans and a tee shirt that was lying handy on the floor. And by the time I toddled into my own damn kitchen there she was. That old lady had done found my can of coffee, the filters and square of chicory, and the greasy machine was already spurting it out like thick crude.

"I see you like chicory, Mr. Stubbs." Now she was running some water in my sink, was washing up a couple of stained cups. "I've always been partial to it myself. Makes your coffee last."

I sat at the table. She washed them cups, disinfecting all the diseases and all, and then rummaged around for spoons and napkins and such. I let her, seeing as how she didn't look to be stopped.

"Where do you keep your sugar?"

"Don't use it," I said.

She stopped and turned to look at me, me sitting there good as a baboon without a shave or a shot of whiskey to his name.

"Never?"

"Never much," I said, feeling kind'a oddball about it, about why this here woman was in my kitchen cross-examining me about goddamn sugar.

"Oh, Mr. Stubbs. You want something so bitter, you just got to have a little sugar. Didn't you know that?"

I shrugged.

"Maybe down there."

I pointed to the low corner cupboard where there was baking stuff and muffin pans, a place I don't think I'd opened since Marleen left. For all I knew, the roaches had done made a motel out of the Bisquick box.

Sure enough, the sugar was in there. Half a sack wrapped in clear plastic with a big rubberband holding it tight. Sugar all done up like a suicide.

She unwrapped it, kind'a attacked it with a spoon to break it up, and then poured some into a little bowl that I didn't know I had. And by then the coffee was done dribbling and she poured us some in fresh washed cups and set them on the table.

Then that old blue neighbor lady set the sugar bowl down, down right directly between us, two spoons sticking out. . . . The hell. . . . I reached over and put a dollop in my cup, right where the whiskey should'a gone.

We sat in silence for a spell, sipping, listening to the dawn birds twitter outdoors. Been a while since I had heard anything

80

but hoot owls. I got to wondering just why that old lady–
Cecilia Guffins–why she wanted that big pecan tree down.
The branches of that tree reached out far, out over my roof as
well as hers. When the wind blew and Marleen and me was
lying in bed, we used to hear them nuts fall and roll on the
roof. Sometimes we'd hear the scuttle of squirrels chasing
after them pecans. . . . That was a hell of a thing for me to
think of: Marleen and me in bed, the rattle of pecans and
squirrels. . . . The Guffins never did pick that tree. Marleen
and me never cared for pecans either.

But I got to thinking of that old woman with that lumberjack-
ax out my window. She up before the starlings and doves to
take swings at some tree trunk thicker than my own belly, let
alone hers.

And I always thought I was the crazy one on the block.

"Now," I said, breaking our little peace across the table,
"why is it you want to chop down that tree for?"

She looked up at me with them calm eyes of hers that about
favored her dinosaur-blue hair.

"For my late husband."

"Mr. Guffins?"

"Yes. You see, he was always a light sleeper and the falling
of those pecans in the summer tormented him... I was all for
paying some young man to come and chop it down, but Jeffrey
refused. Mr. Guffins was always saying he'd do it himself."

"And he never?"

"He never did get around to it. Never did. He was quite
sick for a few years. . . . So I took it upon myself to do it for
him."

"Why don't you let me do it for you."

She took a look at me, me barefoot, my pants stained, my
ugly tee-shirt riding up over my red gut, showing my bandages
and wrap along my hurt ribs. I looked at her look.

81

"Soon as I heal up," I said and pulled my shirt down. "I'll heal up quick and chop that tree for you. I can start in the morning and have you a stump by nightfall."

I felt a mite proud for offering.

"No thank you, Mr. Stubbs."

"No thank you?"

"No," she said and gave me a smile. "I intend to do it all myself. I don't care how long it takes. No one is touching that tree but me."

"You ain't gonna chop down no tree. You're about ninety-nine years old and. . . ."

"I'm seventy-three, Mr. Stubbs. That doesn't mean a thing. The tree is on my property and I can do what I please with it. I apologize about your window and will pay to have it fixed, but if I want to chop down a tree, whatever my age, it shouldn't mean a thing to you."

She had a lot of spunk for a old woman whose parents was probably oil deposits about now. I figured that tree to be on the property line, but I wasn't gonna argue that. Truth was, I just couldn't ever see her felling that pecan.

"But how you think that thing is gonna come on down? What if it smashes through your roof—or mine—just because your old man couldn't bear the sound of a pecan or two."

"It doesn't matter how it comes down, or where," she said, a mite angry all of a sudden. "All that matters is that it does come down. . . . And as for Mr. Guffins—God rest him—don't think he didn't hear you and your Tom-cat ways over here. And you drinking like a fish all the time. No sir. It was more than falling pecans that kept him awake at night, Mr. Stubbs."

That got my hackles up.

"You do what you want and I do what I want. Like you said, it ain't none of no one's business."

I got up and poured myself more coffee, this time reaching under the sink for a squirt of whiskey. No sugar. She watched but didn't say a thing.

"I got my own problems, lady. You want to kill yourself over a tree, go on ahead. Just don't drop it on my property or I'll get me a lawyer."

She got up and poured her own self some coffee. Put in two spoons of sugar. But she didn't sit down. She went and stood by the door.

"You know, Chester Stubbs, I saw you that night out on your garage roof, with that woman. It was but three days after my Jeffrey took ill for the first time and was in the hospital. I was alone in the house. I heard you and saw you howling like some animal, drinking your liquor and carrying on with that woman. I saw it, you know. I saw your wife come home to find you. And I saw enough. Then I went on back to bed, alone, and I tell you now that I cried. And I don't cry much, Mr. Stubbs. But I did cry that night and I don't think I was crying for my husband, either."

And with that she turned and opened my kitchen door. I was struck dumb and felt about as low as ironed dirt. And before she left, she looked at me, she held up my cup with my coffee in it and almost smiled.

"See you tomorrow, young man," she said, then shut the door.

CHAPTER ELEVEN

And I did see her tomorrow.

Only, not till after spending my evening chewing over that night in mention. The night Marleen finally caught me in the act. And what a goddamned act it was.

I mean, after Cecilia Guffins left, I went and did my usual nothing. I got through the afternoon and hit the whiskey before evening come. I went on up to the Junior Mart and got a new case of Blue Ribbon Beer, a pack of bologna, white bread and a onion. That was dinner. And after that I took my pain-killers and my don't-give-a-damn-killers: my whiskey and my smokes. Then I sat down to watch the teevee for a spell, or what I come to call the opium box.

Though I never had smoked a thing other than cigarettes, the teevee was what I figured it'd be like. Smoking drugs. Only a little less interesting, I reckon. So I settled on down in front of the opium box, half gone as usual, but this time it wouldn't play its trick. I just couldn't get myself all numbed-up and dumbed-up, so that them Hollywood shows that was so funny or interesting before just came off as plain stupid.

That night they did.

And so I turned the damn thing off and listened to the muffly traffic noise from on down the block. And pretty soon I wasn't listening to nothing but my own fool self, and that's when I come about rehashing that night Marleen found me on the carport roof with Trisha-Lee, the grocery store girl.

Like I said before, it was a full moon night. And there was a while that I blamed it on the moon, on that big reckless yeller ball up there, because I weren't willing to blame it on myself. Not yet, anyways.

We'd been married near four years, Marleen and I. She was a R.N. and I was finished with the service, the Navy, which I hated every damn second of. So I wasn't working but was thinking of maybe doing some construction work, like I'd done when I dropped out of high school way back when, when I was seventeen and doing concrete work in Montgomery. Doing shit work. And after three years of that I got smart enough to earn my GED, but then I was fool enough to turn around and sign up with the Navy. Anyways, Marleen was going through a spell working nights then. Graveyard shift kind'a crap. She was sleeping most of the day and so it got to where I was doing the grocery shopping and other stuff all by myself. And that's how I come to meet up with Trisha-Lee. At the damn Winn Dixie store.

She was a plump little thing. Plump in all the right places. And I got to admit I was noticing her right from the start. She was a cashier, and it was about the third time through—with me making sure to get in her lane—that she started to talk to me. She talked the kind'a talk it took a while for me to catch on to. The kind'a talk where what she'd said wasn't what she was talking about. Not at all. But once I caught on, well, I learned that language awful damn quick. We was flirting bad as a couple of pimply teenagers—which Trisha-Lee almost was.

Anyways, I was always a drinker and with Marleen working nights I got to where I was hitting the beach bars when she was gone. I didn't want to drink at home and didn't have no real friends other than Crow, and I knew he either wouldn't or couldn't of gone, so I asked Trisha. Winn Dixie Trish, I called her. And she was just dumb enough to think it was cute.

And it was but twice, two times of us out together like that, that we ended up screwing in my car. From then on, we had us a regular parking spot out by the bayside and she'd have to climb on top of me while we done it. She didn't mind none and I was right satisfied. And I thought I was so damn smart, that I was getting the best of two women. I was a man of gusto, I believed, a man who could have any ol' thing he wanted.

It must'a been going on for a whole of two months before I slipped up. Surprised it went that long, really. I mean, between the drinking and the fucking around and my own general don't-give-a-shit attitude, well, maybe I was a hankering to get caught. Just maybe.

It was that flat full moon night when we went all out. We was down at the beach, on a Sunday of all nights, at a fast-times bar called The Docks. . . . I can still recall it: "The Docks Rocks: Rum and Reggae every Sunday." It was as good as religion. . . . And we got all fucked up, Trisha-Lee and me. We was wild as a couple of bandicoots, whatever they is, and weren't paying any attention to the time or how much we was drinking. So we about closed the joint, on a Sunday night, and I was so tired of just fucking in the car. We'd been plowing through rum and cocolas at the bar, but I had me a full bottle of tequila iced down in my car-cooler—and I always had a cooler in the car in them days—and so we drank at it straight and I figured to drive her on to the house, screw her till the porch light burned out, then get her gone before Marleen got off work. That was the plan I had.

The hell. I didn't have no plan. I doubt I even thought about Marleen.

All I liked was the feel of that cold tequila on my tongue and the feel of Trisha's chubby little hand in my drawers as we drove down the road to Warrington. The moon was out over the waters and she was hot as a fresh oven biscuit, mauling me as we drove and drank and I was trying my best to rearrange her undergarments one-handed, in between drinks from the bottle. And by the time we was in my driveway and stopped, both our clothes was already off and I don't know what damn thing possessed me—other than the drink and the natural sex of the situation—but I flung ol' Winn Dixie Trish over my big shoulder, doing a fireman carry up the driveway, her ample behind pressed against my unshaved face, and commenced to toss her on up onto the carport roof. Like King Kong or something, I just jotted her up there on the building top. I was tall enough and strong enough I could raise her up and more'less roll her on to that dirty roof, her giggling the whole while. I set that bottle of tequila up there too. Then I took hold and pulled myself up, easier than I suspected. And there we was.

There we was indeed.

There we was, the two of us, me a married man of four years with my wife at hardwork, and she but some twenty-one year old grocery clerk; there we was with a full sticky moon shining down outta the bright night sky; there we was naked and excited and drinking from the bottle. And then she went right on down on me, her hair-sprayed head slipping and bobbing and slipping on me and I let out a howl. I screamed me a wolf howl for no other reason than I felt like it. And then I laid her on down, right near the edge and we was screwing up there with her ass getting all scraped up by the cinders and pecan shells and regular sticks and shit but us not caring, me still pulling off a howl now and then because she seemed to like it so, us just gone mad-fucking-mad till some car lights swung in the driveway and there was Marleen below us.

Spotted like coons in a tree, we was.

I could see my Marleen's face in the windshield, looking up, a face more astonished and pained than anything I'd ever done seen in my life. And then she was out and slamming the door, standing below and cursing and yelling and I didn't know what Trisha-Lee was saying but all I knew was I'd done come to the edge, I'd led myself to the edge of something and it was a hell of a lot higher and a hell of a lot steeper a fall than the one from that carport roof.

And that was how it happened.

I was living a life of cartoon grandness one minute, the next I was done banished to misery. Real and hopeless misery.

I denied it and fought it all best I could, but that's what it come down to. I know I was between jobs with too much time on my hands. I know Marleen was working nights and we wasn't seeing each other too often. Sure, that girl was no innocent and I was drinking heavy. Sure, there was the full moon. I knew all that. Know all that. Marleen knows it all too, because that's what I offered up as a excuse.

I guess the truth was, I was just bored. I was bored and I forgot what good things I had, forgot I had Marleen and that if I'd got off my ass and found a job right away—like Marleen wanted me to—then I wouldn't of fallen so damn far.

Maybe.

Though I probably never will damn know.

Truth is, I just fucked up and I couldn't go back and undo it. That's what it all boils down to.

Marleen and I tried to make it work again, both of us in the house. But it didn't. Couldn't. So we separated and I moved out of the house and to the beach. I lived in a little efficiency above a bar, signed up for the Reserve, and I tried to hook back up with Trisha-Lee. But by then she was gone. She'd done taken off with some kid in his van, moving out west somewheres, to one of them coastal states where they talk more about orgasms than they ever have them.

And as damn sorry as I was, I thought I could handle it. Or maybe I thought Marleen would always be there, that she'd–that we'd–come on back together.

Her moving outta the house didn't throw me much. Not even the actual divorce didn't do it. Nope. It wasn't until I knew she'd gone to Alabama, and then later seeing that picture from Conettycut, that's when it finally hit home on me. That's how I knew it was over and I was alone again. Maybe for good.

And a man shouldn't have to be alone, if you think of it right. Seems there's enough people in this world that you shouldn't have to be alone if'n you don't want to be.

Seems like it, anyways.

So that's what I recalled, that night, in the house, sitting there with the teevee off and the night quiet enough to make you sick.

CHAPTER TWELVE

It got so that every morning I'd get woke by the sweet whunk of Cecilia Guffins putting ax to wood. She had done had my window fixed and I had got her to swing away from it. But my window was always open for the fresh air, and before the sun could shine she was out there, lopping that blade into the flesh of that pecan tree. The sound of it was about softer than a sparrow's call, it was, but it was enough to get me up. And she didn't seem to care none. She was making her own idea of progress. And she was at it early enough and quit soon enough that, except for waking me, she never did attract much attention or cause no concerns in the neighborhood—not that there was much of a neighborhood left around us anymore.

There I'd be in my bed, dreaming my bad whiskey dreams, my ribs only paining me now at nightfall or when the air dropped for a squall coming in off the Gulf, so I'd be half-assed asleep and then her soft chopping would commence and wake me. It was a good wake up. Then sometimes I'd take a peek at that old lady out there, shake my head, get dressed and washed and go make the coffee. Because she always come in for coffee. It was between us now, a regular thing as long as I was at home, not working, convalescing for being such a fuck-up.

I even had me sugar in a bowl.

One such morning, I woke up and looked out to see here there, going about her self-appointed role as pecan tree killer, looking healthy there in the grey light, moving slow motion while hauling that big ax upward and then letting it fly fast against the trunk. And so, since she'd be in soon, I went ahead and got going and made a pot.

While the coffee was chugging, I sat down and fingered a cigarette. Never did care for smoking in the morning, but I didn't let not caring about things stop me too often. I had a little shot glass of whiskey there with me and sipped at it and considered smoking and just kind of ruminated on how things had gone lately.

I hadn't heard shit from Crow. My mail would come and I'd see my medical bills was paid except for my share. I was getting past-due notices but still could not bring myself to write a fucking check. I was also about out of sick pay and was told that I'd be laid off soon if I didn't come on down to the warehouse and talk to so-and-so and do such-a-such in the fucking personnel office. I guess what I figured—and what I wanted—was I'd get laid off and could live on unemployment for half a year or so.

That seemed like a damn good idea to me.

Also I was afraid to see Crow.

Not just Crow but the whole lot of them, even the two Vietnamese brothers in the freezer. I didn't want them to see me so ugly and broken. I don't know why I gave a damn about that, but I guess I did. It was Crow most of all. Like I said, I had not even heard a cuss word from him since I kicked him out of my hospital room.

But other than that little worm of grief, I was fine all shut up at my house. Fine enough. I could drink and eat and fart and listen to music and watch the trash on the opium box. I had me my crazy neighbor lady for morning companionship and my nights were for drink and smoke and as little thinking as possible.

That was good enough for me.

Mrs. Guffins came in the door, wiping her old prune of a face with a white hanky. She was plumb worn down after going at that tree for a hour or so.

"Mr. Stubbs," she said

"Hey, Cecilia," I said.

She smiled at me. Then she glanced at the pack of cigs and my wet shot glass on the table. She kind'a made a sound in her throat, a soft little chit chit like a squirrel being smothered with a cotton ball or something. I guess she couldn't help it none. But other than that, she never said much about our different ways.

We sat quiet for a bit while she composed herself from her morning activities. I sat listening to the damn birds and the beginning of morning traffic and all those other early sounds I'd not heard much in a while. Then Mrs. Guffins kind'a sat back a bit, stirred her coffee a little and placed her spoon along side the cup, moving slow like a turtle or like one of them tree sloths I seen once on teevee.

"Mr. Stubbs, did I tell you how Mr. Guffins was wounded?"

"In the war?"

"From the war," she said.

Her husband had been in World War Two. A Army man. She had done told me a bit about that, about him being in the second wave after D-Day and going to the German front and him being involved in the Battle of the Bulge. Nothing too specific, but making sure I knew he'd taken part in the history of the world.

"You mean he took some shrap or maybe he was. . . ." I put my hand up to my temple and googled my eyes.

She didn't like that. She gave me that distasteful look like when she done saw my whiskey.

"He was shot, Mr. Stubbs. Through his arm." She grabbed her own white biceps to show me where. "It was in Amsterdam."

"Amsterdam? Where the hell's that? France?"

"Holland."

"Shot in the arm protecting windmills, huh?"

She was losing patience with me. I was being a ass, even with old Cecilia Guffins.

"I'm sorry, Ma'am," I said. "Go on."

"Mr. Stubbs, he was shot after the war was over, when the Americans were effectively the police in the city. You see. . . Now, I'm telling you this for a reason, Chester. This is unflattering toward my late husband. But he was a young man and had just been through a war, a horrid war you understand. . . He was a Sergeant then and one of his men had guard duty that night but the man's girlfriend was coming to visit. And this man, one of Jeffrey's men, made sure to tell them all to leave this girl alone. I suppose he had good reason to worry, as these women were no saints."

If they was saints—I wanted to say—no one'd ever had anything to do with them. I poured us some more coffee. She stirred hers up and commenced with the story.

"Well, maybe you can guess it. But Jeffrey, he knew his man was on duty, late, and so he went to visit this woman. Now, Mr. Guffins and I were acquainted at this time. We were young sweethearts and though we were not engaged we both had promised. But, how shall we say, he being a young soldier and I a long way away and not that we ever would have, well, they ended up in bed. And who should come in but the girl's supposed boyfriend. And though Jeffrey was a fellow soldier, his own Sergeant no less, that private shot him. He shot him with a pistol."

She rested her spoon with that.

"In the arm?"

"That's right. It went clean through and left him with a scar, a permanent reminder of his indiscretion. It was forever an embarrassment for him, to have gone through a war like that and be wounded afterwards, in such a manner. That scar was also something he had to explain to me, a thing I forgave him for, when he got home and proposed."

"I see," I said, but I did not.

I mean, the man had been in a war and had the tough luck to pay for a little hanky-panky. A tough luck story, was all it was. I just hoped that little Dutch girl was good enough in the gunny sack to get shot for. . . . But thinking of it, I couldn't recall seeing no scar on that man. Not that I ever looked at him too close—he was about ugly as a man's ass. But I think I'd of noticed a thing like that.

"This was right after the war," she went on, "back when a man's honor still meant something to himself, it meant something to one's fiancee and one's family. Especially a Southern Baptist family, like ourselves."

She looked at me, wanting me to see something that weren't there.

"Chester, a man can bring himself low and confess to his mistakes. He can then rise back up and live a life of honor. Do you see?"

And she was still looking at me. So I sipped my coffee like I was thinking that one over.

"Yes Ma'am," I offered up, serious like.

And she let it go at that.

But there weren't nothing on my mind but the thinking of a naked lady in a bed in Holland.

Mrs. Guffins went on home before nine A.M., in a good mood and ready to rest up for tomorrow's murder attempt on that pecan tree.

As for me, I had other things to attempt.

Turned out I'd done run out of them pain pills. The doctor said last time he wouldn't give me no more. I tried to get it on with the nurse over the pay phone down the block, told her I was a vet and all—even if the only blood I ever spilled was in a boxing ring. But she didn't buy it. She said that the doc said enough was enough.

So I went over to eat eggs and grits at the Awful-Waffle House for lunch and, seeing how I couldn't get no pills, I invested in a jug of George Dickle and a carton of Camels.

The day's air was about like walking through wet moss, it was so heavy. When I got home I closed all the drapes against the sun, stripped naked and took a cold shower. And I never put any clothes back on. I just spent my afternoon naked as a shelled shrimp, smoking and sipping whiskey, walking circles into my ratty carpet, the radio on for noise.

As I paced I did think some about Mrs. Guffins, trying to figure why she went and told me about her husband. I mean, we'd got to where we did talk some about each other, but it weren't much. That was the most she'd ever said about him, or about herself really. I reckon it made her feel good to confide in me and maybe she wanted me to return the favor. Not that I never thought she was trying to pick my brain, but maybe she wanted me to tell her some pointless facts from my past or something. . . . Well, if so, I wasn't about to oblige her any.

I wasn't even about to oblige myself.

Past suppertime, when my ribs was usually beginning to ache, when most folks was all home and settled and traffic had slowed and dogs was getting quiet and snoozy, I was calm with the whiskey and nothing to eat but a can of boiled peanuts. Anyways, I thought I was calm, but within a few hours, my mind began to gnaw at my skull. Some recollection, a thing long ago, was coming into focus, whether I liked it or not.

The memory was fetched up out of my mind. Don't know why it come, but it did. Like a air bubble rising from deep water, it come up and up, trying to break the surface.

It was from when I was a kid.

It was when my Mama sent me down to see my Daddy's kin one summer. I must of been maybe ten or so, hell, maybe just eight, and she and I was living in Jackson, Mississippi then. We was right in the city, in a apartment, where all I had was the streets and a burnt grass park to play in. So I guess she figured she should send me on down to Vernon, Florida—which was where my Daddy had been born, where most of his folks was still at—so I could see some other side of life.

I'd never known my Daddy. Maybe I had some recollect of him sometime when I was a kid, some idea of a voice, but by the time I went down to the little town of Vernon, those recollections was all mixed up with friend's fathers and teevee show fathers and such. I had no real memory of him except for pictures, which were few. But the pictures was just a face, a body, and I had no memory of who the man was. And maybe my Daddy was a fine boy, a good young man, but he wasn't much of a father from what Mama said, and anyways, he was killed in a knife fight outside a saloon, drunk, over money bet on cockfighting. I was but three, I think. Maybe it happened in Alabama. Or maybe it was in Jackson, and that was why we was stuck there.

Anyways, my Daddy was not the memory that come on up.

What I remember was taking a Greyhound ride to De Funiak Springs with my Uncle John, who was my Mama's younger and only brother, a man finishing up as a grunt for the Air Force down at Eglin. In De Funiak was where my Aunt—my Daddy's sister—met me and took me on into Vernon.

I sat up front in the car with her and saw for myself how green and neat a town it was, full of them big ol' oaks all scrambled with vine, houses with grass yards and no weeds, flowers, dog's houses, and cats staring out the front screen porches. And there was a clean flat river flowing on the north side of town. Fed from a cold spring, my Aunt said. Such a pretty river, water clear and good enough to drink, the far side all banked thick with tall grass and trees.

Come to think of it, I don't know if my Mama wanted me to go. Maybe it was them relatives that wanted me to come and visit, to see me, the son of their son who had gone out and got himself killed over some chickens. That's probably it, because my Mama didn't ever mention them, and she sure as hell didn't go with me. Anyways, I didn't stay long myself.

I was rightly perplexed by it all, being in that town and meeting all these sudden cousins and aunts and a uncle. Even a grandmother in there, I believe. That first night I laid on a strange bed, not sleeping, everything smelling unusual and too clean for where I was from. And the next day, after lunch, they sent me out to play with all the little yokels, a third of them some blood of mine one way or another.

We started playing in the yards of the town. I was with a couple of first cousins of mine, Doug and Tommy was their names. Doug was about my age, I recall, and Tommy was a good two years ahead of me. Anyways, we played whatever the shit we played and the gang kind'a kept growing and we kind'a kept making our way along the road, till we was up to where the river cut in and there was a big grassy bank. And where there was a huge ol' oak tree. It was the biggest damn tree I'd ever seen, its roots going out into that shallow sand bottom, catching things, making a kind'a grey pool out there, where elsewhere you could about walk across, water up to your chest maybe in the middle. And the boys all stripped off their dusty tee-shirts and commenced to clamber up on this tree.

It was deep into summer and hot as ticks on a hound dog, so that water was awful inviting. These little town kids had a thick rope tied to the tree limb, a brown rope frayed some where they took a hold of it, where they swung themselves out like little Tarzans and Janes to plop down in the soft pool of the river. They'd been doing it all summer, the boys and most of the girls, because they had all these different branches and different styles they was doing, different twists and flips and different ways to come splashing down and swim back to the dirt and grass, laughing.

I stood and watched. Struck dumb.

I just watched those bastards swing off that tree into the water, not even thinking to take my sweaty shirt off. It was a whole new world to me. I never thought folk could live like that, I guess. And maybe I got to thinking that that was what I should'a had, what I should'a been: just some careless kid spending my summers swimming in that easy river, sneaking smokes behind the weeds, scaring girls about cottonmouths or copperheads, shit like that. Maybe I thought that, as I stood there in the heat watching my brand new cousins show off and play and go about their boyhood business. All I know is my mind went from a state of awe to kind of bitter-like. My mean streak got set in my brain. The same kind'a blind mean I'd use someday to step into the ring to box. Even way back then I guess I had it.

Of course, it didn't help none that they began to tease me.

Tommy and Doug wanted me to get up and jump from the highest branch. They wanted me to swing way out and show off, or make an ass of myself. But I wasn't gonna. I wasn't even going up that tree. And so they began to tease me because of it, saying I was afraid of heights, afraid of snakes, I was like some of the girls who only got the river sand between their toes. And all it did was make me directly meaner and madder, straight at them.

I wasn't scared of that tree. It was the water. I couldn't swim.

I hadn't learned how to swim yet, what growing up in Jackson. And here was these guys, blood cousins to boot, giving me shit for not plunging into the river. And maybe I would have gone and done it, because I wasn't really that scared of water, but because they was riding me so hard and I was already pissed, it just plain set me against doing anything they wanted me to do. I was stubborn as the trunk of that oak. Anyways, I wasn't about to drown either, just to prove something for them two idiots.

"You're scared, Chester. Plumb scared."

"You're afeared of climbing this tree."

"He can play with the girls. He's afeared. Chester the molester is afeared. He can go molest the girls."

So they hung from that tree and called me Chester the molester. Where that came from I didn't know, but they seen it got my goat and so I got called it by about everyone there, me new in town and standing there and being called names, all of them happy and safe on their home ground. Just another day in their long summer.

"Come on over here," I finally said. "Come on down and come over here."

That got everyone's hopes up. My cousins smiled and came on down. All them little kids gathered around, agitating us, begging us to fight. Kids are a lot like adults. They like fights. Only difference is, they ain't ashamed to like them.

There was this little building made outta logs, like a shelter, open on a side, that was built along the riverbank. The three of us went in there, not saying a thing, each of us waiting for someone to make the threat stick. The other kids blocked the open side, bunching up and closing off the light, waiting to see Doug and Tommy teach a lesson to their little lost cousin.

They came up on me slow, arms out, ready to wrestle me down to the damp dirt. I don't know what they thought. Maybe get me down, twist my arm, kick me a little, spit in my mouth. I don't know. But I busted them in the chops. Both of them. I was bigger than Doug. Tommy had a couple years on me, was a good size taller than me, but he wasn't no wider. I took them by surprise by smacking them. First I hit Doug and he fell. Tommy'd been so cocksure and wasn't expecting me to use my fists, maybe that's why he didn't move, so I poked him in the jaw, once, twice, and he fell too.

Doug got up and ran, cutting right through the wall of screaming kids. They parted for him, laughed and yelled, and then closed the hole back up, like blood turning to scab. Tommy got onto one knee, then up, and he took a swing at me. A kid's swing. I think maybe it hit me, maybe not, but it didn't matter. I felt cold and calm and everything everybody did was slow and turtle like. I could smell everything and taste my own spit like it was sugar water. I could hear all them individual kids, each yell and scream, the girls from the boys, and my eyes looked at Tommy but they also saw everything else plain and simple and focused like a photograph.

Goddamn I could feel it. And I took my fist and buried it into my cousin's nose. Almost straight on. Blood flew and he crumpled down. And as I watched him fall I could see the kids behind him as they rustled about with mighty surprised faces, and I remember that—past Tommy's head and over and behind them kids, outside of the dust and shadow of that little shelter—I could see where that river ran flat with sunlight and the dark shading of the full trees on the opposite bank and there were some older girls playing in that shade, some little southern sweethearts looking around in the mud for clams or fossils or whatever, their skirts bunched up over their bumpy knees. I honestly saw it and took it all in, right past ol' Tommy's sinking headbone. . . . And even then, I knew I'd never make it over to that shady bank on the other side of that river, where those girls was. Especially now, I knew it, now that I had gone and beat-up my cousins who I'd just known for a day. I would never have Tommy's childhood. Never. And I jumped on him and punched him and broke his nose in two places.

There was plenty of screaming which got plenty of attention. I don't recall being pulled off, but I was. Tommy had to go down to Panama City to have his nose set, his Mama and Daddy near wanting to kill me. I was sent on back to Jackson the next day, riding the bus by myself with a note pinned to my sleeve saying who I was and where I was to go. Sent away, never to be called upon to return to my father's home town again.

But I can still recall that river like a dream, long and sweet with its current curling down them low banks and flooding the far tall-grass and trees. And those young girls. I was just a redhead freckled kid, but even then I had some inkling about those girls in their drooping summer dresses. Even then I had a idea about what would never be mine.

That was what'd come bubbling up: Vernon, Florida, a good twenty-five years ago. My pummeling my only cousins I ever knew. And look at me now, pacing around my shack of a house in Pensacola, alone, in the dark, a naked man drinking whiskey from a jelly jar. Think of that.

I did.

And it left me cold.

I put my glass on the window sill. Put the bottle under the sink. I put on some boxer shorts and a tee-shirt and went to bed.

CHAPTER THIRTEEN

The next day I was up with the worms. Weren't even a bird call to mention. My ribs was smarting like it was gonna rain and I got up to look-see out my window. It was a mite misty, but I didn't think it was gonna storm none. I was up so early that Mrs. Guffins wasn't even out yet.

I went to the dusty mirror on my dresser, undressed, and removed my bandages, looking at the black and green bruises where my ribs'd been mashed. It was a mite better, despite the coloring and the weather-ache. I was debating whether to fit myself up with some new wraps when I heard that familiar whock. My alarm clock of ax against tree.

I went to the window again and there she was, dressed in her long loose pants and tennis shoes, wearing a plastic jacket against the mist. I saw her take her little snail swings against that tree trunk, poking out wedges and splinters, exposing

102

white tree flesh from where it had discolored from the morning before.

That old lady.

And it dawned on me that, providing she didn't croak trying, maybe Mrs. Guffins really would fell that big pecan tree. And maybe I ought to concern myself with not only how that tree was gonna come down, but what the hell she intended to do with it afterwards. . . . Like I said, she and her late Mister Jeffrey had a long piece of property. It extended on way back to the block behind us, skinny, but a double lot. There weren't nothing on back there but a ratty old chain link, unkept banana plants and a midget forest of sea oaks and magnolias growing all over, where the mice and lizards and a armadilla or two lived. So if'n she could drop it that way—and the angle she was chopping at looked like that's what she was shooting for—if she dropped her that way, then the tree could lie on down and our roofs would only have the tail-end of the branches to contend with. But that was asking a lot from old Cecilia Guffins, like asking for a royal flush at the bottom of a deck. So, I knew I'd have to do something eventually, even if it meant finishing it off myself.

But even as determined as she was, steady as a bullfrog call on a moonlit night, I probably had a lot of time till I needed to worry. She'd hardly dropped a twig after all that chopping, let alone a whole goddamned tree.

Mrs. Guffins and I had our usual coffee and chatter, only—when I thought she weren't looking—I dripped some whiskey into my cup. But when I turned around, she was staring right at me.

"What?" I said.

She lowered her eyes, slow, like one of them electric garage doors closing down.

103

"Nothing, Mr. Stubbs."

I sat and took a few sips but then she was staring at me again.

"You know, I had an aunt who liked her whiskey. . . ."

Oh boy, I wanted to say, but just sat and took what was coming.

"She was a fun aunt, the mother of my two favorite cousins, Ruth and Aaron. But some of that fun in her was due to her drinking, though I didn't know it till later. By the time I was old enough to see it, she was not so much fun anymore. She was ignoring her own wonderful children, drinking during the day and smoking, always off finding some hidy-hole where she kept herself a bottle. She liked it sweet, with cola or Bubble Up, but then she got to where she liked it any old way. Straight from the bottle even. Her husband tried to get her to stop. So did her mother and father, her minister. But she turned her back on them all, just like she did to her children. And by the time she was forty, she looked about sixty. And by the time she was fifty, she was almost insane, Mr. Stubbs. They had to put her away, in what we then called a sanitarium."

She ended her story there, unfinished-like I thought. So I asked.

"She ever get on out? Of the nuthouse, I mean?"

"Yes, she did."

"Quit drinking?"

"Yes."

"And now she's a church-going grandma who won't even allow the mention of whiskey in her house."

"No, Chester. She died on her fifty-second birthday."

Okay, I figured. Folks die young all the time. Maybe cancer, maybe a train wreck, maybe plugging the damn radio in the wrong way. Mrs. Guffins just wanted to scare me, but I weren't scared. No sir. So I shrugged, wagged my head like it was a shame and all, and then I went back to my cup of spiked coffee.

She didn't say much more either.

Mrs. Guffins seemed a little down, though. Maybe because of me, or maybe she was realizing how far she had to go on that tree, seeing how crazy the whole idea was. But whatever the case, she wasn't gonna let me in on it.

After she left I moped around a bit. Ate some grits with bacon, cheese, garlic powder and red pepper all mixed in. I got to thinking maybe I'd get out of the damn house. Maybe I'd go on over to Gulf Breeze and visit the zoo, stare at some animals in cages or something. But that plan was shot right quick, as quick as the fucking ping of my doorbell ringing.

At least I was dressed.

I had to wonder who the hell it was. A bill collector, I suspected most. It wasn't Mrs. Guffins—she would'a come in the kitchen. I had a kind of hope maybe it was Crow, coming on over to see me and I could offer up some half-ass apology and thank him. But it weren't any of that. Because when I opened the door, there stood them two Asians from the warehouse, Duck and Wayne, standing there in the heat, smiling and holding their baseball caps in their small hands.

"Chester Stubbs," the older of the two, Duck, said.

Wayne stood and grinned, a new-lit cigarette in his fingers.

I was right surprised and just kind of stood staring, my big shoulders blocking up the doorway. I think they thought I was mad or something.

"Maybe we should have call?" said one.

"A bad time?" said the other.

I remembered my manners, at least what was left of them.

"Oh hey. Nah. Come on in, c'mon."

I stepped out of the way and held the paint-peeling door for them. They gave me that slight bow of theirs, like they

105

had at the hospital, which always made me feel kind of embarrassed or something, and walked on into my living room, the one of them putting out his cigarette on my front step, as if I gave a damn about smoking in the house.

I closed the door behind me and went to the trouble to open the curtains, letting the first light in for what seemed like months, sending dust motes all about like a cloud of lovebugs. They didn't say nothing, they just stood there with their heads tucked in their shoulders waiting for me to tell them to sit down.

"Sit down. . . . Right yonder, on the couch."

They did.

"Ya'll like a drink? Whiskey? Beer? Iced tea?"

They looked at each other, then at me.

"Tea. Ice tea."

"Okay. Be right back."

I went in the kitchen and made a couple glasses of instant. It looked like lousy stuff so I threw in some bottle lemon juice and stirred in some sugar. I grabbed me a coldbeer.

I went back on out.

"Here you go."

They took their drinks, looked at them and set them down on the coffee table without so much as a sip, then looked at me as I sat in my broken-down chair.

"I hope you don't mind us stopping," Wayne said. "We have been thinking of you at work. We wonder if you are okay, if you are coming back to work with us."

I took a sip of the beer and acted like I was thinking it over.

"Well, my ribs is still a mite sore. Don't think I could push all that frozen shit around yet, let alone do Marty's work besides my own." They smiled. "Can't rightly say when I'll be back. Or even if'n I'll be back. . . . Why, you guys miss me?"

I was joking, but they smiled even wider.

"Yeah," they said, like they actually meant it. "It get very boring without you."

"You are a funny man," Duck said and the two of them kind'a cracked up. "You keep things going."

Then Wayne got up from his seat and put his arms out from his sides, looking like some orangutan, and he mussed up his hair and I realized that he was doing a imitation of me.

Duck just sat and laughed a silent laugh.

Wayne walked around, pretending to load things or push a pallet-jack and he pointed at me.

"Ah, shit this, fuck this. Marty you got a tomcat in you ass." He was laughing, the two of them just right yucking it up in my living room. "This work for fucking penguins."

He went on for a little while longer, making fun, and I couldn't help but let a smile come on me. I'd never seen these men act this way and it'd been a long while since any-one'd gone to the trouble to laugh in my house.

It broke me up too, for a bit.

Wayne sat back down and he and Duck, maybe trusting me since they'd seen me laugh, took drinks of their tea. And that took some of the trust outta them, by the looks on their faces.

I laughed some more.

"I could put some damn George Dickle in there to smooth it out."

"George Dickle?"

"Whiskey," I said. "Bourbon. Sour Mash."

"Ah. Sour Mash. . . . No thank you. No thanks."

I nodded, fine with me.

"So," I said, leaning outta my chair, "did you two really come on over to chat or is there something else going on here?"

107

They looked at each other again, said something quick in that tin-pan lingo, then turned to me. Duck raised his eyebrows and wrinkled his brown brow up like a train wreck.

"Chester Stubbs, we think, we are here to tell you you need to come back to work."

"I do?"

"Marty say you will be lay off, say you don't come to see him like you are suppose to, that you don't answer telephone calls, that you are a loose."

"A looser," Wayne jumped in.

"He called me a loser?" I asked.

"Yes. A looser."

They both looked to see if maybe I was gonna do something, like rip a chandelier from the ceiling and do a hat dance on it. Of course, I barely had shades for my table lamps, let alone some chandelier. But I didn't budge none, though it did rile me for a dumbfuck like Marty Skipps to be calling me a loser, even if it were true.

"And why's he say that? Just because I got my ribs caved in and don't feel like coming back to push canned beans around the joint?"

"No," Duck said, looking serious. "He say because you are a alky."

"Alcoholic," Wayne said, not looking at me.

"Drunk," Duck tried again.

I sat back in my chair. I looked at the ceiling a bit, checking to see if there was a chandelier that I could bash, maybe one I'd just plumb forgot about. No such luck, though.

I finished my beer.

"Well Marty ain't got a brain to spit on. . . . Don't mean much, anything he says."

"That's why we came. You come on back and show him. Come back and get your job. Make things not so boring for Wayne and I."

I sat and didn't look at them, sat with my fist on my cheek and a empty in my other hand.

They stood up, fondling their hats again, seeing I wasn't gonna answer.

I put the can down and got up.

"Thanks for checking in on me," I said. "I ain't had much visitation."

They seemed happy I was glad to see them and we all kind'a hustled to the door.

Outside, we stood on the steps for a spell, looking at the burnt yard and trees. There was something I wanted to ask, though.

"You two wouldn't know how Crow is getting along, would you?"

"Yes, Mr. Dupree."

They both smiled and went to nodding.

"He is promoted. A supervisor now, which is very good because of the baby."

They waited for me to say something.

I looked at a airplane busting by above us, tilting away into the clouds.

"Promoted," I said. "Good for him," I said. "I almost forgot about that baby. Almost forgot. . . . Well," we shook hands and they put on their caps, "thanks again for dropping on by. Maybe I'll see you."

I turned to go back inside.

"Chester," Duck said and touched my shoulder.

I stopped and turned.

"Wayne and I want to invite you over for dinner. Next Saturday. Night. You come. My wife and we will have a big meal. We want you to come, you come spend a night with my family."

"Well, I don't reckon. . . ."

"Saturday night," he repeated. "We will expect you and my wife will set a place for you at the table."

"That's awful nice, Duck, but I don't. . . ."

Then Wayne handed me a card. It was like a business card but only it had a address and phone number and names scribbled upon it, shit like that. I had to take it.

"You do not have to call," Wayne said. He was the younger of the two. Not married, I took it. "Just stop by. Five o'clock, six o'clock. Come have dinner with us."

I just looked at him, then looked at the card and nodded.

The two of them walked out of my yard and down the sidewalk and I never even seen which way they'd gone, because I was still standing there on my front stoop, staring at a paper card I'd already done read twice.

CHAPTER FOURTEEN

That evening with the sun somewhere low and me in my easy chair, it started to sink in some. So Crow had gone and put on a tie and become a supervisor. Management. I was surprised a bit, but guessed I should'a seen it coming. Not that it mattered much. I imagined he was still the same old Crow, even if he was a boss man; just like I'm still the same old fuck of a duck I always was. But something about the day had done disturbed me. Maybe it was the mood old Cecilia Guffins was in this morning, or maybe it was them boys' visit: them telling me I was gonna lose my job, or that Marty Skipps thinks I'm a gone drunk. And then there was the fact they was expecting me for dinner. I couldn't quite finger it out.

All I had was my whiskey and my cigarettes, my teevee and my memories. And I say memories because things was coming up in my brain right often now. Childhood things. Thoughts that I could keep down during the daylight, but come night—come the time of owls and bats and cockroaches in your kitchen sink—then them thoughts would come out to play.

And thinking about that, about dreams and drinking, that got me to think about the time my Mama and me went to see Uncle John when he was in jail.

This must'a been when I was about thirteen years old, because Uncle John—who like I said was my Mama's only brother—Uncle John had been out of the Air Force for a few years but had managed to get himself shanghaied into a institution again, this time with the Mississippi State Penal System. I don't know what the trouble was or why. I was too young to know then and had never thought of it enough to ever ask my Mama, not even before she died of lung cancer when I was doing my at-sea stint for the Navy. But though Mama said he was in jail, it wasn't no jail. It was a prison, but more like a work farm than anything. A labor camp, just south of Tupelo.

By that time we had done moved to Montgomery, where my Mama and Daddy had been married and lived before I was born. Anyways, it was springtime when we come on over, a fine green spring with the kudzu reclaiming all its ditches and fenceposts and the magnolias blooming like pink sex as we crossed the Mississippi line from Bama, headed for Tupelo.

In Tupelo, my Mama stopped at a store and bought a carton of cigarettes—Uncle John's brand—and one of them extra big bottles of cocola. Then we was off again, she following some directions written on a tiny matchbook. But before we got close to the prison, she pulled off the road and we got out of the car.

"Go ahead and sip some of this here Coca-Cola," she told me.

We was standing in the gravel because the grass was new-green and dewy, everything smelling clean and rain fresh like a southern spring should. I went ahead and drank quite a bit while she smoked. She never had much call to buy me cocola, and though it right burned in my throat, I reckoned I had might as well take me some while it was offered.

"That all you can drink?" she asked when I quit and handed it back to her.

"Yessem."

Then she commenced to pour the rest of that bottle out, into the yeller-green grass. I was a mite surprised, but even more so when she pulled a milk bottle of dark whiskey out from under the car seat and began to pour that into the empty bottle.

Now, I knew what whiskey was. Even at the age of thirteen I'd seen some drinking done. And I even knew that it was shine whiskey, because it was in that milk bottle. Mama was a gin drinker, gin and Bloody Marys with lots of Tabasco, I recall. But the men she'd entertained more often than not drank whiskey, even moonshine, and I'd seen the bottles and smelled it. I'd even had my tastes of hard liquor and beer. Had smoked cigarettes so that they didn't make me sick anymore. But here she was, my Mama standing along some Mississippi roadside putting dark still-mash into a cola bottle. Then she took the old cap and pounded it back onto the bottle using a rock. I just watched, silent as a grass snake.

Then she handed it to me.

"Chester, you hang onto this the whole while. Understand? It's for your Uncle John, so don't you dare drop it. You just lie quiet until we get into the jail yard and give it to him, you hear me."

I took the bottle and nodded my head.

I sat in the car, the front, holding that bottle with two hands and my legs. I could smell it plenty, and even then it smelled good to me. The sweet taste in my mouth, left from the cocola, seemed to me like what the whiskey would taste like.

She drove on and we come onto long cotton fields bordered with stands of blue pine in the distance. At the end of one of them cotton fields laid the prison. We came on up to it and parked in the asphalt lot. My Mama took the carton of cigarettes and had me carry the bottle.

"Hang on tight, now," she told me. "Don't let no one take it from you and if anyone asks, it's Coca-Cola. Right?"

She looked at me with hard eyes, or as hard as they got on a woman who kept a bottle of gin on her bed table.

"Yessem," I said.

I really wasn't that good a child, that polite. Hell, most of the time I was left to myself, shooed out the door of our apartment across from the bus station at any old hour. And I was a bit of a terror with my pals, a problem kid at school. So with my Mama at least, I was quiet and polite. Never gave her much grief because, for her, there weren't much grief to get into.

There were some other folks getting out of their cars with sacks and baskets and things, getting ready to see whoever inside the yard on visiting day. The prison didn't look right bad, really. There were some long old buildings about a football field away, low and grey, but the rest was open grass with a few shade trees here and there, trees all full of new leaves. Of course, there was tall fencing around all of that as

113

far as you could see. Barbwire on top. There was some towers
in the corners where, I imagined, men had guns aimed at
everyone.

We lined up with the others to enter a chainlink gate where
one guard stood sweating in his uniform. Mama was nervous,
I could tell that. I'm sure she could smell the whiskey plain as
I could. But we went right on up and right on through along
a gravel path without but a glance at the carton of cigs for our
trouble. I held on tight to the bottle and before we knew it we
was walking on the soft mowed grass, looking for Uncle John.

"There he is."

She took my elbow—I still had both hands on the whiskey—
and hurried me on with her. She was happy to see him, but I
think it was because of getting rid of the bottle and not much
else. Uncle John was a less reliable person than even my
Mama, I do believe.

"Hey Janey, hey."

Uncle John took the cigarettes and they smiled but didn't
hug or nothing. Then he looked at me. He looked a mite
different from when he'd taken me on the Greyhound bus.
He looked older then he should've.

"Well looky here. That you, Chester? Hell, Janey, you got
you a linebacker there. You brung something for your ol'
Uncle John?"

I handed him the bottle and he uncorked it with his thumb
and finger, no problem. He smelled it and looked around. I
looked around too. No one gave a shit. He took a pull and
didn't even smile, just closed his red eyes.

He handed the bottle to her so he could open his cigarettes.
Mama handed it back to me. They both got one lit and stood
with their backs to the guardhouse. Uncle John took the bottle
and had him another.

"Shooo."

114

He took another gander at me.

"How old are you now, boy?"

"Fifteen," I said.

"Thirteen," Mama told him, matter-a-fact like.

"Damn if you ain't big for it. . . . You drink?"

He held the bottle out, smiling, showing some black teeth up front.

"John."

Mama protested, of course, but she wasn't gonna win. Was never gonna win.

I shrugged, not wanting to show how curious I really was, and took the bottle.

I drank.

It burned hard, not exactly like I was expecting, but I didn't react much. Maybe flinched. Hell, I liked it. I was ready for another and took it.

"That'a boy. There's a Stubbs, just like his Daddy," Uncle John said and took it back.

Well, as the visitation went on and the sun rose up into afternoon, me and John traded licks with that coke bottle of shine whiskey. We had us a fine time and like I said, no one gave a shit. No guards came around, nobody paid us no mind from the other inmates or families. I think it was accepted that come visitation day, the men was gonna get something, be it liquor or handjobs under the trees or whatever. I reckon it was just what was done, unwritten, like a lot of things are done in places like that.

And so there I was, getting drunk for the first time in my life, right there in a prison yard in Mississippi. And I loved it. Mama, I think, just kind of accepted it, expected it. I didn't know. I didn't care. But suddenly old Uncle John was a damn good Uncle in my pigged eyes.

Anyway, I don't much recall what was said or done other then us laughing our fool heads off and Mama being quiet and smoking and me seeing everything in a new spin. Then we said our goodbyes and Mama and I headed on back to the car, me just floating, where I sat up front smiling like a six week old puppy.

Down the road I had to walk across a small cotton field, stumbling some over the budding plants, and into them pines so as I could take a big piss. Boy I thought that was funny. I even thought my Mama was funny.

And then we drove on back. Maybe we stopped to eat or something, I don't know. But I do remember falling asleep, sleep coming into me so fast like quicksand, the red light of sunset burning the back of my neck through the car window and then I was out.

And I guess that was my initiation into liquor, if not the ways of men. It wasn't long after that that I'd drink around the house when Mama was out. I'd steal cigarettes for me and my pals, too. But I think I knew, and what my Mama knew too, was that, Uncle John or not, it was something coming to me anyways. I was gonna do it sometime or another and maybe she was even surprised that I'd taken as long as I had.

And I've been drinking ever since—not counting my first year boxing and when Marleen and me was first married. Seemed like maybe I should think about quitting. Get shut of the whiskey at least. Maybe get shut of it all.

When I got in bed I couldn't sleep none, so I got myself up. I had a urge to pour a little George Dickle, but I put that urge aside and went outdoors instead. I went to the backyard, my little square of property covered with bad grass and sandspurs.

I treaded around out there, in my boxer shorts and slaps, kicking around in the broken soil that'd been Marleen's flower garden at one time. It was but weeds and anthills now, though on occasion a flower would spurt up, some spot of color that'd catch my eye if'n I bothered to look out the window. But there weren't no flowers this year.

I stopped and looked upward, where the sky was tarpaper black because the moon was gone. But the stars was out, a huge scattering shining fierce and dagger bright. I stood and stared at them, leaning back in the midnight dark of my own yard. I looked at them stars so hard, so long, almost gone crippled by the sudden understanding of how many there was, by the jumping whiteness of them.

The world was a awful big place. Makes a man think he don't count for shit within it, that there weren't ever a God except on paper. And in folk's minds.

Then again, who the hell knew? Maybe that's where He was supposed to be all along, in your own damn head.

I kept on looking, bent backwards, thinking about God and other weird things, knowing full well I was gonna fall on my ass.

CHAPTER FIFTEEN

I didn't wake to Cecilia's whippings at the tree, but to her knocking on my bedroom door.

"Mr. Stubbs? Chester? You there, you all right?"

I sat up and rubbed the crusty shit from my eyeballs.

"Yeah. I'm here."

"I'm sorry for coming on in," she said, from behind my half-closed bedroom door. "I shouldn't have. I mean, perhaps

you weren't alone. But I was just a slight worried, you know
...I...."

"It's all right, Mrs. Guffins. I don't mind. Go ahead and get
the coffee going and I'll be along."

"Okay. Good."

I heard her shuffle off down my worn-wood hall.

When I got to the kitchen she was already sitting down,
waiting, rubbing her grey hands together. She didn't hear me
walk in and I watched her for a second or two and she didn't
look too good. Her face looked to have added a Interstate to
the roadmap of wrinkles that was already there, and the way
she rubbed her sore hands and stared at them while she did
it, well, it looked plain pitiful. I coughed and she looked up
and I tried to smile for her.

"Guess I was sleeping hard," I said and poured the coffee
and brought it to the table. The sugar was already there,
lumping up in the dish from the humidity.

"I reckon," she said.

I smiled again. Was hard to do it because I didn't feel so hot
myself. Had me a hangover.

"And I do apologize again," she said. "I shouldn't just walk
into a man's home."

"You can come on in anytime. You ain't gonna see or hear
anything you ain't seen me do before."

And so she smiled.

She picked up her coffee cup but her fingers slipped. She
shook them like maybe she had a leech on her thumb and
then had to use two hands to lift the cup to her lips, shaking
the whole while until she set it on the table again.

"I do believe that pecan tree is as stubborn as I am, Mr.
Stubbs."

"Say the word and I'll fell it."

She looked at me.

"I'm feeling better," I said. "I'm about as healthy as I let myself get nowadays."

"Well, I just said the tree was stubborn. I still plan to be the one to chop it down, even if it takes ten years."

"Yes Ma'am."

We had us our coffee and began to talk, our little table chit-chat, and she seemed to improve some.

"Oh hey," I said after she done told me about her flowering plants and the armadillas that she'd seen rooting up her onions, "I forgot to tell you. I was invited to dinner."

"Is that right?"

"Yeah, these here Vietnamese boys from where I work, or worked, they come on over for some damn reason or another and then invite me on over to their house for a Saturday night dinner."

"I saw those men. I was wondering about it. But I went back to my business. . . . Do they have children?"

Children? Sometimes her train of thinking seemed to be about all cabooses.

"I think, maybe older kids. Maybe one. Them two is brothers but the older one has the wife. The other, he ain't married."

"Children at any age are a blessing," she told me.

"Well anyways, I ain't gonna go."

"You're not?"

She gave me a disappointed grandma-eye.

"Nah. What do I want to go on over and eat with a family I don't know. Hell, they don't even look like me."

"I don't recall anyone looking like you, Mr. Stubbs."

"You know what I mean."

"I would think it would be good for you. Get you out of the house. Get you a taste for family life, perhaps. Something new."

I sat and chewed the idea a little.

"Maybe you ought to come with me then?"

She seemed pleased, but didn't want to.

"No, I'm not going to hold your hand. I was not invited anyway. . . . My days of family are over and I accept that. But I really think you should go."

I got up for more hot coffee, sat down, and gave her a blank stare. But she wasn't gonna have any of that.

"You should go, Chester. A man who has had no children, like yourself, who has let a marriage slip away from him due to his own antics, I'd say it's in your best interest to spend a night with a family at dinner."

I almost laughed. I thought of my Mama, of a Daddy I never knew. I thought of Uncle John who disappeared long before I knew what disappear meant. But I wasn't gonna tell her none about that.

"Just because they call it a family, that don't mean it's something good. You watch too much Teevee. These folks could have so many skeletons they might be a living graveyard."

"Perhaps," she said, "perhaps. Yet, why are they still to-gether? I can tell you that a family may have its troubles, but their house is their home. Especially if there are children. At any age, a child is only at home with its family."

I didn't say nothing. I was used to her preaching about this and that, shit, about me. But it looked like the old lady might cry if I made fun of her, if'n I didn't go on to this dinner.

"I'll think about it," I said.

She looked like she done won some game of checkers or something.

She got up and rinsed her empty cup in the sink, like she always done. She looked like her old self as she headed for the back door.

"And bring a gift," she said, over her shoulder.

"A gift?"

"A house gift. . . . And don't make it a bottle of whiskey, Mr. Stubbs."

That night I took a few stubborn drags on my whiskey, but my stomach wasn't having none of it. It wanted beer if it wanted any alcohol at all. So I obliged it. Drank me a little beer and ate bologna and pretzels for dinner.

I always ate one good meal a day. Usually breakfast: grits and a egg sandwich, bacon maybe. My money was running way low. I was still paying for my electric, but there wasn't no more paychecks. All that was gone. All my money was done pissed away. Hell, I didn't even know why I'd done it, not anymore. Maybe just to prove to myself that I could.

I guessed, as I sat in my suffering chair there at night, I guessed the time had come for me to get up and get going. The shit had hit the fan a long time ago, was hard on the walls by now. Reckon it was about time to scrape it off.

Maybe, come Monday, I'd get me a haircut and go on down and make a surprise visit to the warehouse. Go and give Marty a jolt. Maybe even see Crow and congratulate him. And after that I'd quit drinking, maybe. Give it a rest. A nice long one.

But before any of that, I had me a Saturday night dinner to attend.

PART THREE

Sunlight & Storms

CHAPTER SIXTEEN

I guess you could'a called me a nervous wreck. I was trying to get myself ready for dinner but I kept sweating through my shirts and kept worrying how I was gonna ruin it, about how I was gonna make a ass of myself in front of them all. I'd pitted through my best button-down shirt, one of the few left from my Navy days, and I had to go through the damned closet looking for another.

But all I found was one of my old Hawaiian shirts, some green and yellow number with pineapples and hula gals all over it. It weren't too wrinkled though, and it was cool. At least it had all its damn buttons.

I put it on. Put on my cotton pants that didn't have no holes in the knees or rear. I even wore underwear. I put on some white socks. Tied my tennis shoes with a grunt. Then I stood in the mirror.

And I looked terrible.

I really needed a shot of whiskey, but I'd quit for the day. A practice run.

Needed something to calm me down, though. So I drank beer instead, two of them.

I combed my red head and checked my nose hairs. I grabbed my car keys and pocketed my fold of dollar bills and license, then headed for the door feeling awful dumb, but feeling half good too.

Had my hand on the knob when I recalled what Cecilia told me: Bring a gift. . . . A gift? What was I gonna do, stop at a men's room when I got gas and buy some glow-in-the-dark condoms? I didn't even have a unopened bottle of whiskey.

I went to the hall closet, the top shelf where all the junk was put, and I started to yank it down and have a look-see.

I found a box of old stationary, found my old seaman's cap and some letters from people I'd done forgot about on purpose. I found a big ol' conch shell, a packet of wood screws, some crazy glue, a road atlas, a bra, some candles, four paper party hats and the Pensacola *News Journal* want-ads from three years ago.

I found a lot of crap.

At first I was gonna take the candles. But I looked at all that shit again, it scattered on my hall rug like so much litter from a hurricane, and I gave up.

Then I remembered Marleen's boxes, tucked away in the shadows behind my easy chair.

In there I found a box of windchimes from some gift store on the beach, a thing Marleen had bought but'd never hung. It weren't big, a handful of gold stars, suns, moons and little curlicues hanging from some purple ring. And it looked damn tacky enough for something I'd buy. . . . So I grabbed the chimes.

I felt a mite guilty, but at least they was still in the box.

So with a gift in my paw and two beers in my gut, I was out the door and on my way to have dinner with a family of foreigners.

Duck lived over near the sound. When I'd read that card he'd handed me, I found out his name weren't Duck, like everyone called him at work, but something like Ngoc. And Wayne's name wasn't all too close either, it was Quang. As far as their last name was, shit, I couldn't even try to get that off'a my tongue. I'd just call them Duck and Wayne like always, unless they didn't care for it none. But I did know the whereabouts of their house and so I steered my beat up ol' car thataway, still nervous as a kitten in a car wash.

They lived in Gulf Breeze, past the beach bridge some. Their neighborhood was kind'a thrown in off Highway 98, behind a Junior Mart, a bus stop and some two-bit real estate office. There was a number of homes back in among the dark pines, homes up on stilts because the soil was sandy and swampy, homes looking like beach houses yet they weren't. Anyways, Duck's place wasn't so bad. It was painted and had some right colorful things hanging from the porch, which was up above the gravel drive where I parked.

I got out and looked up, trying to pull the sweat-creases out of my shirt at the same time. There was lights on and my ears picked up some oddball music that was playing, like somebody pulling a dog's ears or maybe trying to stuff a porkypine down a toaster or something. But after I stood a while and listened, it weren't so bad. And I could hear voices too, none of it in any language I understood.

The beer had all drained down outta my brain, so I set my boxed windchimes on my car top, slipped over to the bushes, and took a piss. And before I was done, I heard my name.

"Ah, Chester? That you?"

It was Wayne. I could see him on the top porch, looking down at me.

"Yeah, it's me," I went ahead and answered. "I'll be up soon as I finish peeing in your palmettas here."

"Okay," he said and walked away. I thought I heard him laughing.

And I just knew the rest of the evening was gonna go like that.

But when I got up the steps and into the lights, out come Duck and Wayne, all pleased to see me, and they led me on into their house which was full of curtains and low chairs and pillows with dragons and tigers stitched on them. There was a wild food-smell in the room, smells of peanut oil and fish and spice, like cloves and pepper maybe, and there was just the smell of people who was strange to me. There was Duck's wife, Mai-hingsomething was her name, but I could call her May, an easy name for me to get and remember, and there was a boy, some skinny teenager with round glasses who was sitting at a desk punching at a computer, Duck's boy doing his electronic homework while the food cooked and both the woman and the son done give me big smiles and did their little bow and Duck kind of scooted me along to sit down at the table, and I sat, feeling weird and smiling too much and then the wife done poured me a glass of something from a little tea pot, warm green tea, about too-weak when I sipped it, but I was as glad for it, for something to do with my hands and throat, as much as any goddamned whiskey I'd ever had.

The boy, whose name was Lon, shut down his computer and come and sat across from me. Duck and Wayne was finishing some conversation, standing by me, but talking in their Orient-lingo. May was back in the kitchen, stirring and frying food.

"You were in the Navy?" the boy asked.

"Some years ago."

"I'm thinking of going into it."

I drank some more tea.

125

"How old are you?"

"Sixteen."

"Sixteen," I said, meaning nothing, but the boy smiled.

"He's going R.O.T.C.," Duck said. "College."

"Well, I ain't gonna say anything one way or the other," I told them. "When I joined up, back then, things was different. They'd take any old fool."

And that was the truth. And though I would'a told the kid to become a high school janitor instead, he was—and they all was—smiling too much for me to say anything bad.

Then Duck sat down at the head of the table and Wayne sat next to me. There was a place for the wife at the other end, I reckoned, and there was one more spot laid out next to Lon, but I hadn't seen no sixth. But I was just glad they sat at a regular table. I mean, I was half expecting some little coffee table with no chairs where I'd have to sit on the floor and have my knees cramp up on me. My leg joints was bad from all the road work I'd done when I'd fought, not to mention the fights themselves.

"You like seafood?" Wayne asked.

"I'm living in Pensacola, ain't I?"

Just then, May, she brought out a big ol' tray of deep fried stuff. It was long brown-battered things arranged around two small bowls full of two kinds of sauce. She set it down and Duck motioned for me to take some. I wasn't too sure and so he went ahead and grabbed some and then Wayne did and the boy and then May put three of them deep-fried things on my plate, before she took one for herself.

I stared at it for a moment.

"What is it? Octopus?"

They laughed.

"Shrimp."

It was shrimp, all done up with lots of batter and their tails cut off.

"Shrimp. . . . I like shrimp."

"Try this sauce, Chester," Duck said and held out one of them bowls. There was a load of thick brown sauce in there. The other bowl had green stuff.

"What's the green?" I asked, pointing, because it looked a mite more appetizing to me.

"Oh, very hot. Hot," May said from down the table. "That shutnee," she went on about the other, what Duck held. "Shutnee, you like shutnee, Mr. Stubbs?"

"Chester," I told her." But I don't know. . . ."

But she'd done got up and disappeared into the kitchen, coming back with a little dark bottle that had a label with a damn parrot on it.

"This is," she said. "This it."

I looked at it and it was a damn bottle of Pickapeppa sauce. It was chutney she was talking about. Store bought at that.

"Oh yeah," I said. "Chutney. Hey, I like chutney . . . but that ain't, you know, that ain't Chinese or nothing."

And they all smiled again.

"We ain't Chinese," Wayne said, and they laughed.

And that was how dinner started, me feeling my way along like some blind man whose dog was dead. But they made me feel damn welcome, and it went okay.

After the shrimp, Duck and May brought out some kind of dish that looked like a boiled salad or something, full of colorful vegetables I ain't come across too often before, and there was gobs of rice. They did use them chopsticks to eat, though me and the boy used forks. They all spoke American good enough–hell, Lon spoke better'n me, just a regular kid, he was. With Duck's wife it took me a while to get a hold of what she meant, but I got used to it. So we just ate and talked and shit like that. They never asked any about me working and I didn't figure it'd make good table talk anyways.

It wasn't until after the meal, when May and Lon was cleaning up, that Duck and Wayne invited me out on the porch to smoke, drink some beer and have us some personal conversation.

I turned down the beer. Told them I was resting up on the drinking a bit and they took that with a smile and we had us some cocola instead.

It was a fine night, dark, with the swamp bugs singing in the palmettas and light traffic clicking on the highway past the pines. The porch was screened and Wayne burned some citronella to keep any extra skeeters away. Duck sat himself down in a hammock that was strung in the corner–looking right cozy there–while Wayne sat up on the porch rail, pushing against the screen. I sat down in a plastic lawn chair, which was just about my speed.

We settled in with our cigs and thoughts for a bit, sipping the cola. You could hear May and Lon in the house, soft-talking, cleaning, leaving us alone on the porch.

I was right comfortable.

"I'm gonna go on down to see Marty, come Monday," I told them, breaking the peace.

"Good, good."

"Can't say I'll still have my job, but I figure I'd better get it straightened out, now that I'm feeling a mite better."

"That's good, Chester," Duck said. "Now Marty will have someone to be afraid of again. Maybe he will do some work."

"He's goldbricking on ya'll, huh?"

"Goldbrick?"

"He ain't doing his job," I said.

"Well," Wayne said, "we have never seen him work enough to know what his job really is."

We all laughed.

"He does not tell us what to do anymore. He is never there, unless Mr. Cotton is there."

"I reckon I know where he's at and with who, and if his old lady ever finds out, I reckon I know where he's going. . . ."

They looked at me.

"Down the tubes, boys, down the tubes."

I don't know if they knew what I meant, but they didn't laugh. They nodded and lit new cigarettes.

We listened to the bugs some more and then I asked them how the hell they ever came to Pensacola.

"Ya'll had contacts in the Navy or something?"

"No, no. . . . We stayed in South Vietnam after the war, but it was terrible." Duck spoke, Wayne sitting silent. "We paid to get on a boat and sailed. Many days. That was horrible too, but we get to Thailand and the U.S. agree to take us.

"They send us to Pensacola. I know of Florida, you know, but not Pensacola. I know of Miami, Tampa. . . ."

"Fucking Disney World," I said.

"Yes, yes," they both said.

"But this is nice. Very pretty. Opportunity for us to stay together, work together. There were two other families with us, though we did not know them from Saigon. But one family go to Texas, to be with relatives who have a fishing boat. The other family, they go back to Vietnam. Homesick."

"Local folks give ya'll a rough time?" I asked.

"Yes and no. . . . Depend upon the folk."

They both smiled and nodded.

"Ya'll didn't have careers in frozen vegetables over there, in Saigon, did ya?"

"Ah, no, no," Duck said. "I work with flowers, a florist. I had a shop with flowers. My wife, she a doctor assistant, she help with sick, dying, births–until Lon was born. But he was our only one, only child. . . . Wayne, he was a professor."

I looked over at him, sitting there in the shadows of the porch, stubbing a cigarette into the railing, sending the red coals all over the place.

"You a teacher?"

"Yes. University. I teach History. French history, our own history."

"And now you toss frozen turkeys for a living," I said, not expecting an answer, but he looked up, fixing his black eyes like some stone arrowhead at me.

"Yes," he said, "but at least there is a living to be had."

Well, I couldn't figure that, so we sipped a little more and sat back in the warm night with them candles flickering like jars of orange jelly. And the candles made me think of them candles I'd found in my closet and that set my brain to recalling why I'd done looked in the goddamn closet to begin with.

"Hey," I said and jumped up, near scaring the two of them. "I plumb forgot. I brought ya'll a gift. . . . You know, a house gift or something."

Then I clomped on down the steps and got the box with them windchimes in it, still sitting there on top of my car.

I went back up the steps where Duck and Wayne was now standing, waiting.

"Here," I said and handed the little box to Wayne. "It really ain't nothing, you know. I just figured, I mean, I was kind'a told that it's polite to bring ya'll something. . . ."

They was both listening and I was feeling a mite foolish. Wayne opened the box and held up them chimes, the metal of it catching the candle light and the tubes and figures tinging and tanging.

"Tell the truth," I said, "them was my wife's. I don't think they been used, but she did buy them, and left them, but I want to give them to you. . . . Kind of stupid, maybe."

"Oh no, no," Duck said, putting his little hand on my shoulder. "Thank you, is very nice. Very."

He seemed pleased.

"You are married?" Wayne asked, him still holding up the gift, letting it tinkle tinkle as he talked.

"Was," I said. "We split. She's up in Montgomery, in Alabama."

Then I remembered that she weren't in Bama, but was up in Connettycut. I didn't try to tell them that, though.

"Something of your wife's," Wayne said, holding the chimes up higher and staring at them tubes and the little gold moons, suns and stars clinking around under the purple ring.

He hung it up on a rusty nail, not far from a orange kite that was strung up along the rafters. Then he excused himself.

"I will get more soda," he said.

I nodded. Duck and I lit cigarettes when he left. Then Duck sided up next to me, like he was fretting over some secret or another.

"Chester. . . . Wayne, he lost his wife on the way over. She die on the boat."

I stopped smoking and kind'a held my breath for a moment.

"That a fact," I said.

"She die of sickness, here." He grabbed his gut. "And the men, the captain, he have her body thrown over into the sea. Wayne at least want to bury her, but the men scared they get what she get and so. . . ."

I looked up at him.

"Didn't know that," I said. And I didn't know what to say, but figured I ought to try. "Now all he's got is your family?"

But Duck didn't get a chance to answer, because along come some big-dick pickup truck with rock music blasting out it's windows like advertising for a school for the deaf. I mean, that shit was just thumping. You could feel it in your blood. It even rattled the windchimes, not that you could'a heard them any.

We both looked, seeing it was a big four-wheel drive monster with its headlights shining too bright and there was a couple of dumbfuck kids in there. But what was so surprising was that the truck done pulled into Duck's driveway, parking right behind my ol' Super Bee, leaving the music still whomping and the lights on while the passenger piled out and headed for the steps.

And that passenger was a girl. Some pretty girl with straight black hair wearing cut-offs and a green tank top and not much else. Duck's girl, I figured.

Both Duck and me stood there, dumb as wood, as she come on up and pranced right past us, not even looking, not saying "howdy" to her father or nothing. The truck's speakers had gone to another song, though it didn't sound no different than the last crap, and whoever was sitting in it—a boy, I reckoned pretty easy—wasn't planning on changing that tune.

I looked at Duck.

He got a grip and went on down the porch to talk to the boy.

I watched him go, saw his shadow leaning in the window past them bright lights. The music went down, but not off. Duck was still talking but I couldn't hear what.

Then the noise came from the other way, inside the house.

It was Wayne and the girl. They was yelling, or he was yelling in his own language, but the girl wasn't answering him. He was hot and it wasn't until he talked in American that she done yelled back.

132

"You no go!" Wayne yelled. "I don't care what night, you out too late, you out with wrong people! Wrong! Wrong!"

Right then and there, I got the distinct impression the girl was Wayne's, not Duck's.

"Take a damn pill," the girl said, calm, cutting, the way teenagers must practice it in a mirror or something. Or maybe they teach it in school nowadays.

I didn't know if she'd come on back to eat or to get her cigarettes or IUD or what, but she was set to go back out with the boy in the stereo-on-wheels and Wayne weren't for it.

They yelled some more and then the girl bust on out to the porch, stopped for a second to stare and give me a sneer, then she was down the steps, passing Duck who was on his way up, paying him no mind like he was a invisible cabbage. Though, when she'd stopped to look at me, just for the second, I'd seen through that sneer: tears was gonna come sometime tonight.

Duck came in and stood with me. We watched her hop back in the car and the boy backed her up, keeping the music low this time. Then Duck looked at me and I was feeling pretty low, for him and Wayne and knowing they was probably embarrassed about it all.

"Nice girl," I said, deadpan. "Carries herself well."

I busied myself with a cigarette and he went in to see the family.

We talked a little bit more and I said my thank yous to May and Duck and Wayne—the boy'd gone to his room—and we all kind'a pretended the night'd ended all nice and cozy, like it was supposed to of.

I went down the steps, got into my creaky Super Bee, waved goodbye, then backed out of the sandy drive and into the road. But I didn't get but two yards forward when I came across the boy and Wayne's daughter, them sitting in the bed of the truck, lights and music off this time, parked in a blind of oak and vine. They was fumbling with something and she waved me over when I rolled by.

I parked and got out. They stayed by the truck, so I went to see what was up.

"You got a light?" the girl asked.

She had a fresh cigarette to her lips. Her eyes was moist, her face a little red.

"Sure," I said and got out my cheap lighter.

Then the boy nudged over. He had his hair chopped straight and an earring in one ear. He also had him a marijuana joint he wanted lit.

I lit them both up.

"Want some," the boy asked, holding his breath.

"Not for me," I said. "But maybe I'll have a lick of that."

I pointed to where a quarter-bottle of tequila sat on the truck bed. I guess I figured I deserved it, after turning down the beer and all. And maybe I could help Wayne to boot.

The boy didn't want me to have some but the girl, maybe feeling bad about not meeting me or what happened with her Daddy, gave me the bottle.

"Drink up," she said, smiling at me. A pretty smile.

And so I did.

Maybe I didn't deserve it, maybe I was showing-off, maybe it wouldn't help Wayne out like I thought, but I done drained that thing. I opened my throat up and let her go, with only a smile and a belch to show for it when I was done.

The girl looked at me slack-mouthed and amazed, turning down the joint at the same time.

The boy was pissed.

"Hey," she said, smiling.

"Look," I said to her, lighting up myself now. "Maybe you ought to give your ol' Daddy a break. Just for tonight. He's probably done gone to bed anyways. . . . and I reckon you made your point."

She looked me in the eye, smoked, thinking. The boy was almost saying no, but I was a head taller, a tree trunk wider. I hadn't even bothered to look in his eyes, which spooks them sometimes.

I held up the empty tequila bottle.

"Looks like your evening is pret'near ruined anyways," I said.

She snorted a laugh.

I chucked the empty to the boy, like a football, and went back to my car. I drove off, seeing them arguing in my rearview before I turned the corner to head back home.

CHAPTER SEVENTEEN

I woke up to Cecilia's first choppings at the tree.

I went ahead and showered and dressed and even had me a bite to eat before she come dragging her old self through my door for coffee. She was damned surprised to see me looking like a normal person, instead of like some hungover raccoon.

"Well, well," she said, almost circling me as I stood there with hot coffee. "You are looking a mite chipper this morning, Mr. Stubbs."

"C'mon now. . . . I just showered is all."

"Is that a fact?"

We sat down to the table.

"I'm going on down to the warehouse this morning," I told her. "I'm gonna see about my old job."

She looked at me, saying nothing, but I could tell she was right tickled.

"Don't give me that," I said.

"I said nothing."

"Didn't have to," I said. "I seen it. . . . I seen it."

I drove on up to Olive like I'd always done last Fall. I thought it'd be familiar but it weren't. Seemed like I'd been gone a whole hell of a long time–and maybe I had.

I went into the big parking lot, where I'd coldcocked ol' Charlie Cotton, and parked. Then I went in the back way, through the extra door past the loading dock, so I wouldn't have to see any suits and could talk to Marty Skipps first.

And I got lucky—or unlucky, depending on how you saw it—because there was fat ol' Marty right there, soon as I come up the concrete steps. He had his back turned to me. I didn't see Duck or Wayne about.

"Hey, possum-butt," I said.

Marty turned around, surprised.

"Stubbs?"

"No, it's Mother Teresa."

He tried to rise himself up some and look important, but it made him look like he had gas.

"You talked to Roger yet? He tell you?"

I scratched my nose.

"Roger who?"

"Roger DeMent. You know, Personnel."

A suit.

"Hell no, I wanted to see you."

I didn't smile none, didn't even take a step closer. He looked around but, other than some boys moving pallets with forklifts back yonder, there weren't no one.

"You gotta talk to Roger, I don't think. . . ."

"Didn't come to hear what you think," I said. "I heard tell you was concerned about me. Heard you was talking about my welfare some."

I watched him fidget. Saw him move his eyes around like hummingbirds. I couldn't imagine he'd figure Duck and Wayne would ever come see me and tell me what he'd been saying. He'd think it was Crow, and he wasn't never gonna say boo to Crow.

"I was trying to find out if you was coming back," he told me.

"I'm back."

"Yeah, no. . . ." he nodded his head and looked over his shoulder again.

This time he was lucky, because Duck and Wayne was coming out of the freezer, wearing their coats and gloves.

"Hey! Look!" He called to them. "Chester's back, boys! C'mon and say hello."

They waved, I waved and they started on over.

"Look, Chester," Marty said, feeling better now, "I gotta get up to the dispatch office. Now you go on and see Roger, ya hear? He's got some forms for you to sign, I think."

He began to walk away kind'a fast like.

"What kind of forms?" I asked, loud enough.

Marty stopped and turned at the steel stairs. He gave me a buzzard's grin.

"Release forms."

Duck and Wayne came on over, smiled, gave me a slap on the shoulder and took off their damn mittens.

"Hello, Chester. You come in and get your job, yes?"

I smiled on back.

"Don't know about the job. . . . Don't look too good."

They shrugged and gave their little bow.

I changed the subject.

"I sure had a fine time last Saturday. Ya'll throw a fine wingding."

Duck and Wayne said something in Vietnamese to each other.

"Oh, yes. I'm sorry how it ended," Wayne told me, looking a mite bad. "My daughter . . . she come home just after you left. Was very nice. She is really very nice."

I smiled to myself.

"I believe it. She's just a teenager, they all get like that— especially when you live near the beach."

They both looked upward, hangdogged.

"Ah, the beach," they both said.

We jabbered a bit more, them saying I was welcome to come on back sometime, but they didn't say exactly when and I didn't offer no visits myself. We shook hands and they went back to work and I wandered on over to the personnel office.

I walked kind of slow, got a few stares, nodded to a few familiar folks. I was kind'a hoping to run into Crow and also kind'a hoping not to. I wasn't gonna go look for him, though I knew I should. But I made it to Roger DeMent's office without seeing him.

I walked right on in. If he had a secretary, she was gone, maybe she was gone with Marty for a threesome or something. Anyways, Roger was behind a desk.

"Can I help you?"

"It's me, Chester Stubbs."

"Oh yeah. Okay. Sit down, Chester."

I sat.

"We've been trying to reach you. You should answer your mail."

"You could'a called," I said.

"We tried. It seems your phone's been disconnected."

"Oh yeah. I forgot."

I wasn't much interested in what he had to say, but I figured I'd best get it done with.

"I'm sorry, but we've had to lay you off, not only for medical reasons but for lack of commitment on your part. You need to sign this release, to confirm that, and then you need to sign your unemployment insurance form."

"What's that about unemployment?"

He looked kind of pissed but was trying to hide it, maybe like a magician whose rabbit'd gone and shit in his hat in the middle of a show.

"Yes. This is to say you won't receive unemployment but that you can contest it. One of our new managers, not your manager, deemed you eligible for unemployment, but his suggestion was put down."

I knew he meant Crow. That man was still looking out for me. I didn't know if'n that was good or just plain pitiful. Pitiful for him or for me, was the question.

"Okey-doke," I said and scribbled my name on all his pink and yeller papers. He gave me some copies of this and that, which I shoved in my pocket, then he said this and that and got off his ass and showed me to the door.

"And I suggest you contact the hospital, Chester. Our insurance program covered about seventy-five percent of your bills, but they told me you've ignored their requests. They've retained a collection agency, I believe, to handle it."

"Awww," I said.

"So, I would pay the bills, maybe on a payment plan," Roger told me.

"And unemployment?" I asked again, just to see that look on his face.

"If that's what you want, I suggest getting a lawyer."

And he smiled before closing the door in my face.

What the hell.

I went on home.

The next morning, when she was done flailing at the pecan tree, Cecilia came on in for coffee and found me sitting at my table going through the mound of crap that was my mail. At least what I hadn't already thrown away.

"I never took you to be a man for spring cleaning," she said.

"Ain't that," I said. "I just come to the conclusion that you can't escape reality, that's all."

I shoved the shit aside and we had us our coffee.

"Did you get your job back, Mr. Stubbs?"

"Nope. And looks like I owe a lot of folks a bit of money too. They said maybe I should get a lawyer."

She looked sorry.

"If you need one, I know one. A good one. He was Jeffrey's lawyer."

"No thank you Ma'am." I didn't want to go to some jackass lawyer. Never. As long as I could help it, anyways. "I'm thinking I'll get me a job instead."

"Very good. But why would you need a lawyer?"

"So I can get unemployment."

She didn't say anything, just kind'a gave me one of them grandma looks.

"That's the way I seen it too," I said.

We let the subject drop and talked about the weather and armadillas in her garden. Then she remembered something.

"You never did tell me about your dinner. How did that go?"

And so I told her, kind'a smoothing over the part about the windchimes and me pissing in their yard.

"And the boy is right nice, far as I can tell. Smart kid, I reckon, though he's got a hankering to join the service. But Wayne . . . has him a handful with his daughter. A wild girl."

"A child?"

"Maybe eighteen, I figure. Hell, I don't know."

"A child," she said.

"You had a kid didn't you?"

She nodded and stirred her coffee some.

"Have any trouble?"

"Some, but our boy was always good. Polite. He and Jeffrey were close, very close."

Now, I couldn't quite recall seeing their son over there, ever, and she seemed a mite bothered about me asking. Not upset, like I done put a spider in her oatmeal or something, but I got the impression she didn't want to talk about her own kid, just other folks'. Maybe something had happened to their boy and I was bringing grief back into her old age. Or maybe she just didn't like me making comparisons with her child and Wayne's girl.

Whatever the case, I let it drop.

"So, when you figure that tree's coming down? Next Tuesday?"

She blushed a bit. That old lady.

At noon I went out to the beach, to Sun Ray's for some Gulf-Mex food. Looking over my mail had given me a poor outlook on things and I felt like I needed to do something different. I sat outside, on the boardwalk, with a damn tuna taco, some hot-sauced shrimp and a iced tea. I read the want ads in the newspaper.

The wind kept coming in off the bay, blowing the pages, and I gave it up after reading about halfway down. I had a urge to scramble on over to the Sandshaker for a tall Dickle on ice, but I let it pass. This no-drinking thing weren't too bad so far. Of course, I did have them beers and that tequila, but that was it. The thinking of it kept me on my toes. So I put away my urges, had me my sweet tea and watched the gulls fight over food wrappers and dead crabs on the bay shore.

I took my newspaper and sad mood for a drive, on out towards Navarre. I drove into the National Seashore, a place me and Marleen used to go to a lot, where she'd sometimes swim and sun naked and, in the off-season, we'd fuck in the sea oats. But as I drove through that white sand land, the dunes tall and sloping, like frozen waves on the moon, I couldn't muster up much for the scenery or old times. My mind was thinking about money-owed and money-needed and how much my tuna taco just cost and how much gas and oil my Super Bee was burning and how I was getting damn tired of eating grits every day.

It wasn't like I needed a whole hell of a lot of cash to live on. And I figured I could pay the hospital bill if'n they let me piece-meal it. The power bill was okay. I owed some for water and some for old phone bills. I had taxes to pay on my property. Had to eat. Had my smokes. But if I could quit hitting the bottle, that'd save me some. Could even save up for a damn tombstone somewhere. Or maybe I'd just have my ashes scattered over the liquor stores of Pensacola.

But I didn't want no unemployment. I really didn't. So all that was left was to suck it up and find me a job.

I stopped at the Tom Thumb Store before the Navarre Beach bridge, dumped three dollars worth of gas in the car, bought a roll of Spearmint Rolaids and turned the car back in the direction I come.

I chomped on them Rolaids like they was party mints, got back into beachtown and then took the road towards Fort Pickens. I headed for the only place I seen in the paper where I figured I belonged, employment-wise that was: One Leg Lafitte's Oyster Bar and Grill. A bartender's job.

Sounded kind'a stupid, I know, me having gone and quit drinking. But I loved the beach and I loved bars. I reckoned I could handle it.

I sat in my car, parked there in the crushed-shell lot, just broiling away, working up the courage to go on in.

Lafitte's was a local's joint, mainly. It was a upstairs place, with some real estate office beneath it. It weren't too big a tavern: just a short bar, a cramped kitchen and a big ol' rectangle of space where they put the tables and chairs. The property was on the wrong side of the highway, away from the beach. Not only that, it was west of the main drag, out of the way down a winding road past a few no good motels, the only bar on your way to Ft. Pickens–if you didn't count the goddamn Holiday Inn–which was why locals hung out there. It did have a view of the Bay, past some hairy dunes on one side and fancy new homes built on a man-made islet along the other. There was a long dock, too, with a few sloops for boats, should any happen their way. And, there was a big pit of sand with a couple volleyball nets strung up, where young folks who had more energy than brains could play some.

I already knew the owner of the place, Jimmy James. He knew me from the days I'd lived on the beach, right after Marleen and I decided to split and before she gave up the house. I spent a month in a rental on the beach, a little crab-hole of a room above what was called the Tiki Club at the time, what was later called The Right Stuff Saloon and what now was called a abandoned building. Those was some hazy days. Anyways, Jimmy James was the Mayor of Pensacola Beach. But he was about as much a politician as I was a protector of the American Way when I was in the Service. Don't know how he got the job. By default, probably.

Finally I had about enough of the sun and worried guts, so I stepped on out of my Super Bee and climbed the stairs to find me a job.

And I got it. On the spot.

Luckily, Jimmy didn't know me well enough not to hire me. It made me damn near dizzy, like I was standing in the ring in the eighth with one of them chicken-boned heavyweights who was too tall and fast to K.O., but didn't have no power to ever return the favor. Just made a man tired to fight him. But anyways, I took the job. He told me to start Friday. Night. No training needed.

I thanked him. Shook hands. Then was out the door and on my way home before either of us could change our minds.

CHAPTER EIGHTEEN

The next morning, Cecilia wasn't none too happy with my choice of employment.

"I don't know, Chester. . . . I was thinking you could find yourself something more promising, something steady and with benefits. Like up at West Florida, the University."

I don't know what she thought my qualifications was, to get a job at a damn university. Maybe as a janitor or something. And I could tell thoughts about night-life and alcohol was preying on her mind. But I wasn't gonna let her sly grandma ways get me to scrub toilets for a living. Shit. I'd rather be on the beach, even if it was on the working-side of a bar. Even if I was trying to stay dry.

"Beats hiring a lawyer," I said.

That afternoon, I got myself tidied up some and went out to take on the world, or at least my little cobweb corner of it.

I went to the bank and took out what cash I could, without leaving my account empty as a open tuna can in a house full of cats. Then I went to the phone company and paid what little I owed. They said there was a hook-up fee and I now needed a deposit before they'd flip a switch so that my phone could ring again. I told them to stick it, I didn't want one. Fuck a telephone. I mean, who the hell was I gonna call and who's gonna call me?

I went to City Hall just to make sure my property taxes'd been paid for the year. They was. I hadn't remembered for sure if I'd done did it—had other shit on my mind at the time— and at least Florida didn't have no state income tax for me to worry over.

Then I went on down to the hospital. I found the cashier on the first floor and told her I owed them money.

"Name?"

"Chester Stubbs."

"You know your account number?"

"Don't even know my phone number."

"Your account's been given to a collection agency, Mr. Stubbs," she said, looking at a computer screen.

"I got the cash right here. Most of it anyways."

She quit looking at the computer and then looked at me.

I smiled for her.

She smiled back.

"Okay," she said. "I think we can work it. Let me talk to my supervisor and we'll try to get it straightened out. Please wait."

She went off and I stood there at the cubbyhole like a idjit. A responsible idjit, at least. And as I was waiting I heard the cashier at the next little booth talking to her customer.

"Dupree?" she said. "Mr. Crow Dupree?"

And then I heard a familiar "Ah-huh."

I backed up a notch and took a look.

And he was looking straight at me.

"Hey, Crow," I said, quiet like.

He turned back to the lady and said something and handed her a paper or two. Then he turned back to me.

"Chester," he said.

"Uhm, what'cha doing here?"

"I'm sorting out some insurance, for Della's pre-natal."

I had to think some.

"The baby," I said.

"That's right."

"I'm paying my bills," I said.

"That a fact."

"Here you go, Mr. Dupree," his cashier said and handed him back some papers. "Those are for your records and your HMO will be billed."

"Thank you," he said.

He folded them up and put them in his pocket. He turned to me again and I didn't say nothing. He stood for a second or two.

"See you, Chester."

And he was on his way.

I watched him walk.

"Hey, Crow," I said, wanting him to wait up.

But I'd said it too quiet. He was already gone.

The hospital had taken my hard cash and was gonna let me pay the rest month by month. But as I sat in my easy chair in my living room, I didn't care too much. I'd had a chance to talk to Crow, to thank him, to congratulate him on the job, on the baby, hell, on just being a good man. But I'd blown it. I was still a asshole in the end.

Friday night came and I had me a supper and put on some long pants and a button down shirt before driving out to the beach to go to work. It was good to see the old WELCOME TO PENSACOLA BEACH sign lit up at the head of the bridge in Gulf Breeze, that old Vegas-blinking orange green and blue billfish, his marlin spike pointing the way to fun and money.

On the other end of the toll bridge I pulled away from traffic and headed on the narrow road west, passing the Holiday Inn and the tourist cars, past the red white and green Tom Thumb store and into One Leg's parking lot.

I checked myself in the rearview, hearing the box music and drinker's noise coming from the bar, stubbed out my Camel and got out of the car to go to work. And as I headed on up the steps, I felt awful damn weird, just like you always do when you start a new job.

I walked in the door, where the light was bad and the place was half-full of customers. I stood a minute by the pinball machine. The employees gave me a look-see, maybe wondering if I was wanting to eat or drink or pull my dick outta my pants. Finally I asked where Jimmy was.

They went and got him.

"Chester!" He was all smiles as usual. "Come on, I'll show you around a bit before we get you started. . . . You eat?"

"I did."

So he drug me back into the office where the time cards was, where he had me sign a W-2 form and had me sign something saying I wasn't no illegal alien, then he showed me the kitchen and the bathroom and the supply room. He took me behind the bar and introduced me to all the employees.

"This here is Sammy. This is Brad. That's Lynn and that's April at the cash register by the door. Jack there is our cook tonight."

I said my howdy-doos and didn't remember a name to a face. They all looked friendly enough, though a mite younger than me. And they was all dressed a sight sloppier, some with aprons spotted with remoulade and grease and juice from shucking oysters.

"Here you go," Jimmy said and threw me a tee-shirt. "Go on and wear this One Leg's shirt and Brad will train you some."

I went to the Men's room and put on the shirt and it didn't fit too good, even though it was extra-large.

"Tomorrow I'll get you a extry-extry large," Jimmy said, and then I was put behind the beer taps with Brad.

"I ain't never really done this before," I told him.

"Nothing to it," Brad said while making drinks, smiling good as Jimmy.

In fact, pret'near everyone was smiling. It made me damn nervous. No one ever smiled much in the places I'd worked, especially the Navy, unless they was about to get discharged that is. But seeing all them teeth did make me think some of Wayne and Duck's house.

Brad showed me how to run the taps and what sizes and kinds of beer they had. He showed me the bottles of coldbeer, imports and Americans, and the wine coolers and he had me do the beers while he handled the drinks and the cash. The sight and smell of it gave me a pang or two, but I was too nervous to give a damn.

Customers came and went and stood around like garden snails. I met the regulars and talked a bit and poured beers and even learned a bit on the bar register. The night got pretty busy and I did this and that and cleaned a few tables and spilled drinks and ate some fried shrimp the cook gave Brad and me, and then things began to really rock, the diners all gone leaving only the loud music and a crowd of happy drunks busying themselves with talk and machine-games they'd never have a interest in if they was sober.

Then Brad told me Jimmy didn't care if we drank, so long as we could do our jobs and he offered up a beer. But I said, naw, not tonight, and things went fine.

Until there was a row out on the porch. Some short-haired ass was picking on two guys. Small guys who didn't want to fight.

The folks in the bar sensed it and, even with the rock and roll music, it got a bit quieter as they all turned their heads to see out the screen windows. Even Jimmy, who was still around, must have sensed it because he come out of his office to see.

There was some shoving and yelling and it looked to be getting bad.

"Is that dickhead back again?" Jimmy said to no one in particular.

He turned and looked at Brad and me. Then he just looked at me.

"Go sick'm, Chester."

"Me?" I said.

He was smiling again.

"Why do you think I hired you? Haha!"

So I went on out to do my job.

That boy had his back to me. One kid was already on the porch-wood and the other was being held by the shirt, not looking too happy. The big guy was cussing at him. There was a little circle of outside drinkers gathered and I walked through them. The troublemaker had pretty wide shoulders and arms like bologna loafs. But he wasn't my size.

I came up right behind him and stood.

"Better let go, boy," I said.

He did let go, without looking, then turned and threw a punch. He swung where he must'a figured my face would be, but he hit me in the chest. It hurt. But it didn't move me any.

The hangdog on his face was pretty damn precious, when he looked upward into my hard face.

I didn't have to do nothing but grab him, turn him around and take hold of his back collar and waist-pants. Then I hoisted him up like a sea turtle and walked him to the stairs.

I got about half-way down before I tossed him into the crushed oyster shells of the lot.

He scrambled up and called me some names and then took off into the parked cars. But a minute later, I saw him screaming down the road on a motorcycle, his red tail light like the ass of a firefly.

There was some hoots and handslaps as I went back on in to One Leg's. Everyone was looking at me and I felt a mite embarrassed. I got behind the taps and most of the employees said a little something. Jimmy laughed, gave a thumbs-up, and went back to his office.

I tried not to feel too good about it.

"First day on the job," Brad said, like he understood.

"Guess so," I said.

Here I was, still beating people up for a living and other folk's entertainment. Guess some things don't change in a man's life.

After the bar was closed I stayed for clean up.

First I took me a break. The cook and I sat outside and smoked, where the lights of the island was low and all was latenight quiet, the bay water still as a owl's wing. Inside the bar, though, it weren't so quiet. The music sounded near twice as loud as before, all them young employees was jamming along as they cleaned up, not talking to each other, stoned to the gills for all I knew, just lost in the noise and their last job of the night.

151

Jack and I went back in and I did my clean up though the music was getting to me. Somewhere down the line I'd done lost my taste for Rock and Roll. Maybe I just didn't have the energy for it no more.

Jimmy was still around but getting ready to leave. He took me back into the office before I was done with my chores.

"You did fine, Chester," he said. "You come on in tomorrow at about three o'clock. Okay? It's Saturday, but we'll try to get you out a little earlier than tonight. Then I'll pencil you in for next week. You did just fine."

He handed me a fifty dollar bill.

"What's this?"

"Tips," he said. "And that ain't anything, you'll be making between a hundred to two hundred on nights like tonight. . . We split all the tips here, straight out even, but since you're new you got to wait till next week to get a share. That's just policy. But I wanted to give you something after the way you took care of that sonofabitch tonight."

I stuffed the money in my pocket.

"Thanks," I said.

I figured if I was gonna be his goon, I'd may as well get paid for it.

Later, when I was done but still sitting around with a sweet tea and smoking, everyone was gone except Jack and Brad. They'd let the loud music burn out and I was near burnt out too. Tired, I was. But I felt good. And then Jack set on some new music.

It weren't loud and it weren't rock. It was some old Bob Wills playing. I like Bob Wills.

So I sat a little longer. Smoking. Sipping my tea. Staring out yonder at Pensacola Bay where the moonlight hung. And listening to that old music made me think of my poor Mama, her sitting by the windowsill on one of them so hot

Montgomery afternoons, she maybe doing her nails and drinking a gin-and-something, the ice cubes always melting too fast on her, the fan blowing and the huff of the Greyhound buses always coming and going across the street, my Mama listening to her record player, humming along to Bob Wills or Hank Snow and getting ready for I didn't know what, maybe getting ready for nothing, maybe for another man, maybe just passing the time till her lungs took her. Shit, I could remember that.

"You okay, Chester?"

It was Brad. He was fixing to close up. Jack had gone.

"Yeah," I said. "Sure. . . . Guess it's just been a while since I've been up this time of night. Been a morning person of late."

"Well, this job'll cure you of that. Right quick."

"Good," I said. "Good."

We went out the door and into a peaceful night, the sky pretty enough to make your teeth ache.

Saturday afternoon and I was back at One Leg's. That morning I'd done slept through Cecilia's chopping. In fact, she'd had to wake me up for coffee. Which was fine. I'd told her about the night before but said nothing about throwing that rascal into the oyster shells. And I'd told her nothing about my not drinking—guess I was shy of giving her any credit for it, or maybe I didn't want her to know if'n I failed. Though so far I was holding true, even if I did have dreams of dancing whiskey bottles at night.

Anyways, she still weren't whole hog about my new occupation. But I was back, ready for a new night of work.

I could see why Jimmy wanted me in for the afternoon. It was just as busy as the night before and the crowd was a mite

153

younger and a mite more active. There was a few families eating inside but the sand volleyball courts was just singing with people, all of them drinking like thirsty dogs.

Brad wouldn't be in till night time. Jack was there and a couple of others whose names I didn't remember. Jimmy was there at first, gave me a bigger shirt like he promised, but he left within the hour. And after that I worked the bar by myself, kind'a cold turkey.

And it went fine. I smiled and did a little talking. I asked questions when I needed to. It was a beer crowd. Hell, One Leg's didn't have a liquor license, but they sold this drink made with Mad Dog wine, malt liquor and pineapple juice called a Pirate's Punch-Out. Sounded right disgusting to me, but I sold plenty.

The day was sunny as could be, warm as always, and seeing the young women coming in and out of the joint and down there flipping around in the sand wearing their bikinis and shorts, well it surely interested me. My sex drive had been in mothballs since I had my ribs busted, it seemed, but I reckoned it to be dusting itself off now that I was back at the beach.

So I kept at my job, doing okay and near enjoying myself. Then me and Jack took a dinner break. We sat outside in the hot dying sun, eating our grouper sandwiches and hush puppies, drinking cocolas and admiring the women in the sand pits.

"I got to get out of the kitchen more often," Jack said, giving me a grin like a teenager.

I just nodded. Ol' Jack wasn't exactly a lady's man, probably spent a good deal of his nights alone. I wasn't much better, but I knew I was a old man, in them girls' eyes at least. I reckoned I'd already used up my wild nights on the beach.

"Whoever invented the thong bikini, I'd like to shake the man's hand," he said, still grinning.

But there was one thing about the beach I had to admit, that no matter who you was, if you stayed long enough and kept at it, you'd always find some one-night stand waiting for you. Maybe it weren't the law of averages, but it was the law of Pensacola Beach.

And I certainly didn't mind the view as we sat on the porch, looking down. Right then I was looking at a girl in particular, her back to me, her hair long fine and shiny, black as a crow's wing. She wore a thong bikini, her skinny yeller rump just hanging there, collecting the sun rays. But when she turned profile, I saw something else.

I saw that I knew her.

It was Wayne's girl.

And suddenly I felt bad. Not for him, but for myself. I guess I felt near ashamed.

Jack and I went on back to work, but I kept my eye on Wayne's daughter the whole while, just seeing what she was up to. She was with a different boy than the first night. This guy was older and he was buying her drinks. From me.

The next time he come up, I eyeballed him. He was having beer in a cup while buying her them Pirate's Punch-Outs. He was a skinny kid, college age, good-looking I reckon, but with a dirty brown goatee growing there around his mouth. I didn't see much use in it, other than to keep cocktail sauce from dribbling onto his crotch, maybe.

I didn't say nothing to him, but I did to Jimmy when he come back.

"Hey, Jimmy," I said.

"How you getting along, Chester?"

"Not bad," I said. "Jimmy, you see that girl down there playing volleyball, the one with the long black hair? I reckon she's underage."

He looked out the big window.

"In a green bikini," I said.

"The Oriental?" he asked.

"Vietnamese," I said.

He looked back at me, funny like.

"You ID her?"

"Her boyfriend's been buying her drinks," I told him. "But she looks underage."

"I don't know," he said. "She hasn't bought none herself?"

"Nope."

He kind'a laughed.

"C'mon, Chester. . . . You got to remember, this is the beach. The beach, man."

He smiled, did a little whirligig with his hands, and then went back to his office.

The beach. . . . I reckon he was right.

Still didn't feel good about it, though.

I went back to work and put it out of my mind.

Later, while washing up some glasses and beer pitchers, I felt someone staring at me. I looked up and there she was, her black eyes sparkling with wine.

"I know that dude," she said, pointing at me.

Her boyfriend-for-the-day was behind her, playing pinball.

"Name's Chester," I said.

"I know you," she said. "You work here?"

"I do now."

"You were at the house. You know. You gave me a light."

Her friend was done with pinball. He stood next to her and looked at me.

"Come on, Tam," he said.

"I know you," she said again. "Chester?" she said.

"That's right," I told her.

"Come on, Tam," the boy said again and he led her to the door, ready to leave.

"That man can drink," she told him and then they left.

And I was feeling shameful all over again.

Brad came on to work and I was let off. He offered me a beer, and though it sure sounded good I held myself and said no.

"Think I'll go home and rest some," I said.

But when I got to my car I wanted that beer. My body had been rumbling for a drink for days now—getting a touch shaky in the mornings. I'd been a good boy, so maybe I should have me one, I figured.

I stopped at the Sandshaker. Ordered me a beer. I let it sit in front of me while I stared at the whiskey bottles for a while. I smelled it, ran my fingers along the wet glass. Lifted it up, then set her down. Undrunk.

I left the full glass there at the Sandshaker and got back in my car. I drove on over the Beach Bridge, to Gulf Breeze, then over the long Bay Bridge, to Pensacola and on home, crossing little Navy Bridge to my dark house in Warrington.

CHAPTER NINETEEN

Working the weekend at the beach kind of shook the webs out of my brain. Even the thing with Crow, and me feeding drinks to Wayne's girl, couldn't shake the good feeling I had to be back out in the world. It was almost nice talking to folks who were a damn sight more normal than me.

Come Monday morn, Cecilia said she could tell a difference in me. And I suppose there was. I didn't tell her about the fight or about the girl, Tam. I just fed her the positive stuff – except for me not drinking so far.

"You're like one of those reborn Baptists, Chester. . . . In your own way, of course."

"Don't go comparing me to no Baptist," I told her.

"What should I compare you to?"

"I don't know . . . maybe a snake, like a snake getting shut of his old skin."

On Tuesday, I went on out to the beach to check the schedule. Brad was working and I said howdy, saw that Jimmy'd penciled me in for Thursday, Friday and Saturday nights, and then I was out of there.

I stopped in at Chan's Market for some lunch then took a walk up a motel sidewalk just to see the surf. Pretty day. Pelicans was having a good time shitting on the swimmers.

I went homeward, stopping at the Delchamps for groceries before getting back. I needed to rest up for work or it'd cure me of sunrises for sure.

Getting up at the crack of noon sounded right nice, but Cecilia wouldn't like it.

When I got home, I come in with the sacks when I noticed some note stabbed onto a loose nail on my front door.

I set the bags down and sat myself down on the step and read the note. It was kind'a half-scribbled, in pencil, and I finally figured the signature at the end.

It was from Wayne. He'd come on over to talk to me. I was gone. He wanted me to stop over at his place some night this week.

Shit.

That was all I needed, to catch hell from some irate Daddy about his girl drinking, even if it was good ol' Wayne.

Damn shit.

I crumpled the note up and tossed it down into the dead bushes along the house. It just melted in there with all the cigarette butts and rusted beer cans, with the candy wrappers and plastic and Styrofoam. All that crap that I either threw down there in the last two years or that blowed back in there with each storm.

I fried up some bologna on the stove-top. Had that with bread and mustard, and some of them damn pork rinds that I can't figure out why I keep buying, and I had me some sweet tea. Then I settled in front of the ol' opium-box and just plain frittered away.

Thursday night I was back behind the beer taps at One Leg's. Jimmy was there, Jack was in the kitchen, April was taking in the cash and there was only one waitress working. Iris was her name. I'd never met her before.

It weren't too busy. Jimmy'd told me there was some big digs down the beach at The Docks. Something to do with nickle beers and women in wet tee-shirts, so he wasn't expecting much of a night. Even the locals fell for things like cheap drinks and moist tits. Come to think of it, so did I.

Either way, I was getting a hang for the job. Pouring beers and making them drinks was easy. I didn't care none for running the cash register. It weren't that I was bad at math, I was just fucking terrible at it. I had the math skills of a treed possum. But the machine did most of the work and I made change my own way, slow, and soon it didn't bother me none.

Iris was a right funny girl. She liked to joke around and tipple a little wine, especially while Jimmy was snoozing in his office. As the late night rolled in there wasn't much call for a waitress and so Jimmy gave her the night off. But she hung around for a few free ones.

"Hey, what do we have here?" Iris said.

She was sitting in front of me, looking out the back window at the bayside.

I took a gander.

Some boat was motoring in the lagoon. A sailboat with all its sails and boom tied tight and its little putter of a engine glub glubbing in the moonlight. It had its fore and aft lights on and it looked to be coming for One Legs' dock.

When Jimmy come out to see how much money he was losing, he saw us looking at the boat. He took a look himself and smiled.

"Aha. Money ahoy, mates," he said.

That boat cut its motor and sure enough slid on into the dock. And I mean INTO the dock. The starboard side of it more'less crashed up into the spare tires slung around the poles like some drunk kid taking his Daddy's car into a rail guard. Then the motor was on again, in reverse it looked, and then it was off again.

"Damn," Jimmy said. "Looks like he's already off to a good start."

"Who is it?" I asked.

"Fob the Slob."

Jack came out from his hole.

"Fob? Are you sure?"

Just then we heard some crashing and crunching and saw some small man clamber out of the boat and try to tie her down. He was dressed pretty slick and pretty dumb, by beach standards at least, and he kind'a wandered around by himself having hell trying to get his damn sailboat hobbled up to the dock, even though the night was calm as a glass of baby milk. But that boy was weaving around some and before we knew it, he'd fell plumb backwards into his boat, like a chicken into a stew pot.

"Don't see how it could be anyone else," Jimmy finally answered.

He and Jack laughed. Iris and I just looked at each other. And when I got around to looking at April, well, she just looked plain mortified.

Guess she knew him.

And it wasn't long later I found out I knew him too.

Fob Langtree.

Now there's a good ol' southern name for you.

When I knew him he was a helicopter pilot out on the base. He did mail duty on the same carrier I was on, then was a copter trainer for a spell before leaving. Didn't know what happened to him after that. Didn't much care.

Fob Langtree. Don't forget a name like that. But his name was about the only recollectable thing about him. So I didn't recognize him when he finally stumbled up the steps and into One Leg Lafitte's.

But he recognized me.

Folk's may not remember my name, but they never seem to forget my face.

Soon as he let the screen door slap his ass, he gave one big smile-around and then fixed on me with a drunk's grin. He shuffled towards me, poking his finger like he was testing the breeze and he kept shuffling and pointing and grinning until he stumbled up onto a bar stool without looking, like he'd sat there so often he done knew it'd be there to catch him.

He leaned on the bar and looked at me, not blinking, his hand still up but now the fingers snapping. He snapped about a dozen times and then brushed back his flat gold hair, showing the bald spot he'd grown it to cover.

"Stubbs. Stubbs," he said, things clicking slow up in his pickle brain. "Chester Stubbs. Heavyweight champion of Pensacola Naval-Air Station."

And that's when I recognized him.

"Ex-champ," I said.

Of all the assholes to walk into all the beer joints on the Redneck Riviera, Fob Langtree had to make this one his home. The one I'd done found a comfortable job in.

"Damn, Chester. Chester Stubbs. . . . What can I say?"

He was happy as a peeing puppy.

"Say what you want to drink," I said.

He got a big kick outta that. But he didn't tell me what he wanted. He just went on saying my name and started pointing that finger again.

So I poured him a beer, set it in front of him, and he took it without looking. Guess he didn't care what he drank, so long as it was within reach.

Then he took notice of Iris sitting two stools down.

"Well now," he said. "Now there's a treat. There's something new under the hood."

I looked around and saw April turned towards the door, sideways, looking outta the corner of her eye now and then. I saw Jimmy peeping out of his office, his face cracked bigger than the door, him trying so hard not to laugh and give himself away. And Jack was standing right behind me, evidently wanting to be noticed.

And he was.

"Jack! Hey Jack-O!" Fob said and he shot upwards, spilling half his beer, reaching to shake Jack's eager-beaver hand.

"Hey, Fob. Good to see you back."

"Jack. Fried shrimp. Fried shrimp for breakfast."

"I'll leave it on the boat for you."

"Good. Good. Nothing like fried shrimp for breakfast."

Then he stood all the way up, grabbed what was left of his beer, and started for the exit. Guess he plumb forgot about me and Iris. He staggered a bit, ran nose first into the screen door, then looked back. At me.

"Don't go thinking I forgot you, Chester Stubbs."

Then he was tripping down the steps to his boat, spilling the beer he hadn't done managed to spill inside.

We all watched him disappear into the boat and saw a light come on in the cabin.

By the time Jimmy come up Fob was out pissing off the bow of his boat. Jimmy watched him go back below deck before he said a thing.

"Get that beer on his tab, and the shrimp, Jack. Fob the Slob is back." Then Jimmy slapped me on my shoulder. "I didn't know you knew that ol'boy, Chester?"

"Knew him way back when, when I didn't have much choice."

"Well, you ain't got much choice now, either. Fob will be here all summer long for our delight and entertainment."

"You charge him rent for the slip or something?" I asked.

"Hell no. No one uses that dock much anyhow. No, he eats and drinks here like it was his own house. Runs up a big old tab. That's why we put up with him. Yes, runs up a big old tab."

Jimmy was a happy oyster. He pumped his arm like a slot machine and commenced to make cha-ching cha-ching sounds all the way back to his office.

No one else looked so pleased, except maybe Jack.

Iris looked at me.

"This looks to be an interesting summer," she said.

I rolled my eyes for her.

"Reckon so," I said.

The next morning I heard Cecilia's weak whacks on the tree. Heard them in my deep-sleep like something familiar and important and my brain dragged itself awake.

I went ahead and got up and made the coffee. I was damned tired though. Even as quiet as it'd been at One Leg's, I hadn't got home till three in the morn.

Old Cecilia noticed.

"You are looking poorly, Chester," she said. "You aren't back to your old ways, are you?"

It was like she knew I was taking a rest from drinking, like she knew it was always on my mind to start up again, too.

"No Ma'am," I said. "Just can't seem to reconcile my nights with my days is all."

She shook her blue muffin of a head.

"I advised you to get a real job."

That she did. But it was getting to be that my job was looking more real than her. And, I was thinking, if something had to give, it was bound to be my mornings of small-talk.

"I'll get the hang of it," I said.

But it wasn't gonna be easy. Because Friday night turned out to be the most worst of them yet.

I rolled in Friday night and relieved Brad at the bar. There was a tide of people jamming the joint, inside and out, and I went right to work, pouring and mixing and saying all the right things when I had to.

Brad come on back in about an hour and we worked together, even taking some food orders. Iris was working her pretty legs off, running oysters and fried fish and hushpuppies all over the place. Jimmy was gone on some Mayor business—or so he'd told everyone. Brad was managing for the night, and helping me too.

Around mid-evening, things slowed enough for me to take a break and I sat on the ice chest with a sweet tea and a cigarette. That's when Brad told me that Fob had been asking for me.

"Damn," I said.

"He'll be back. He went on down to Sidelines, but he'll finish up here. Always does. Unless he picks up some poor woman."

"Fob with a woman?"

"Like I said, he'll finish up here."

But it weren't Fob I had to worry over. Because no sooner did I get back to the job, I saw her again.

Wayne's girl, Tam.

She was with the same young turd, standing at the curve of the bar, drinking, bouncing to the loud music, and looking at me. At least she didn't appear as far gone as last time.

She smiled when I looked back and I gave her a little wave.

The night slammed on. I was busy as a bullbat around a street light. Sometimes I'd look up to see her, sometimes she'd be gone and I'd think she finally went on home. But then she'd be back, same spot, same look. And it wasn't no special look, really, just a howdy-doo friendly look. And that's all I was giving her in return. Hoped so, anyways.

Then late later, when only the hardcores was still hanging, she come to sit down in front of me.

"Hello, Chester," she said and she laughed a bit, putting her hand in front of her mouth like her Daddy and Uncle always did.

"Hey, Girl," I said. "Where's your boyfriend?"

"He went home. . . . He's jealous of you."

I felt something then. But it was something I didn't want to feel.

"You want to call your Daddy?" I asked. "For a ride home?"

She looked pissed, then. Guess I'd said the wrong thing.

"Sorry," I said.

"I'm going to a party. On a boat."

"A boat?"

"With him."

She pointed to the end of the bar, the very end around the curve, and there was Fob Langtree. Who else. Fob sitting there with his big white-tooth mouth open, laughing with some other drinkers.

I shrugged.

"You got to watch the company you keep," I told her.

"My name is Tam," she said.

"Just the same," I said.

"There's going to be others. . . ."

She was gonna explain her reasons, I guessed, but she didn't get the chance. Her old boyfriend had come on back into One Legs.

"Tam," he said to her, but was looking at me, "let's go. You come with me."

He reached out and grabbed her shoulder. She shrugged away from him.

"No, Brian. Leave me alone."

He looked at me some more, trying to figure what was up, what I was about.

I went back to work. It really weren't none of my business.

"How are you getting back, Tam? You better come with me. Come on. Come on."

But she refused. He tried to take her hand. They was making a scene.

"I'll take her home," I said.

I didn't mean to say it. I didn't want to say it. But I said it.

"I brought her," the boy said. "She's going with me."

"I said I'd take her on home."

Hell, I didn't know if'n she even wanted me to take her home. But I knew she wasn't gonna go with him.

He stood still and stared at me. He was afraid and was having a hard time sticking up for himself.

"It's all right," I told him, letting him off the hook, letting him get out. "She just don't want to go, is all. I know her Daddy. I'll get her on home."

He didn't say nothing more before he left, but he did throw a chair across the floor, smacking it into the legs of the pinball machine.

That brought Brad out of Jimmy's cubbyhole.

"What's going on?" he said, looking at me and Tam because everyone else was too.

"This girl needs to get home," I said, giving him my best look.

"And he's going to take me," she said, staring at Brad with that all-out stubborn face she had.

Brad was smart enough to figure he wasn't gonna win.

"Go on," he told me. "I'll finish up. Take her home."

167

"I'll be back before closing," I said.

"Just take her home. This once."

I didn't wait. I came round the bar, got her off her stool and we went to the door.

"I'll be back quick," I said.

And then we was out, down the stairs and into my old car without another word.

It wasn't till we was off the beach bridge, headed for the sound, that I even looked over at her.

"How old are you?" I asked.

She gave me a snort, like it was the dumbest question ever, but she answered.

"I'm nineteen."

"You ain't in school no more?"

"No."

"You ain't in college, you working?"

"Work," she said. "I work at the Cordova Mall: How do you like this shirt, Sir? This dress, Ma'am? Would you like it giftwrapped?"

She stuck out her fist and gave my windshield the finger.

We drove on, not talking for a spell.

Finally I tried to tell her something that maybe'd be of use to her.

"Listen, I ain't your Daddy and I ain't your boyfriend, but I can tell you that you'll be saying yessir and yess'm for a long while, if all you want is to be wild on the beach."

That didn't sit too good with her. She crossed her skinny little arms and wouldn't look at me.

I handed her a cigarette. She took it and lit it herself.

"How would you know that?" she finally asked.

I waited a bit, till we was turning down her street and up to her drive.

"Because I'm a thirty-five year old man working in a beach bar," I said.

I stopped the car in front of the house and put out the lights.

She got out, not saying a thing, and I watched her jump up the steps, the coal of her cigarette blinking.

I lit my own as she went in the porch door. I sat a bit, smoking, making sure she got in okay. Then when I was about to pull away, I saw someone coming down.

It was Wayne.

He was kind'a jogging across the sandy drive, wearing some silk drawers and no shoes or shirt. He had his hand up and was looking at me and saying my name.

"Chester. Chester. Chester."

I put my gear in neutral and hung my head out the open window. I was gonna have to talk to him sometime and it might as well be now.

"Chester, wait," he said and came up next to me. He leaned against my car, picking the sandspurs out of his bare toes.

"I'm sorry, Wayne," I told him. "She come around and I just brought her on home."

"I know, I know. Didn't you get my note?"

"Yeah."

"I just wanted . . . I wanted to say, she, my daughter, she like you. She tell me she think you okay."

I pulled my head inside and he moved over to the window.

"I want to ask you, Chester. . . . She and I, we don't get along. You know that. So maybe, you. . . ."

"Maybe I what?"

"You work at the bar now, so maybe you can look out for her? I ask you that. I ask you to look out for her. . . . When you can. Maybe?"

He stood there looking at me with them black eyes, his brow wrinkled up like a bloodhound's. He wanted me to look out for his girl, just because she'd taken a shine to me somehow. He wanted me to do it. And I didn't want to do it.

I finished my cigarette, butted it out against the door of my car and dropped it into the sand. He was still staring at me. I spit into the palmettas. He was waiting. I put the car into reverse. And he still waited, silent as a fed cat.

"I'll try," I said. "I'll do what I can."

His brow come undone and he put a hand on my arm.

"You look out for her," he said again and dropped his hand because I was pulling away.

He was still standing there in the dirty sand when I turned my wheels and my headlights left him.

I headed back towards the beach, paying my dollar at the bridge and taking a right at the intersection on the other side.

Look out for his daughter, that's what Wayne wanted me to do.

Shit.

Seemed to me I already was.

When I got back inside One Legs, Iris and Brad was shooing the last of the hardcores out the door.

"I already punched your time card, Chester," Brad said. "I'll clean up for you, this time."

I shrugged. Thanked him.

"Come on over here," I heard someone say. "You look like a man who could use a drink."

I looked over to the end of the bar. And there he sat, his face tan as a cowhide and his teeth shinning white as a cold glass of milk. Looked harmless enough, friendly even. And what with the crazy night and Tam, what with the way the summer was playing out, I figured I could give-in a little.

So I went on over and let Fob Langtree buy me a beer.

CHAPTER TWENTY

"Chester Stubbs, I do believe it has been a long time."

"Could'a been longer," I said.

He laughed.

We was sitting together, drinking bottle beer. My first sip went down guilty-like, but damn if it didn't almost taste better thataway. The rest of it was awful good, too, and before I knew it, we was on a second round.

Brad and Iris finished their chores. Some gal named Minnie was cleaning the kitchen because she'd cooked. Jack had the night off. They'd let me hang on, even though I wasn't working. Brad let Fob stay too, as he was a special case. A irregular regular, maybe.

But as we talked, no matter what I said, ol' Fob thought it was funny. He was pret'near drunk, but not dead drunk. He was still the same from what I could recollect about him, still acting like everything was funny so he could treat folks like shit and never get in trouble for it. Probably the only way to piss him off was to refuse to drink with him, but as long as he was buying—and he sure seemed to buy a lot—not too many ever turned him down.

On any other night maybe I would've declined, but I felt like drinking tonight. And anyways, it looked like I was gonna have to talk to Fob all summer, so I figured to make the best of it. He weren't a good excuse to drink, but he was my excuse.

"I thought you was gonna have a party on your boat?" I said.

He made a quick look around him, though he knew there wasn't no one.

"Seems they all had other plans."

He laughed again.

Brad came by and gave me my tips. Over a hundred. I tried to give some back, seeing as how I'd skipped out, but he wouldn't let me. He and Iris wasn't ticked off anymore, but they was ready to close up right soon.

"Chester," Fob said, seeing that neither Iris or the cook had any plans to come to his boat, "why don't you come on down and I'll pour you some gin."

"Beer."

"Beer it is," he said.

Hell. Where else was I gonna get beer at that hour, and now that I'd started I wasn't ready to quit.

Don't know what I'd done if he'd offered up whiskey.

We wandered out into the warm night and down to the dock. Weren't no one up but us and the stars and a few cars passing the Bay bridge in the distance. It'd been a while since I'd been on a boat, and even though the little inlet wasn't more than a bathtub, the rock and slaps of the water caught my attention some.

It was a nice ol' boat, a forty-some footer, with all the sails down and capped and the boom tied up. I sat outside as he went below for the beer.

"Come on down, Chester. I'll show you around."

I went down the tiny steps.

It wasn't a bad cabin. He had him a little stove and a fridge and sink and next to that was the bar with lots of bottles of this and that in roped-off shelves. There was two little rooms from there, both of them with single bunks and porthole

172

windows. There was a skylight in one that you could pop open for fresh air.

But just the same, it all looked pretty cramped to me, like a floating coffin or something.

He handed me a bottle.

"You live here all summer?" I asked, looking around, having to hunch because I was too tall, whereas Fob could stand up straight with a little headroom to spare.

"Not the summer, all the time. I live on this boat all year."

"Shit."

I took a gulp of the beer. It weren't no Budwiser. It weren't even American, best I could tell. Some kind of beer that they don't stir-up too much so's it stays thick and ugly. Still tasted good, though.

We went back out top. I liked it a whole lot better under the stars. He brought two more bottles up with him.

"So, Chester, what have you been doing all this time? I knew you wouldn't stay in the Navy."

"Damn near did," I told him. "I even recruited for a spell— but that's when I knew I had to get out. . . . You?"

"Went to Auburn."

"Alabama?"

"The university. I used the GI Bill and went on to Dental School."

"You're a fucking dentist?"

"Almost," he said, thinking I was funny again. "But I switched to Pharmacy. I'm into pharmaceuticals."

"How's that?"

"I sell drugs to dentists and doctors."

"And you live on this here boat?"

"Well, Chester. I had a house, in Fort Walton. I had a wife too. I don't have the wife or the house anymore. But I kept the boat. I sell pharmaceuticals from Pensacola to Port St. Joe, just slipping along the Intracoastal Waterway."

I looked over his rig again.

"Do all right, I take it."

"Take my summers off."

"And you spend them here?"

"I like Pensacola Beach. Reminds me of my Navy days sometimes. Lots of sun and water. Lots of pussy."

Pussy. I ain't heard a grown man say that in a long long time. Of course, maybe it was me that'd said it. Can't right remember.

"Shit," I told him, "seems to me, with a boat like this, I'd just take her to open water and be off. You know, head on down to the Carib'. . . or on yonder."

He started to laugh. Maybe laughing at me.

"It's what I'd do," I said. "Better then sitting around One Leg's, getting your arm pits wet."

"Well, Chester," he said, "I would too."

"Then why don't you?"

He a started to laugh again, burbling some in that heavy beer of his when he took a drink. Then he come up for air, looking damned amused with himself.

"I don't know how. . . ." he started.

"Don't know how to what?"

"I don't know how to sail," he said.

Well shit. The boy don't know how to sail. And then I had a picture of him in my mind, ol' Captain Fob just a put-putting his way along the Intracoastal, a laughingstock to all the goddamn sailors along the way.

I grinned into my own bottle.

"I suppose that does hamper you some," I said.

"I suppose so!"

And he was laughing again.

"And how about you, Chester Stubbs? What brings you to working at a beach bar?"

I guess maybe, a month back, I'd of told him to mind his own fucking business, or maybe I'd of slopped him in the mouth just for the feel of it on my fist. But, especially after he'd done fessed up about his lack of sailing expertise, I figured I'd let him know. A little bit, anyways.

"Well, I was working up at a warehouse with ol' Crow Dupree—you know him?" Fob let his eyes swim for a spell and shook his head no. "Don't matter," I said. "So I was working up there and got in this here, well, a boxing match kind'a, with one of the big shots and. . . . Ah, shit, Fob. I just pretty much fucked-up, okay?"

He nodded and raised up his beer.

"Okay with me."

"I'm just going with the flow right now."

"Who isn't? I thought you married, though?"

I kind'a shifted my weight, took a look up at the night and then the water before I looked back at Fob Langtree.

"Was," I said. "We split about two years ago. I reckon its been two years now."

Fob's baggy eyes lit up for a second.

"Aha!" he yelled. "Another man set free upon the earth!"

He opened up the other bottles, splashing some as he handed me one. I drank the other down just as a gust of sea-wind blew on in from the Gulf of Mexico, and then, to the side of us there was a peculiar sound, a rustling in the dunes. We turned to see a owl, some moon-grey owl sweeping into the sea oats after mice or something, darting in and then off again, disappearing the same way it'd come, like a magic trick.

Then it was just the breeze and the water lapping at the boat hull and the sound of the surf snuffing in on past the highway and the dunes, and the sound of us two men, us two divorced men breathing and drinking ourselves drunk under a sky done caked with stars.

CHAPTER TWENTY-ONE

I slept hard and I slept in. When I woke, about only two things felt worse than my beer-soaked head. One, was that I had to straighten up, go back to One Leg's that night and do it all over again. The other, was that I'd missed my morning coffee with Cecilia Guffins.

When I finally wandered out of bed the sun was already out of the shadows of the trees and was baking the thin roof of my house. In the kitchen the coffee was in the pot and there was a note propped up against the sugar bowl on the table.

Dear Chester Stubbs,

I could not rouse you from your bed and I apologize for trying. I hope you do not mind, but I made coffee and had myself a cup. I have been feeling quite poorly as of late and believe I will take Sundays off from chopping at my tree. Perhaps I will see you on Monday.

Yours, Cecilia Guffins

Well, I did feel a mite sorry for her. Maybe the old bird was running out of steam. Either way, I'd see her on Monday. I promised myself.

As I fried up some bacon and had me my coffee, I thought a bit about last night.

All that horseshit with Wayne and his daughter, hell, I'd try to help him out. I didn't know how that would be, though. I believe she was pissed at me, so that might be the end of it right there. I'd keep my eye out for her, I guessed, but I wasn't gonna go around trying to scare off her beaus and drive her around Escambia County like some goddamn cab driver.

Then there was Fob Langtree. I can't right recall all we talked about on his boat. That old boy is more hopeless than myself, I'd say. The only difference is he's got a lot of money. And that's a pretty big difference. I wouldn't mind having me some money like that. I would not. But I ain't never gonna. And to go around wishing, or even thinking about it, that ain't gonna bring nothing but more grief upon me.

After eating I got dressed and sat outside for a bit with my cigarettes. I was kind'a hoping to see Cecilia, but she never did show her face.

I had me a late lunch, looking in the way-back of my fridge to see if a beer was lost in there somewheres. But there was none. I knew the whiskey was under the sink, but I didn't even dare peek at it. So I drank ice water with my sandwich, then showered, dressed and drove on out to the beach for a big Saturday night.

The night started fast and furious and didn't let up none. I was busy as a octopus, pouring beer and serving up coolers and drinks and bottles, even serving oysters and shrimp cocktails and shit like that at the bar, all the while thinking I'd look up and see Tam. Never did though.

Jimmy was still out of town and Brad was running the joint. Jack was cooking and April was up front and Minnie, who'd cooked on Friday, was working the rest of the counter. Iris was doing the waitress chores, snaking around the tables to the beat of that loud juke music, laying plates full of hot seafood in all the right places, coming round with her drink orders for me to fill. She and I joked it up some. I stole a few beers and drags from cigarettes when I could. Iris was right there with me.

It was right hopping. Brad helped me out some, but not much, and he looked pleased that I could handle the crowd.

After enough beer and joking with Iris, I was all smiles and yuks with the customers and my tip jar began to fill up with green bills, big handfuls of it like Christmas wrapping after all the presents had been tore up.

I felt pretty good. All of us was moving along fast and happy, like the crowd, and the night just danced on faster and faster. Ol' Fob even came in and we said our howdy-doos and I was kind of glad to see him. He sat at the other end of the counter, the very last stool, which I figured was kind'a his spot, where he could gander at the women and talk to Minnie.

With all that going on, I didn't think much of my not seeing Tam. I was half-dreading and half-looking forward to seeing her, I think. But it wasn't until late night, after the crowds had gone on home to their hangovers, that I thought about it much.

So she hadn't showed.

Just as well, really. Just as well.

Fob had him his own little corner of attention over there. There was a mix of folk, boys and girls, all of them a mite young. But he was buying and so he got to tell all the good jokes and he must have been tipping good, because Minnie was right in there with them.

By closing time he had set up a after-hours party on his boat.

"Chester, Jack, now you all be sure to come on down when you finish. Minnie is coming. April?" He gave her his big white-tooth smile but she got a fright on her face and declined. He laughed it off, like he laughed it all off. "Okay, but Iris is coming, ain't you darling?"

Iris looked at me and I shrugged.

She shrugged to Fob, and he took it as a yes.

"Good, good. See ya'll in a while. But hurry up."

We got the joint closed and Jack put on some real ugly rock and roll and I guess we all felt our energy draining because the night was about over. All that high-time of work was catching up to us a bit, so we started to drink heavier to make up for it some.

By the time we caught our second wind, Minnie had already gone to Fob's boat–with a case of coldbeer he'd paid for–and Brad was jingling the lock-up keys in time with the music.

Iris and I took a to-go cup of beer and our cigarettes and sat on the dark porch. The bar was closed and Brad, being smarter than the rest of us, had gone on home. Jack was already down on Fob's boat. Iris and I could see him there guzzling some kind'a liquor or another from a bottle as we sat and smoked.

There was about six or seven folk on the boat. There was some music, not too loud, and lots of laughing and talking, all of it carrying off over the quiet water. The green and red aft lights was on, giving a nice glow to the whole scene.

"What do you think?" Iris asked.

She and I had taken a shine to each other, nothing big or horny, but enough of a liking to think we understood each other.

"Ain't no harm in going down there, I suppose," I told her. "Fob's not so bad, if you ignore him."

"Yeah, but he's not trying to jump your bones."

"He ain't?" I said and gave her a face.

She laughed. We was about drunk.

"You stay by me then, Chester. We can drink up all of Fob's good shit."

I didn't know about that. I'd seen the man's liquor cabinet. "What the hell," I said.

We got up and ambled down the steps to the dock.

We came upon the small crowd in the boat, me holding Iris' hand so she could jump into it, and Jack greeted us with a howl. Then Fob came up from below, his hands full of open beer bottles. He looked right pleased to see us.

"Chester! Hey! Why I knew you wouldn't let me down. Iris. Darling. Here ya'll go."

He handed us a beer each, handed more to other folk and then went below again.

We stayed and partied with them, laughing, listening to Fob talk about dentists and doctors and flying helicopters, him telling them about me and my boxing and them wanting me to tell stories but I wouldn't. Not much, anyways.

Jack was passing around marijuana joints and a bottle of vodka. Iris took from them both, but I didn't.

"I know what old Mr. Stubbs wants," Fob told them. "I remembered and got it just for you."

Then he was back with George Dickle whiskey, a whole bottle.

All I could figure was I must have told him what I drank, the night before, though I didn't recall it none.

I was feeling too good to turn it down.

I took a hit right from the bottle: the old, familiar, wonderful stab in my gut.

The night went long and the stars reeled up in the black sky. Folks drifted off and there was a bit of a chill coming off the bay until all that was left was us One Leg's crew and Fob.

And so we all went down below, Fob and Minnie and Jack and me and Iris. We drank a little slower, us dumb as manatees as we put a few more smoke stains and butt-burns to his cabin wood.

"I got to go talk to Ralph," Jack said all of a sudden.

We stared at him and he had a look of consternation on his face.

"Ralph?"

"Gotta go talk to Ralph about feeding the fish," Jack said.

He stumbled on up the short steps out of the galley. We all looked at each other until we heard him up there.

"Raaaalfff-raaaallfed-raahhh-fff.."

You know, like that.

He went on for a spell, puking his guts out, and we all just kind'a shut-up and listened and almost laughed. Then he was quiet and I went up to check on him.

There Jack was, his tee-shirt all stained and stinky, lying curled like a puppy-dog at the back of the boat. He was as asleep as a possum at noon. I went back down, got a blanket from Fob, covered the poor sonofabitch up and went back with the others.

And the others was just Minnie, Fob, me and Iris. And that quickly split up to just me and Iris.

Without saying nothing, Fob and Minnie slunk off to one of the bunk rooms. They didn't close the door and Iris and I just sat there, looking, as they went at it like a couple of doomed teenagers.

"Maybe we ought to go," I said.

She threw up her hands.

"Can't believe she's gonna fuck ol' Fob," I added.

"Yeah," Iris said. We was done drunk for sure now. "I guess we should leave them."

We didn't go anywhere.

We poured ourselves some more whiskey, opened more beer.

When we looked next, we could see Minnie's brown legs with Fob's bald ass between them bumping along, kind'a slow and methodical, like a white bobber on a cane pole.

Iris and I looked at each other and rolled our red eyeballs. We guessed we ought to go.

Instead we went into the other bunk.

I don't know if we said nothing or not. All I know's is she and me went in there and commenced to slobber and suckle up to each other. She took her shorts off and I got mine down and we went at it. Man, we went and went and it seemed like I ain't done it none in so long and like Iris was what you dream about when you dream about screwing when you ain't done it none too long and, truth was, I hadn't done it none in too long. It all come on back to me so easy, come back sweet and mean and natural as being hungry.

Goddamn we screwed. We licked and squirmed around, slippery nasty-like, until it was done, until I lay back on that little metal bed with my head up against the wood wall and my big legs sticking all the way out, about into the galley, and Iris was rolled onto my red chest, eyes closed, and neither of us giving a damn about the what-next.

And after I finally did get up, after falling asleep for a bit, waking and waking Iris up too, we got dressed, grabbed a couple extra beers that was warming on the counter, then re-ambled up them steps, said our goodbyes and went on our ways home. Our own ways.

And I got to my little lonesome house, put the unopened beer in the fridge, went into the bedroom, took out my tips for the night from my pocket, threw them on the dresser, me stripping down naked just as the first low low raylights from a Sunday sun was coming to my window sill. Naked in the sheets, I laid there, seeing all that hard cash on my dresser, thinking about a woman's flesh under me, feeling the first hang of a whiskey hangover coming on before I just had to close my eyes and I just had to get some sleep, and, and well, all that bad goodness in my mind and body made me think it was just like the good old days.

Like the old days.

And no way could I think if'n it was right or wrong.

CHAPTER TWENTY-TWO

Sunday.

Goddamn Sunday afternoon with one of them aching hangovers and nothing to make it better. I was out of cigarettes, didn't feel like coffee and didn't have no cocolas or juice or nothing. No headache powder either. I did have me a can of Squirt that I found sitting in the back of the fridge, all lonely-like. Squirt. The hell with that. I grabbed the beer I took from Fob's boat, cracked her open and drank it all down without stopping.

I didn't see Mrs. Guffins. Not even a note. Maybe she took the day off, like she said she might. Reckon that's a good idea. Reckon I ought to do the same—especially from the whiskey. But first I had to get me some smokes.

I got myself dressed—tee-shirt, shorts, slaps—and went out to greet the fucking day. A day hot and slimy, the air thick enough to think Pensacola had done sunk into the sea. The sky was beating hell on my head as I walked along the street, past the bus stop to the Junior Mart around the corner. Inside I bought me a chocolate milk, a quart of yeller Gatoraid, a box of powdered dog-nuts, two packs of Camels and one of them Goodies Headache Powders. I swallowed down the powder with Gatoraid before I even got out of the shade of the doorway. Then I tramped on back home.

I didn't leave the house the rest of the daylight. I just sat in my favored chair and sweated. Killed a few flies. Had some noodle soup for dinner and I began to feel a mite better. When night came I thought about Iris for a spell, horny thoughts, and I began to wonder what she was doing that night. I began to wonder what ol' Fob was up to, too.

And even though it was my night off and I still wasn't feeling all that bright and shiny, I thought maybe I should drive on out to the beach and see what was jumping.

Something to do with my time, anyways.

I bought a can of beer to drink on the drive over.

The beach weren't all too busy, it being a Sunday night. I stopped at One Legs for a coldbeer, hoping to catch Iris. But she weren't working. Jimmy was there, though, back from his weekend away.

"What are you doing here?" he asked when he saw me sitting by myself at the counter. "You ain't working tonight, are you?"

"Nope. Just got bored, I guess."

Jimmy gave me his smile.

"Chester. You're out catting, ain't you? You're back in the groove."

I took my beer on down to the dock. The bay water was all glassy and clear, like a pond of plastic. I stepped onto Fob's boat, tried the little door to the cabin. It was locked. No one home.

I finished my beer and left the empty bottle, like a calling card on his deck, and went back to my car.

I figured to try the Sandshaker, or Dirty Joe's or Sidelines. I could go to The Docks—which got a crowd on Sundays—or Boy On a Dolphin or even the damn Holiday Inn bar. I was bound to run into somebody. You couldn't hide too good on Pensacola Beach.

I was on my third try, at the little dance club next door to Dirty Joe's called The Islander, when I found someone. Problem was, it wasn't no one I was looking for.

It was Tam.

I was sitting at the bar, drinking and smoking, taking a half-look at the crowd when I saw her. She was out there dancing with some yahoo or another, moving her skinny body around like nobody's business. And she was looking straight at me.

She was giving me a mean little look, something saying she was both pissed-off but glad to see me. I didn't want none of it, though. As much as I liked Wayne and felt for him, I didn't need no trouble from his girl. She had eyes for me, I could see it now for sure, but no way was I about to enter that ring. I wasn't never gonna win there, no matter how many rounds it lasted.

I drank the beer, stubbed out my cigarette and was about to hit the door when she come on over.

"I'm still mad at you," she said.

Right then I wished I had a coat or something, or a hat, something to put on and let her know I was just on my way out. As it was, I put my cigarettes in my shirt pocket. She watched me.

"Can I bum one?"

I took them back out.

"Here you go."

I lit the match for her. The bartender come round and Tam ordered up, for us both. I gave up and lit my own.

"How's your Daddy?" I asked her.

She frowned.

"Uptight."

"You still working at the mall?"

She rolled her eyes and asked, "You still at One Legs?"

I smiled, notched one up for her.

"Life is grand," she said.

She laughed at herself and sat on down next to me. The music was going again. I took a glance at the dance floor.

"You got another boyfriend out there?"

"Nah," she said. "Maybe they're all my boyfriends."

"Never can have enough of them," I said.

She laughed for me.

"I came in with some girls," she told me, looking on over at a table so that I looked too.

There was about four of them there, young things all, sitting at a table giggling at us.

"We got Monday off."

"They work at the mall, too, huh?"

"They go to West Florida. But they work summers."

The way she said it, I figured maybe she wanted to be a college-girl too.

"Well," I said, making to leave. "Good to see you. Give a holler to the family."

She put her hand on my arm.

"You give me a ride? Home?"

Hell. I weren't expecting no cargo, but. . . .

"Okay," I said.

I went to the door, still feeling like I ought to have me a coat or hat or something, and she went over to the table of girls. She said something to them, got more giggles, then came over to me.

We went out together.

We made it to the top of the bridge, with the lights of Gulf Breeze and the lights of Pensacola itself sitting near-pretty to the west, before she said anything.

"Maybe you want to get a bottle and park by the Bay and talk," she said.

"Talk?"

"Yeah."

I thought about it a bit, but probably not long enough. I stopped at the Del Champs liquor store and got a six pack and a couple of them little airplane bottles of tequila. At least I didn't go and buy a pint or nothing.

We went on into P-cola, through downtown, down Palafox and onto the big wharf, where the auditorium was. Across the way was the Pensacola Port Authority and the city docks, where the big rigs came in. We sat in the car with the windows down, drinking our canned beer and tiny tequilas, both of us smoking and looking at a big freighter loading up across the water. I could see the longshoremen working hard under the lights, see the cranes going and a few of the crew on the boat moving around, some of them standing and looking out at the Gulf, maybe hankering to ship out. Then again, maybe the opposite. We could even hear us some voices, coming across the water when the hum of the winches wasn't drowning them out. The sights and sounds of it made me a mite anxious to be at sea myself.

"Used to be on a boat bigger than that," I told Tam.

"You were in the. . . . in the Marines?"

"No."

"Not that, I mean in the, what do you call it?"

"The Merchant Marine?"

"Yeah."

"No, no. The Navy. I was a swab in the Navy, on a carrier for a bit."

"Oh yeah? What did you do?"

"Do?" I had to think for a minute. "Hell, I didn't do shit. Didn't do shit."

I was a gunner's mate at that time—after being a shoreman—but I never were good at it.

"I don't like boats much," she told me.

"I thought everyone liked boats."

She turned her head and looked out the other window, where there was some trees. And then I recalled what Duck had told me, about how they got away, about her Mama and all.

"I reckon I better get you on home," I said and started up the car.

She grabbed my arm.

"Wait a minute."

The smile was back on her face, the shine in her black eyes. She moved closer to me, pulling herself in. I knew what she wanted, and though it took me twice to think it, I wasn't gonna have none of it, even if it was nothing more'n a kiss. I moved back some, took her pretty hand off my arm.

"Look, Tam. Like I say, I ain't your boyfriend."

She moved back quick to her side of the car, close to the door. She was mad for a start, but then looked sad-like. We sat there with the car running.

"And you're not my Daddy," she said, not even looking at me anymore.

"You got yourself a damn good Daddy," I told her.

"I don't want a speech."

"That's fine," I said, thinking what I should say. "I ain't good at speeches anyways. . . . But your Daddy, he's worried about you. He even asked me to look out for you, to keep an eye. . . ."

Now she looked at me, at me with all the hellcat back in her eyes. I guess I'd said the wrong thing again.

"Is that why we're here? Are you looking after me? Is he paying you or something?"

"No, no. It ain't like that."

"You just doing your job?"

"No. I never said I'd keep track of you. I didn't. . . . Listen, I don't know, maybe I don't know what I'm doing here with you."

She settled a bit.

"You ain't my Daddy," she said.

"I know."

"You ain't my boyfriend."

"Nope."

"Then why are we here? How come you give me rides home? Why did you buy the beer and park here?"

It was my turn to look out the window, out at the ship across the way, all lit up and loading, a whole floating city of folks waiting to cast off and be gone.

"Maybe I'm just a friend," I told her.

"A friend?" she said, looking up at me, her eyes still hard.

"Yeah," I said. "It's a sight better than a enemy, ain't it?"

She didn't say whit.

I took her on home and then went home myself.

Come morning, I missed Mrs. Guffins again. I got up late with a cloudy head, sat on the edge of my bed and scratched my balls. The night before was a odd one. I couldn't make outsides or innards from what Tam and I was up to. . . . I got up and took a peek out my window, at that there pecan tree. I wasn't expecting to see Cecilia out there or nothing, but I thought I'd at least have a look.

Nothing much going on. The day was grey with a little rain falling down. Maybe she didn't chop on account of it, though it ain't ever stopped her before. Poor old woman. She didn't look to be making much work on that tree. Here it was, hurricane season, and that thing was shedding pecans like a dog scratching off fleas.

I went out to the kitchen to see if she'd been in.

No note. No coffee. No nothing.

I felt a touch bad about it. Seemed like a long time since we'd had a morning together, though it'd been but a few days. I figured I owed that woman something, though I couldn't right say what it was. I didn't want to go on over, though, knowing she'd give me her old grandma stare if I told her what I'd been up to. I'd catch her on Tuesday.

I made my coffee and settled in for another day of whatever.

I twiddled through the day okay, till about nightfall. Then I started to get bored as a wingless bat and had a hankering to go to the beach. I poured me a whiskey under the kitchen lights—just the one—looked out the window some, tried to shake it. I played the radio.

I smoked through my pack of Camels and was about to go get more—to go get in my car and take off and probably not stop till I was on the beach—but then I recalled I had some in my bedside table. So I didn't go nowhere.

Eventually I fell asleep in my chair with the teevee on, getting up in the middle of the night to turn it off and get myself in bed.

I did wake up early, and was ready to roll over and sleep some more, when I thought of old Cecilia. I made myself get up and take a look out the window.

There was that tree, tall and lively in the early light. There was more pecans than ever, for all I could tell. But there was no old lady. No Cecilia Guffins.

I thought I was early enough. Reckon not though, since she weren't there. So I put on my boxer shorts and went to the kitchen.

Nobody there but the roaches. The bugs scurried on off to wherever they lived when I flipped on the light. I made the coffee, sitting and letting my head clear as it dripped and burped. Maybe that old lady had given up. Didn't seem too likely, really, but I know that the impossible can get the best of anyone. And I reckon her ever felling that there tree was on the impossible side.

I drank some coffee, waited, expecting to see her. If not, I guess I'd go over and say my howdy-doos. Later maybe.

When later-maybe came, about eleven that morning, I went on over and knocked on her front door. I knocked and stood like some kind of farm animal on her stoop, dumb and fidgety, waiting, knocking again and no one came.

Maybe she was out with that son of hers that I'd never seen, or maybe out with some other old fossil doing whatever it is they do. Shopping, playing cards, square dancing, maybe going over the obituaries with a magnifying glass. But I made my way round the back door just the same, beginning to feel a sweat creeping onto my neck. I even heard my own heart beat.

I knocked on that door. I tapped the bedroom windows. I tried the knob on both doors again, but they was fixed shut. I wasn't right sure what to do. If'n I broke in, she wouldn't be too pleased to have to put a new jamb on her door. Or I might get myself arrested. . . . I reckon I could break a window. As I recall, she broke one of mine.

191

Maybe I could break a itty-bitty one.

I busted the back door window with my fist, then reached inside and opened her up.

The lights was off in the house and I didn't hear no teevee or radio or nothing like that. It was hot and things didn't look like they'd been moved around much. I wandered into the living room, calling her name, not too loud but loud enough. There weren't no answer, not even a cat. She ought to have herself a cat.

I went down to where I figured her bedroom was. I didn't know the house. It was a two-bedroom house, the front one being a guest room, I reckoned, because the bed didn't look like it'd been used since maybe the nineteen seventies or something. I tried the next room and could tell it was hers.

"Mrs. Guffins?" I called. "Ma'am?"

The curtains was closed and no lights was on. Her bed was a bit mussed but it looked like no one was there. That was, not until I saw the feet sticking up from the wall.

"Mrs. Guffins?"

The bed sat close to the wall, with one little head-table there for distance. In that little space there was definitely a pair of legs–calves, ankles and bare feet–sticking up near the bunched covers, not moving at all. And they was Cecilia Guffin's feet.

I went on over to see the rest of her.

And there she was, her old body kind of twisted and stuck down in that space between the wall and the big wood bed. Her head was facing up, her face powder-white and her eyes closed. She looked done dead to me.

"Cecilia," I said.

I was gonna call, call someone, figured I had to, was supposed to call someone.

"Goddamn," I said, my breathing getting hard. "Cecilia . . . goddamn, Cecilia!"

And then a eye opened. One eye that didn't look to be seeing a thing.

"Chester? That you?"

It was her voice, low and almost not there, but it was her.

"Cecilia, I'm here," I said.

"Chester," she answered, still sounding further away than the one foot I stood from her. "Chester, I was so hoping you would come to call."

CHAPTER TWENTY-THREE

I rode with her in the ambulance to Baptist Hospital. The folks there asked me a whole hell of a lot of questions but all I could say was what her name was and where she lived. I didn't even know her phone number. I told them I thought she had a son, maybe, but maybe he didn't live in Pensacola. I had to tell them my name and all that crap and how I had found her and why. All the while she was laid out on a table in the emergency room and there was some nurses and doctors buzzing around her but not really seeming to do too much.

I had a few questions of my own. Like, what the hell happened? Was she okay? Was she gonna live? But they didn't answer them any better than I answered theirs.

The hospital people took her away then. I didn't know where and they wasn't gonna tell me, so I just kind'a wandered the hallway for a spell, checked out the waiting room where a teevee was playing, then went outside and stood against the wall and smoked. Finally, when I went back in, there was a doctor who'd tell me a thing or two.

"Mr. Stubbs?" he said.

"That's me. Is Cecilia gonna be okay? She all right?"

"I think so," he said, like that was real inspiring.

193

"What was it?" I asked.

"A stroke, I believe. . . . It's hard to say for sure and we're going to keep her here for a few days, maybe a week, for observation. At her age it could be a number of things. Her heart, maybe. We think it was a mild stroke. She should be fine. She's talking."

"Can I see her?"

"Not right now. No. I don't think so."

There he was, being inspirational again.

"It's good that you found her when you did, Mr. Stubbs. She was suffering from dehydration. Another day and. . . . You said she was caught under the bed?"

"Not under," I told him. "She was kind'a stuck between the bed and the wall. Had a hell of a time getting her up and straightening her out."

"I see. . . . She thinks she was there for two days, maybe three, like that. . . . Doesn't she have someone, you know, family, that visits her or at least calls?"

"Hell, I don't know. . . . I reckon I was the only one she saw, for a while there anyways. . . . I don't know."

"Well," and he paused some, so I'd know he was finishing up, was done doing his talking to me. "She does have insurance. And Medicaid. . . . She gave us the name and number of a lawyer who handles her estate for her. . . ."

I shrugged. I never saw no one nor heard tell of anyone from her.

"Anyway, Mr. Stubbs, she might need some looking after when she gets back home. . . . For now there's nothing, for now you may as well go home. You can probably visit tomorrow."

"All right," I said. "Thanks, Doc."

I had to take a city bus to get home. I didn't even have enough pocket money for a cab.

I wasn't right sure what to do with myself. I couldn't help but to think of Cecilia, her lying there in some hospital room, probably with one of them curtains drawn around her bed like she was a dead lady. Cecilia Guffins, feisty as she was, going at that pecan tree like she had, now she was some lame old lady who had to be looked out for. And I didn't like thinking of her that way, especially because I'd been ignoring her of late, because I'd moved on from waking up to her soft chopping at dawn, to her sipping sweet coffee across the table from me, moved on from her telling me what she thought of this and that, what she done thought of me.

Later, just about sunset, I did spy a car pulling into Cecilia's drive. It was a brown Buick, clean and waxed without even a drop of birdshit, and out of it come some man in a suit. I saw he had some keys and let himself into the front door of the house. I figured he was the lawyer. Guess he was gonna make sure all was okay, maybe block up the back door and window where I'd busted in. Maybe he'd want to talk to me or something.

But I didn't want to talk, especially to no lawyer. Didn't feel up to it none.

I put on my slaps, shoved a handful of tip money in my pocket, grabbed my car keys, and went out the door.

I drove east, away from the low sun, not knowing where I was going but knowing just the same.

I thought I was going to the beach. But when I got to the turn-off, where that old billfish sign was blinking its orange and blue and green, I didn't turn. Instead I went straight, straight on to where that real estate office was and that little orange-dirt road headed to the sound, on to Wayne and Duck's house.

I doused my headlights, pulled on up in the drive, killed the engine and got out. Then I sat there on the hood of my car, even though it was damn hot. I sat and smoked one, trying to figure exactly what the hell I was doing. Upstairs there was some lights on and I could hear that tinny music, like a bunch of strings being pulled at once, and there was the smell of their fried seahorse hearts or whatever it was they'd cooked up, and then, then I looked through the screen and I could see those damn windchimes I'd given them that first night. They was still up there, though I couldn't hear them none unless they was mixed with the music.

I waited around a bit, trying to think what I might do or was gonna say, hoping maybe they'd come out and see me, hoping maybe they wouldn't. And I wasn't sure who I was there to see. Was it Duck and Wayne? Or was it Tam? I hoped it wasn't Tam. Things was peculiar enough as they was.

I decided to go on up myself.

I went up the wooden stairs, quiet-like, hearing some voices as I got closer. I opened their screen door, not letting it slap behind me as I went on in, still quiet, silent as them owls that live in the jack-pines along the bay as I sneaked on across the porch, getting right up to their door before stopping. Then I peeped in the window like some odd fellow or something. I couldn't seem to help myself, couldn't help it none even though I felt damn crazy as I stood there and looked inside. And there they was, the whole lot of them except Tam. They was sitting at the big table playing dominos, Wayne and Duck smoking up a storm under the hanging light, little bowls of eats next to their skinny elbows, all of them moving them white domino chips around and laughing, the boy smiling, the woman with a pencil and paper keeping score, the kitchen behind her all dim with only the stove light on and thick green plants hanging from the ceiling corners and I could hear them in there, hear the laughs and some talk, hear their music muffled and tin-panny and the windchimes behind me on their top-porch tinkling soft as a sea breeze . . . and then there Tam was. I seen her come out of the back hall wearing a robe and her long hair wrapped up good with a white towel, coming out of the shower or the bath and she kind'a stood there, looking at her family, her Uncle Duck's family playing a game together, listening, and they didn't see her but she leaned against the wall and I seen her laugh at it, her pretty face breaking up into a wide grin, her black eyes shining.

And then she looked at me.

She looked over at the door anyways, where I was standing in the moon-dark. And she did a double take, looking again though I didn't reckon she could really see me none. But I wasn't gonna take no chances. And maybe she did see something, because she gave a funny look and took a few steps my way. But I didn't want to see her, I didn't want to trouble their evening, trouble their life. I couldn't. If she was coming to the door, I wasn't gonna be there behind it.

I backed away slow, silent. I closed the screen door with my fingers, went back down them steps and got into my car, quiet as settling dust. I left the headlights off when I started her up. I'd about backed up to the road, under the hang of scrub oak, when the porch light popped on. The light came on and maybe the door was opened and maybe someone called who's there or maybe even my goddamn name.

But if they did, I wasn't there to hear it. I was gone.

I hit Highway 98 and drove back the way I'd come. I drove with the windows down, feeling a sight worse than when I'd started, not listening to the radio, not even wanting a smoke. My head was a big blank, just dumb as a shucked oyster shell, until I got the idea I should go see Crow.

It stuck in my brain like chewing gum. I should go see Crow and apologize and talk to him and tell him what I'd been up to, tell him everything about what a dumbshit I was and about Duck and Wayne and Tam, about Fob Langtree and me working at One Leg's, tell him about poor old Cecilia Guffins.

So I slid on back to Pensacola proper, knowing I was gonna go talk to Crow. Only, I needed some gas. So I stopped at a station, filled it up and went in to pay. I laid down my cash and bought a cocola and went back out and sat on the hood of my car for a spell. I drank from the bottle and watched traffic and I knew I wasn't a gonna do it. I was not gonna go see Crow.

I couldn't get myself to do it.

I got back in and took off and went to the beach, to find Fob, thinking it's what I should'a done from the start.

I didn't bother searching for him this time. I didn't even bother going on in to One Leg's. I bought a fresh pack of Camels, a lighter and a quart of coldbeer at the Tom Thumb, walked over to the docks behind the bar and went onto his boat.

I went behind the cabin, where no one could see me, and made myself comfortable. I sat like a lizard and smoked and drank from the big bottle. I watched the boats out on the bay, listened to the rock and roll noise from the bar and waited. I didn't want to do nothing else.

And along about late-o'clock, here he come.

My beer was gone, my cigarettes half-smoked and I was near asleep when I heard someone clopping down the dockboards. I sat still until I felt the boat tip as he hopped on her and came slipping along the little starboard walk to the deck. And when his flat feet done touched the polished wood, I stood up out of the shadows.

"Hey, Fob, " I said.

He about jumped two miles.

"Jesus! What in the fucking Jesus!"

"Been waiting for you," I said, stepping closer.

"Chester. . . . Goddamn, Chester. Don't you ever, buddy, never do that again. I about peed my pants."

"Sorry."

It took him a bit to catch his scared breath.

"Hell, Chester. . . . I ain't seen you in a few days."

He put his hand out for me to shake. Just a reaction, I guessed, him being a salesman and all. I went ahead and shook it. I looked at him and he looked at me. He didn't seem too drunk or nothing, but I guess I looked damn lousy.

"What's the matter?" he said. "Your cat got run over today or something? You look like a man who needs a drink. I was heading in early myself, even I've got to recoup now and then, but hey, we can have a short one. Come on down."

I followed him below.

He turned on a light and got out some drinking glasses from a cabinet. I didn't feel like slouching, so I sat on a little seaman's chair that pulled out from the wall and hung by chains. We didn't say nothing as he poured a couple, straight up.

Fob handed me one of the glasses, gave a little toast and we drank us some whiskey. It felt near good.

"So, what's up?"

"Nothing much," I said.

"Say, Chester, did you nail that waitress last weekend? Iris? Did you get yourself some of that?"

I didn't say anything. I'd plumb forgot about Iris. Maybe she'd plumb forgot about me, or maybe'd like to. I hoped not, because I wanted to see her again. Me and Iris. But I sure as hell didn't want to talk about it, not with Fob anyways.

I figured I'd best go ahead and talk about what I really wanted to.

"I pulled a dead lady out of her house today," I said.

He looked a mite perplexed.

"Okay," he said.

"Only she weren't really dead, just pret'near. An old lady. She had a stroke or heart attack or something."

"Was she your Mama?"

"No, no. My Mama's been gone a long while. She's a neighbor, next door, but we been visiting regular. We was friends."

"But she's alive?"

"Yeah, she's up at Baptist Hospital, gonna be there a while, I reckon. . . . I guess I'm just shook a bit. Been a while since I seen dead folk, or near-dead anyways."

"Maybe because she was a friend," Fob said and he reached the bottle over and poured me some more.

I didn't even know I'd drunk it down.

"Maybe," I said.

"Friends are sometimes few and far between, for guys like us."

"How's that?" I asked.

"Shit, Chester. Guys like us: divorced, about past our prime, always out looking for something to do with ourselves, looking for a party, some drink, some pussy." He gave me his greasy smile for a second. "We don't have a whole lot of roots. That's what I mean."

I reckoned he was about right.

"Why the hell you think I hole up here all summer? This boat is only my bedroom. The bar is my living room and the whole beach is like my house, like my home. Jimmy and Jack are my pals. You too, Chester. All else I got is a few doctors over in Okaloosa County I golf with and a few doctor's wives I'm stringing along. Shit like that."

"Sounds like shit," I said.

He laughed, slapped me on the back.

"Damn right. . . . Let's have another, then call it a night. You ought to sleep here tonight. Go on and spend the night."

"I don't know," I said. I didn't want to spend the night on Fob's boat. I didn't know why, exactly, but it didn't come to me as a good idea. "Don't think I should."

"Hell, why not? Here."

He poured us another short one.

"Go lie down. Think about it. I got to go up to the bar and take a crap, maybe get some shrimp, but I'll be right back. Relax, Chester, relax."

He plugged up the whiskey bottle and set it on the counter before leaving. I felt the boat shove when he left it, then heard him walk away on the worn planks. I took my glass and went into the other bunk room. I propped a few pillows up and leaned back, taking a few drinks and looking out the porthole at the water and sky and black stand of timber across the way. I drank it all down and thought about the owls and fox and shit living over there in them woods, so close to the road and town. I thought about them and the boat rocked and I closed my tired eyes.

I didn't know what time it was when I woke up. At first I wasn't right certain where I was, until I bumped my head when I stood up. One Legs had closed and it was dark as a coal mine in Fob's cabin. There was no traffic either, boats or cars. Everything had that quiet, that sea-quiet, with the summer waves snuffing in on the beach over yonder only making it quieter.

That was, until I heard Fob snore.

At first I thought maybe he was over there attacking another ugly woman. As I got ready to sneak on home, I seen that his door was open and he was lying on his bed, near naked, his head cocked back, letting big rumblers come out. That might'a been what woke me up.

I looked around a bit, getting my bearings. The whiskey bottle was still there, along with a couple empty beer cans too. There was a ashtray full of dead butts and a neat pile of shrimp shells on a paper plate. Fob was working up some more thunder as I went top-side.

The sky held some clouds but there weren't much wind. It must'a been near dawn, I figured, what with the quiet and lack of wind. I felt like sleeping some more, sleeping like a damn rock, but I still had a creepy feeling about staying on Fob Langtree's boat. Just a gut-wrong feeling. He'd been awful good to me, though, last night. We didn't talk much, but I guess we'd talked enough for me to sleep. I stood there, running my fingers through my hair, having some second thoughts. Then I remembered about Cecilia. And that was enough to wake me up and send me back home.

Back in my own house, I caught some more sleep. When I got up, I dressed myself best I could, took breakfast at the Awful-Waffle and made it to the hospital by ten A.M.

The smell of hospitals gives a lot of folks the willies, but I got different feelings. It reminds me of Marleen, is why. I met her at a hospital and even after we was married she'd have that smell on her after coming home from a long shift. She'd smell that way when we'd screw and screw right when she came home, sometimes with only her shoes and stockings off and her whites all bunched up over her hips, before she had a chance for a shower. . . . Hospitals weren't nothing strange or bad to me, back then at least. Even now, what with my last experience, when I was laid up with my ribs and lung, and even considering what happened between Marleen and me, even now just the smell of one roots up some decent recollections, good and sad. . . . And when I peeked into Cecilia's room and saw her sitting up in bed reading the morning *News-Journal,* it was definitely a good feeling that hit me.

Cecilia was at the end of a three-bed room. The middle bed was empty but the first one had some really old lady in it and she didn't look good at all. That lady was propped up with her eyes shut tight and she had tubes running out of her nose and had I-Vees in both arms and all sorts of mechanical shit affixed to her bed side. I couldn't look long. I went past that woman and over to Cecilia, where she still had her old nose in the newspaper, and she had but one tube running into her grey arm.

"Ain't' you got a tree to be chopping?" I said.

She looked up, threw down her paper, and gave me a smile.

"Mr. Stubbs! Chester, I was hoping to see you. Glory. I thank you. I believe you saved my life."

She put out her hand, the one that wasn't tied to a bag of fluids, and I gave her mine. She held it pretty strong.

"You're looking good, compared to yesterday."

"Oh, I'm all right," she said, taking a look at the door. "These doctors and nurses and whoever are fussing. I'm ready to go home, I am, but they won't let me."

"Well, Ma'am, I can't exactly blame them."

"But they want to keep me a whole ten days! I'm eating and drinking and they got these fluids going in me, but they want to observe me, they say, observe. . . ."

I almost laughed. She was fighting already.

"Anyway, Chester, I can't thank you enough, you know. How can I thank you?"

I didn't know and I didn't want her to thank me any. If I'd been any good, I would've been over two days before. I was almost too late as it was, so the doctor said.

"Don't think of it none," I told her. "Maybe I was just returning a favor. So don't thank me."

She just went back to smiling and fixing me with some new kind of stare, ready to say something.

"Don't thank me no more," I said again. "All right?"

"Oh. . . . I'll do as I please."

"I reckon you will," I said.

And I pulled up a chair and she told me about it, at least what she recalled. She told me she'd dreamed about chopping that tree, chopping and chopping until it came on down, but it come down on top of her, she said, and she'd done woke up and kind'a jumped up, faster than she'd moved in years, only she was in her bed and then she had a hard feeling in her chest and down her arm and then about everywhere and then she was falling again, only it weren't no dream this time. She fell back, conking her blue head on the wall or table or something and then she was out, out black. She told me she'd woke up and it was dark and she was all numb, she didn't know what time or what day it was, but she couldn't move the bed or get up or even roll away from the wall. She tried but she couldn't. She tried to yell for help, but no one heard her or maybe she just couldn't raise her voice loud enough and eventually she was out again, all the while figuring it would be me that'd show up, show up and get her the hell out of that ridiculous situation.

She told it like it wasn't much of anything now, that it was over and she'd already put it behind her. Yet it was almost just the day before–hell, it was the day before. It didn't sit that well with me, to think of it. It didn't sound like nothing I hoped I ever had to go through.

I was glad to see her act tough, talk it through like it weren't much. If she weren't the damnedest most unusual lady I'd ever know, I didn't know who the hell was.

I stayed with her through lunch, talking about this and that, watching a dumb teevee show with her. Then a nurse come in and said it was time for some goddamn test or another. Cecilia didn't like it none, but she wasn't gonna get out of it. So I said my goodbyes and said I'd see her tomorrow and I left, hearing her complaining all the way.

I knew I should'a said I'd come back and have dinner with her that night. But maybe she had other visitors, maybe her son, ol' Mr. X, was gonna drop by or something. Something. But I doubted it. I'd see her tomorrow though, I would, and the next day and after. But I didn't want to come on back that night, something about when I walked by that other lady in the first bed made me not want to. She hadn't moved even one old muscle the whole time I was there.

CHAPTER TWENTY-FOUR

I went through the week slow and sober. In the morning I got up, got ready and went on over to the hospital to see Cecilia, left around noon, then came on back in the evening for a game of cards or some such shit and more talk. I guess I felt I owed her some, guess I felt sorry for her a bit, laid up with no family I could tell of, so I didn't mind it none. Maybe one thing that kept me coming was that the next day I visited, that first bed was empty. I didn't even ask what happened, just figured there was one less old lady in north Florida was all.

Jimmy'd given me my weekdays off, bumping them into next week, so I didn't go back out to the beach. Though I was scheduled in for the weekend, I tried to get out of it too, but Jimmy needed me bad, it being summer and all. And truth was, not only did I need the money, I wanted to see Iris, too.

So I went in like old times but it weren't the same. Iris was working and she and I said the same old shit, tried to laugh like we did before, but we'd crossed some damn line or other—the sex-line, I reckon—and maybe she wished we hadn't done it. We didn't talk about it, anyways, though I promised myself I'd see to it that we did. But something, something was all different with her just the same.

And then there was Fob.

He was there, not saying too much but giving me a look like we was brothers or something, like we was in on something together.

Sunday night was the worst, because he got skunk-drunk and near got his ass beat by a couple of young dicks from the beach. He'd been on over to Sidelines trying to hit on some bikinis, but they was these boys' bikinis. So the young studs followed him on over to One Legs. He made a point to sit right in front of me, where I was working like a monkey behind the bar. It didn't take me long to catch on that he was in trouble and that he was expecting me to stick my fat neck out for him. And I did. Not just because of him but also because it was my job. So when punches was thrown, I threw a good one and cooled the bigger of them right there in the bar. When his head whomped against the bar floor, I felt pretty bad. But that's business. And anyways, it sure made Jimmy happy. It gave One Leg's the reputation where you couldn't get away with that kind of shit, but also I think Jimmy just liked seeing it. And it sure as hell pleased Fob. Now he figured we was blood brothers for sure.

It was that night I finally worked up the nerve and corralled Iris for a talk. It was when the bar'd closed and we was cleaning up. It wasn't like I was gonna ask her for no repeat or nothing. I guess I was gonna ask her out, like on a date or something.

But she said no.

We was sitting at the end of the bar, me with a beer and her with a ginger ale, and she said more'n just no.

"I'm tired, Chester."

"I didn't mean tonight," I said.

"No, I mean tired of all of this: waiting tables, the beach, drinking. Especially the drinking."

I nodded.

"You need to rest up a bit. I did that. Down to mostly beer now."

She shook her head.

"It doesn't work like that, Chester. I need to quit for good. I'll be thirty-one come September and I'm killing myself. The party's over, for me. I need to grow up."

That hit me somewheres where it counted, but I shook it off.

"We don't have to get drunk, that ain't what I'm saying–"

"I like you fine enough, Chester. I do. But I've fallen off the wagon before, and I know I can't hang out here or see the same people if I want it to stick. Not for a long time, maybe."

"You ain't going to. . . ."

"Join A.A., baby," she said. "This is not working at all."

And I didn't have no more to say and neither did she and but a day later she done quit and wasn't seen on the beach no more.

But I got through my work nights after that fell through, drinking some beer but not too much, waiting for my days off so I could get back to the old-lady life with Cecilia at the hospital, so I'd be there to take her on home.

And I was the one to take her home. No one else volunteered. She was fine, best I could tell, though they made her ride in a wheelchair all the way down to the door. And that's when they gave her a cane. I was surprised, because the way she talked I figured she was her old self. I had to help her get to where my car was. But anyways, it was about noon when they let her go. She got in my car, I tossed the cane in the back, and off we went.

"So, Chester, tell me how you've been doing. . . . The truth now."

All the hours we spent together we never discussed me too much, or if she asked I didn't say much more than fine and dandy.

"I'm doing good," I said, seeing if it'd work one more time. It didn't.

"Come now. I asked for the truth. We aren't in the hospital anymore, you can tell me anything. Like we used to."

That seemed an awful long time ago.

"I guess I don't know how I'm doing, one way or another."

"You're confused then," she said. "Working out on the beach has confused you."

"Maybe just working is what's got me confused."

She almost laughed.

"You been behaving yourself?"

Shit. Even my own goddamn mother never asked me that. Never.

"Let me ask you something," I said. "You still got a mind to assassinate that pecan tree?"

"I'm still thinking about that tree," she said, her mind drifting a bit. "But I can get back to it when I want. It's not going anywhere soon."

But you might, I almost said.

"Now you answer me, Chester."

"Answer you what?"

"About your behavior."

We was almost home. I was burping on over the little bridge into Warrington and we was almost to the turn to our street. But I knew I'd have to say something sooner or later, even though later was a mite more appealing just then.

"I was having some good times," I said and then looked over at her, "but maybe them good times come with a price."

"There's a price to everything, Mr. Stubbs. . . . A price to everything."

And then we pulled into my drive.

Cecilia wasn't quite up to par yet, so we started having coffee over at her house in the morning. Not early morning no more either, but around nine o'clock I'd mosey on over to her white kitchen and we'd have us some and talk a little. I had lunch with her a few times and spent a few evening hours on her back porch drinking sweet tea, maybe playing cards and listening to the mosquitoes whine against the screen. I didn't mind. And at work I kept my nose pretty clean. I drank me some beer but didn't spend any late hours with Fob, he and I just shooting the shit when the crowds'd been cleared out at closing time. Iris was gone, but things was all right.

But the slow life only lasts for so long, I reckon. Summer was hot and getting nasty. The beach was having a big season and there was festivals about every weekend: Mullet Festival, Gumbo Festival, Bikini Festival, a Billfish Rodeo, shit like that. And there was the Fourth of July and then the fifth and sixth and so on, right into August. Jimmy was on top of the world, just raking it in.

But for me it all seemed to be getting out of control. Each day come a little wilder, a little longer, feeling that much closer to some disaster or another. I seen it that way, anyways. And I was in demand there, at One Legs. It got to where I was working four to five to six days a week, pouring beers and drinks and serving up shrimps and oysters and breaking up more fights than I knew. It got to where I didn't right know what day of the week it was, almost what month. I just spent my mornings half-asleep with Cecilia and spent my nights jamming at the bar and conversing with all the weird folks I done knew by heart now.

Them old quiet days with Cecilia slipped away damn fast. I couldn't remember them any better than my own birthday.

And then I got to staying late and later after work, drinking beer with Fob and the gang, but still no George Dickle whiskey. I'd see Tam here and there and we'd talk a little, but that was all. And I got to where I was spending a night or two or three on Fob's boat, not driving home till the sun was up and hot as cherry pie. I let my mornings with Cecilia fade some.

I still saw her on my one or two days off. She didn't say much about what I was up to. Maybe that was on account'a I was her only line to the world out there, because I was the one doing her grocery shopping and running to the pharmacy for her old-lady drugs and stuff like that. She wasn't getting any better and still hobbled about with that cane. I even vacuumed her goddamn house a couple times. . . . Hell, I guess she was my line to the real world too, when I thought about it.

But I didn't think about it often enough, I reckon.

And maybe the summer would'a just gone on and played itself out like that, me busy working and drinking at night and acting like a preacher's son for Cecilia Guffins in the daylight. Maybe it could'a. But the night Tam come on in to One Legs, lit up like a firefly in a beer bottle and telling me she was gonna run off to California, well, that about put a ruin to it all.

CHAPTER TWENTY-FIVE

I don't know what day it was, maybe a Wednesday, maybe a Saturday, but I was behind the taps working and yakking, drinking a few beers and loading the tip jar up best I could, when she come in. Tam. She was grinning that big grin of hers so that I knew right off she'd been drinking some. More'n me at least. I gave her a nod and one of my honest smiles, then went back to my job. But she stuck around and wormed her way on up to the counter, looking at me the whole while like she had something important to say. And when a bar stool turned up empty, she sat down in front of me.

"You want a milkshake?" I asked.

I didn't know if she'd laugh, but she did.

I got her a wine cooler, on the house. She sat there, looking at me, still grinning.

"So, what's up?" I finally asked.

I was sweating from arm pit to arm pit and had to wash me up some beer pitchers, so I did that while she talked.

"Chester," she said. "Chester, I am so happy. I am happy!"

"Happy about what?"

"I'm just happy, like, excited. . . . I'm going to California."

I didn't hear her too well and had to get some sonofabitch's drink order. Maybe he weren't a sonofabitch after all, he left me a buck in the jar.

"What's that?" I asked after.

"California. I'm going to San Diego!"

"San Diego?"

I rolled my eyes.

"I'm going," she said.

"What you gonna visit San Diego for?"

"I'm not going to visit. I'm moving. I'm going to go live in California."

Oh hell.

"I'm going with Pauley. We're going to live together."

Oh shit.

"Who the hell is Pauley?" I asked.

She answered but I didn't get to hear. It was too damn busy. I had to take care of all the others who wanted their drinks and goodtimes, their own Californias and Pauleys.

"Hang around," I told Tam, when I got back to her. "Or come on back around closing. I want to hear this, okay?"

She gave me a nod and then was off, walking out the door with her bare shoulders and tan legs, her long hair and her goddamn idea about leaving Pensacola.

So I worked like shit the rest of the night, trying not to drink too much or to smile too hard, trying to ignore that little burn in the pit of my stomach that was telling me something was wrong, damn wrong.

The bar'd done closed and I was cleaning up the joint, with no sight of Tam. Maybe she'd got too drunk or maybe she was out partying with the dawn-patrol drinkers. I sure as hell hoped she wasn't on her way out of Florida or nothing. So I was getting a little worried–like I was her damn Daddy, after all–until I saw her.

I saw her out the back window. Down on the docks and talking to Fob Langtree. Only the two of them.

I finished up and got down there, right quick.

"Chester, Chester," Fob said, sticking his hand out like always, though I'd seen him but a couple hours ago. "I was just inviting this young lady onto my boat. . . . I reckon you'll join us?"

"Damn right," I said.

Tam smiled. She didn't look too far gone, considering the hour. I didn't know what Fob had in mind–hell, I knew exactly what he had in mind–but I was gonna do the talking and be sure to get her on home after. So, we all went on the boat.

I didn't bother asking why she didn't come up to the bar and what she was doing with Fob. It didn't matter none now. Fob was being a right gentleman, or trying to be what I reckon he thought would impress Tam. We sat up topside but he brought up about his whole liquor supply and some fancy glasses with little designs in them. He had a bucket of ice with them salad-bar tongs so you didn't have to get your fingers cold and a bunch of other oddball shit that he lugged up in about three trips. I would'a laughed but I was worried for Tam.

"I know what Chester will have," Fob said, handing me a coldbeer but looking elsewhere, "but what would you care for?"

He stood in front of the display he'd done drug up.

Tam took her time, looking the junk over, picking up a bottle of this and then that, reading labels and fingering the fancy glass. I went ahead and opened my beer while she doodled around.

"Can you make me an iced tea?"

"Tea? You mean a Long Island Tea?"

"No," Tam said. "Just plain tea. Iced tea, you know, instant would be okay."

Fob looked damned silly.

"Well, I. . . . I don't drink much tea myself. I suppose I could go on to the store up yonder and buy some. . . . You sure?"

"Tea. Yes, I'd like some iced tea. That would be sweet of you."

Fob liked her calling him sweet, so he went, giving me a green eye before he left.

"Don't he know we're friends?" I asked, after Fob was half up the stairs.

"I don't know. . . . He's kind of, kind of, I don't know, slippery?"

"He ain't too bad," I said, sticking up for Fob's good side. "But I reckon you ought to stay clear of him about this time of night."

"Why? Does he, like, turn into a werewolf or something?"

"You mean he ain't one now?"

We laughed some.

"Well, I won't be around much longer."

"California," I said.

She nodded.

214

"San Diego," I said.

She nodded some more.

"Johnny."

"Pauley," she said.

"Just checking to see if'n it weren't someone different by now."

I figured that would piss her off, but it didn't.

"Okay," I said, "so go on and give me the details, here."

"Do you know Pauley?" I shook my head no. "Well he comes around a lot, plays volleyball all day and, well, that's why he's going to San Diego. . . ."

"To hang around beach bars?" I asked.

"No. To play volleyball. Sand volleyball, two-man teams, it's really a big deal now. It's on TV and in sports magazines, like professional. Anyway, that's what he's into and I'm going with him, I mean, he's got friends out there, a friend, a guy he's going to team with. . . ."

"When?" I asked.

"When?"

"When ya'll fixing to go?".

"Well. . . . soon, I think. He's got to get some more money together, we're going to pool our money."

"So you're staking Pauley some cash?"

"No. I mean, we're pooling it, sharing it to get us out there, I mean. . . ."

"You gonna feather this guy's beach shack while he plays volleyball all day, is that it?"

She gave me a look, seeing where it was all heading in my mind.

"Look," she said, "I was just trying to tell you, let you know I wasn't going to be stuck here anymore, wasn't going to have to work in the mall anymore or live with my Uncle, you know."

I didn't want her to get mad, but just the same, I wasn't gonna encourage her none. The whole thing smelled like ten day old tuna. Tam didn't need no long-distance disasters. I didn't figure her to have the nerves for it.

"What's your Daddy say?"

She didn't look at me, but was about getting ticked off now.

"I'm not going to tell him. . . . Not yet, anyway."

"You ought to."

Now she looked at me, them eyes full of that coal black.

"Ought to? Ought to? What do you know, Chester Stubbs? Where I'm standing, you don't look like any role model!"

Well, she had me there.

"I'm just giving my opinion," I said.

"Did I ask for it? Did I?"

"I just reckon he should know, before you go way off with some guy who wants to hit a ball over a net for a living."

She kept staring at me, mad, a regular beehive swarming behind them eyes. I stared right back.

"It's my life," she told me. "It is, you know. Mine!"

I finally took a drink of beer.

"Your one and only," I said.

And then she'd done had enough. She jumped off'a that boat and raced on down the dock to the stairs, whizzing by old Fob as he was coming down with a jar of instant tea in his hand. He didn't even have time to try a new line on her, she was gone that fast. I figured I'd better catch her and get her home, late as it was.

I met Fob halfway down the dock.

"Thanks a lot, Chester," Fob said, not even asking me to stick around.

"Anytime," I said.

"Don't get me wrong," he said. "I like your company just fine, but when there's a fine piece like that. . . ."

I turned on him.

"That girl ain't gonna have nothing to do with you, Fob. Never. So don't you go trying to hustle her."

"Goddamn it, Chester."

I got up close and over him, him still standing there with his clean shirt and pants and jar of store-bought tea.

"I said don't. I mean don't. Never."

Then I went on after Tam.

Never did find her, though.

I drove up and down the beach road at least five times before I went on home. She must'a had a ride or some late party or maybe her Pauley lived on the beach and she was shacking there. Anyways, she done disappeared on me and I didn't know when I'd see her again. If ever.

And it bothered me enough that I told Cecilia about it the next day.

"You'd better tell the father," she told me.

We was in her kitchen, having some morning coffee. I'd made it a point to get my ass up and see her, half-early. She was pretty pleased about it too.

"I don't know," I said. "It really ain't my business, but I think she's gonna make a big mistake. I think she's paying for it all, too."

"Her father should know. The earlier the better."

I didn't know what to do. It didn't sit right with me to snitch on Tam. Hell, she was near old enough to do what she wanted. It was her life, like she said. But I knew ol' Wayne would be awful disappointed with me.

"You ever have such a thing happen?" I asked. "With your young'un?"

She looked at me from across her little pink table but didn't say nothing at first.

"My boy?"

"Yeah. I was just wondering."

She didn't say nothing again, so I shrugged, got up to get us some more coffee.

"He did," she said, when I was standing at the counter, my back to her. "He did run away from Jeffrey and me. Once."

"That right?"

"Yes. And there wasn't anyone to tell me he was going. There wasn't anyone to tell me where he went."

I thought she was gonna say more but she didn't. And I reckon she'd said enough. And when I sat back down with the coffee, Cecilia was staring off and away, looking no better than the sick old lady she was.

I didn't know what I was gonna do, but I figured the topic was done dead between us. For now, anyways.

"So, you need me to get you something from the store?"

She come on back then, from wherever, and said she did. She got up, her hands shaking, going over to the fridge to get a grocery list. She leaned on the chair when she handed it to me.

"I'm sorry to bother you with it, Chester," she said, her hands still shaky and her wrinkled eyes getting a mite screwed up. "I know you don't need to run errands for an old lady like me, but I do appreciate it. You're a good soul."

"No, Ma'am," I said. "It ain't nothing."

And the truth was, I didn't mind it a bit. I'd come to admit to myself that Cecilia Guffins was a anchor for me, keeping me sane, keeping me from living on Fob's boat whenever I worked. She'd done replaced my whiskey bottle under the sink, I figured. I still had a half-bottle of George Dickle there, maybe even another one unopened, but I hadn't had a look-see in a long while. For all I knew, the roaches had drunk it up.

It was getting a little too emotional in that kitchen, for both of us.

"It's getting warm early today, isn't it," she said, turning to look at the window. "The air's heavy."

I looked thataway myself.

"Yessum," I said. "I reckon we're in for some storms."

CHAPTER TWENTY-SIX

So I went back to my two-way life: spending my nights drinking and smiling and patching things up with Fob, thinking about whiskey and women, and spending my afternoons and days off with Cecilia, playing gin-rummy and getting groceries and talking about things like the weather and tuna salad. The end of summer was boiling and storms come cracking in about every day from the Gulf, blowing in damn near like hurricanes and then blowing out, giving notice to every sonofabitch on the beach to party as fast as they could. I kept busy, just sliding by, not doing any way-back thinking about Marleen or about Crow and Della and the baby they was having, or had by now; and not even thinking much about Duck and Wayne or if I was gonna ever hear from Tam again.

But of course, I did.

I sure as hell did see and hear from Tam again. And this time she was mad as a string of lit firecrackers.

It was after a Sunday night—a long one—and Fob had him some woman he was entertaining, or so he said. Which was good for me, I was gonna go straight on home that night and

219

get some good rest. I had done closed up One Leg's with Brad, had just said bye to him as he left the lot in his car and was walking to my own car, even had my keys out of my pocket, when she come rumbling out from behind the fence by the Tom Thumb.

Tam come right at me. I just stood there, my keys still in one hand, my other hand about reaching for my door handle. The way she walked and the way she stared at me, everything burning afire in her, I was lucky just to stand my ground.

"You told him! You fucking told him!" she yelled, getting right up under my face and damn near spitting on me. "You fucking liar! You big, you stupid big. . . . You told him!"

I knew what she was talking about, but at the same time, I didn't.

"You fucked it up! Damn you, Chester Stubbs. You told my father and now I can't go. I can't go to California. I can't and Pauley'll go without me. You fucked it up. I told you and you told my father. . . . You're nothing but a jerk-off, you know? A big fucking fat-ass jerk-off, that's you, Chester Stubbs!"

Her eyes was red now and her little white hands was all balled up like she done caught of couple spiders she was fixing to squish. But I think the only death she was hoping for was mine. And then she took them fists and hit me. She pounded me on the chest about three times, then she hauled off and slugged me on my arm. It almost hurt. She slugged me once, twice, and cursed me up and down and sideways. She slapped me in the face. Then she ran back to the Tom Thumb where there was a black car. She got into the back seat and the car drove away, fast, spitting sand and oyster shells as it pulled out on the pavement.

I stood there, big red marks forming on my arms, looking down the road where the car had done sped off.

220

I stood there, in that hot night-slick air, my car keys in my hand, trying to take it all in.

Shit.

I'd never said one word to Wayne.

When I got home, I went to my bedroom, put my tip money on the dresser, my keys and license too, I got undressed for a shower. But I didn't shower. I sat down on my bed and just more'less disappeared. It was like I was no better than some concrete lawn ornament, or a stump, or the goddamn bed sheet. I just sat naked there for I don't know how long, dead to the world, dead to myself, not feeling like doing nothing in particular for a whole hell of a long while.

And the next day I wasn't no better. I didn't move much, didn't go see Cecilia, didn't try and see Wayne or Duck or even Tam to tell her she was wrong. I didn't feel like talking to no one. I didn't feel like explaining no truths. I stayed inside with the shades down, smoked and read old newspapers, had a beer before I went to bed.

And I slept all right. Slept hard and long so that, come next day, I felt like I could at least take a gander at the sun. I still felt stupid. I still felt like I'd done been hit with some kind of a brick and didn't understand why—or how—but at least I knew I was gonna recover from it.

I got myself cleaned up. Had some grits and bacon. Then I went on over to call on Mrs. Guffins.

She was in a right chipper mood, too.

We had us some sweet tea and rolls and sat out back, on her screened porch where she had a electric fan going. Like me, she didn't have no air conditioning. She was old fashioned. I was just cheap.

221

I still didn't feel like talking about what happened with Tam, and anyways, she never got around to asking. She was feeling like herself again.

"Chester, I tell you, I'm ready and raring. You won't have to run anymore shopping chores for me, or help me with the laundry or even mow my yard. I feel one hundred percent."

"You sure of that?"

"Oh yes. I am."

"You ain't thinking of chopping at that pecan tree again, are you?"

She stopped there and thunk a bit. And just then a hot wind blew and the tin of the porch roof clattered with pecans. She looked up and smiled. I didn't like it none.

"You'd best not," I told her. "Why don't you let me take it on down for you, if you're still feeling ugly about that tree."

"No, no," she said. "That's my own business."

"At least wait a while, then. Put it off till winter, or until this here hurricane weather blows away."

She looked at me and grinned like a kid.

"Listen to you, Chester. Ha. I ought to chop on that tree just to devil you. That would teach you."

She never did say what it'd teach me. And I sure as hell wasn't no fast learner.

And I wasn't joking none about hurricane weather. According to the paper, there was one brewing out in the Atlantic right now, spinning around and coming for Puerto Rico and the Keys, looking to fly right on in to the Gulf. There was plenty of places for it to go after that, though I suppose Pensacola was as good as anywheres. And the way the summer'd been, so crazy, it may as well just come on in and slam everything flat. Now that might really teach us a lesson or two.

I knew that at work, Jimmy would be tracking that storm on his cable teevee. He wanted to have a party. He'd already told me that. Told me he can make twice the money on a hurricane party and I could make twice the tips. "People spend money like crazy when they think that any minute they might be swept out to sea," he'd said.

"You just take it slow some," I told Mrs. Guffins. "I don't want no more rides in ambulances."

She smiled and waved her old hand.

"Shoo."

When I got to work the next night, I was right. Jimmy was glued to his opium box, watching them satellite pictures and listening to the same old reports again and again like he was addicted to it all. But so was about everyone else. The whole beach crowd was paying closer attention to that hurricane than to their personal hygiene—which wasn't really saying much. But Jimmy was just smiling when they showed that big ball of wind and waves moving under the Keys, and floating on into our Gulf of Mexico, building back up to hurricane strength. And Fob was right there with him, his arm slung over Jimmy's back like they was in cahoots together with this storm.

I didn't know what the hell Fob was excited about, especially him owning a boat for a home, but he looked to be as pleased as Jimmy. I guess he was just a fellow who liked to have something to get excited about, and it being the end of summer and all, a hurricane was good as anything else.

I wasn't looking forward to it, though.

I'd sat out one hurricane in my life and it weren't even a head-on storm. That was over in Pascagoula, Mississippi, when I was on a three day leave with some drinking buddy or another, after I'd quit boxing but couldn't yet quit the Navy.

223

Me and this guy—Roger, I believe his name was, him being from Pascagoula—we was in this tin roofed oyster bar drinking our minds awful damn numb. There was a whole crowd of other idjits too, including the bar owner. It was the only bar still open on the whole damn waterfront and everyone was having a glorious time, that was until the storm really come on in. Then, those that wasn't passed out—including Roger and me—wished we was.

Like I said, it didn't even hit us head-on. I think she landed around Bay Saint Louis or somewheres, though it didn't make much difference. That whole little claptrap bar shook, it shook like the way a dog'll shake a rabbit its done caught. I mean, the tin roof clattered around like tin foil and the raindrops was shooting at the windows like buckshot, streams of it coming right in under the doors and sills. Just all this weird noise and then the power done shut out and the women started to scream and cry first and all that wind and water just blew and blew for hours. Half the folks either threw up or spent the night on the goddamn toilet. I know I crawled on under the bar and lay on that stinking floor for I don't know how long.

Felt mighty stupid come daylight.

And that's how I reckon all these folks'll feel, if'n they stick around for a hurricane landing. The ones that live, anyways.

But for now they all was following it like some damn football game, maybe hoping to get in on the action. As for me, I didn't want none of it, no matter how much Jimmy was gonna pay.

The next day, I stuck close to Cecilia. We played us some checkers till afternoon, then I walked with her up to the market. I wanted her to use the cane, but she had her little two-wheeled grocery cart that she used and I guess she couldn't take both, besides, she was just plain stubborn. But she weren't no one hundred percent better. I could see the trip'd taxed her some and she laid down to rest after we got back to her house. I put her stuff away in the cupboards.

She fell asleep on the couch and I went on home and got ready for work.

On the way to the beach I tuned in the radio and between the music they talked about the storm. It was still out in the middle of the Gulf, shimmying around like a nude dancer who don't know where to throw her panties. They didn't know where it was gonna go or when, maybe two days, maybe four, maybe Tampa, maybe Galveston, Texas, or anywheres in between.

On the bridge I stuck my head out the window and looked around. The day was pure as cornstarch. Blue and white and the sun beating like a hammer on every damn thing.

Hard to believe there was any danger in the whole world.

When I got to the bar it was high tide with drinkers and I got right to work. Around about sunset ol' Fob came wandering in, on a tear, and he sat by me while I ate a oyster po'boy for my dinner break.

"Hey, Chester, you know, I'm sorry about the other night, with that Chinese girl. You should have told me you already had an interest."

I chewed for a while and he didn't say nothing more.

"She and I is friends, that's all."

He gave me one of them looks, near winking at me.

"Well, anyway, I don't think she's your friend anymore, is she?"

"How's that?"

"Well, I ran into her over at The Docks just last night. . . ."

"She ain't gone on to San Diego?"

"No, no. She was telling me about it, though. I got the drift you told her father and her father cut her off from her money, or just plain cut her off. The old man threatened her with something and, man, she is mad at you, son, she sure is."

I shrugged.

"Did you?"

"Did I what?"

"Did you squeal on that little thing?"

"I didn't tell nobody nothing," I said.

"You ought to tell her that, then," Fob advised me.

I didn't want Fob advising me.

What I should do was go see Wayne and find out what the hell happened, but I hadn't raised the gumption for it yet. I was kind'a hoping it'd all just go away.

"I'll deal with it when I deal with it," I said.

"Well anyway, why don't you come on down for a drink tonight. You can spend the night if you want. . . . Truth is, I've been on a dry spell. You and I ought to go hunting something up. It's better to move in packs."

He laughed at that.

"Ain't got the time," I said and he closed up his mouth. It looked like I'd done hurt his feelings.

"Maybe I could have a drink," I told him. "We'll go out some before you leave."

"Leaving in three weeks," he said. "I don't even know if I want to or not, but I suppose I will. I always do."

"Okay," I said, feeling a little more charitable towards him. "Okay?"

He reached over and slapped me on the shoulder.

"You working Saturday night?" he asked.

"Reckon so."

"I figured you were. Jimmy probably wants you for some muscle for the hurricane party."

That was the first I'd heard of it. Jimmy hadn't been in, or at least I hadn't seen him. I hadn't had no time to talk since I'd first come in and Fob was monopolizing my dinner break.

"So he's just gonna throw the party no matter where she lands?" I asked.

"They're saying it's coming our way," Fob told me. "Didn't you know that? Jimmy just decided to make it official. A big party. Lots of women, I imagine. Women always get horny when they think we might all die."

"That so," I said.

"Sure," he said and laughed and slapped me again before he got up, wandering off like a moth looking for a porch light.

Jimmy's hurricane party. That was all I needed. I'd have to find a way out of it. But the rest of the night it was the talk of the bar. Minnie and Jack was pumped for it and so was all the customers. The young ones, anyways. Jimmy still wasn't nowheres, so I never got the chance to talk to him about it. The official folks on the teevee was predicting the storm to fall somewhere between Gulfshores and Appalachicola. Well, I wasn't having nothing to do with it. I'd drive all the way on up to Huntsville and sleep in my car if I had to.

After work I had my beers with Fob and some other folk on his boat, and though the sky was clean, I could hear the surf agitating up. When I left the beach it must'a been about five in the morning, because as I was going out here come loads of kids with their surfboards, ready to ride big waves along the breaks soon as the sun edged the water.

The next day, Friday, I talked to Cecilia about the storm.

"You can come on with me," I said, "if she's gonna hit Pensacola."

She shook her head.

227

"I believe I'll say put, Chester. We haven't had a hurricane hit us in I don't know how long. Besides, it's not supposed to be a very strong one, they say."

"Come on, Mrs. Guffins. It ain't safe. A hurricane's a hurricane."

She just smiled.

"These old houses are built tough," she said. "You go up north of here and that's where the tornados are. That's where it floods and people get killed. . . . I'm too old to take off every time a storm comes around."

I shook my head.

"If it's gonna hit us, you come with me in my car. We'll get to some high land."

She said she would not.

That night, I talked to Jimmy in his office. He was a mite pissed.

"What do you mean you won't work tomorrow night? I need you. You know how crazy it gets at one of these parties? You know how much money you can pull in?"

"I don't care," I said. "I'm surprised the police will even let you be open. I thought the beach was supposed to evacuate."

"Evacuate my ass. . . . Anyway, that's why this is a private party. Hell, ain't I the Mayor? Anyway, Dirty Joe's is staying open. The Sandshaker's doing the same. No one says it's gonna land right here, at One Leg's. A little wind and water ain't much, considering the profit."

"You're throwing your own private party? That don't sound right."

"Officially, Fob's throwing the party. He's renting it out. But it's not a matter of right or wrong."

"I don't care for it none," I said. "I reckon I'll skip it."

There wasn't much more for him to say. He wasn't gonna fire me over it, but I was probably gonna have to break some more heads some night before I got on his good side again.

Actually, they was saying the storm was likely to slide on east of us, to Destin or maybe even Panama City. But they was still asking everyone from Mobile to Port St. Joe to clear out, or at least batten down for the weekend.

I worked the whole night, listening to most folks joke about it, listening to the surfers talk about the rides of the summer. Listening to Fob say how he'd secured his boat and the only rocking it was gonna do was if he got laid on it that night. But I knew that if'n it did hit Pensacola, it'd rip those docks right off the landing, taking his boat with it. Maybe the water'd take it all the way up to Milton or maybe it'd take it the other way, out to sea, with Fob on it. And if he lived, then he'd better learn to sail right quick.

When I got up the next day, things wasn't sounding too pretty. It was raining near sideways, with the wind coming hard out of the southwest. It was grey as wet lint and the sounds of the trees and feel of the air was right spooky. I threw some clothes and shit into my duffel and put it in my car. I went on over to Cecilia's but she still wasn't worried none.

I had some coffee with her and on the radio they said the storm had done shifted back our way. They was saying Navarre and Gulf Breeze was a fine place for it to come ashore.

"You coming or not," I finally said.

The storm wasn't due till night, but her house was already near shaking. There was branches and leaves and loads of rain splashing down on her roof, not just some lousy pecans.

"No, Chester," she said, calm as a stump, "you go on, though. I'll see you tomorrow, providing you're not hit by a tornado up in Alabama."

So I left her there. I wasn't about to haul her off against her will. No I wasn't. Even though I thought I ought to.

I went back in my house and paced the living room with the teevee on. They still couldn't make up their minds where exactly the hurricane was gonna hit. And now they wasn't even sure if it was still strong enough to call it a hurricane. Just the same, they was advising folks to get on up north, or to fill up their sinks and tubs with good water and to pull their drapes and stay clear of windows, to get in closets or under tables and such. I was beginning to think maybe, that maybe, I was acting like a old fart. I wasn't scared or nothing, really, I just figured I was being normal for once. But maybe I was making a fool of myself.

But then I listened to the wind and got to remembering that night in Pascagoula and times at sea, when I was in the service, the times I'd seen open waters go crazy, and that was enough.

Come about supper time, I went to my car. I gave Cecilia's house one last look, started her up, put my wipers on and lights on and joined a line of other cars with their lights on, heading north on the flooded streets, out of town, a whole damn bunch of us like one big funeral procession leaving Pensacola.

CHAPTER TWENTY-SEVEN

I was about thirty miles from Montgomery when they called it off. I was driving through the black and the rain when on the radio they said it was gonna come in past Mobile Bay, the tropical storm swinging a ways west from where they was predicting it that morning. They was calling it a tropical storm now.

But if I was a fool, there was a whole hell of a lot of other ones too. I tried to get a cheap motel room off I-65 in Hope Hull, but they said they was full. Said everyone was full up to Birmingham. So, even though there was still a lot of rain and wind, and—Cecilia was right—there was tornado warnings, I got gas, turned my car around and headed back to P-cola.

I was gonna have to take some shit from Jimmy and Fob about this one, even from Cecilia in her own way.

It was way past midnight when I pulled in. Though the storm was near fifty miles away and the rain'd let up, the wind was still fierce and our little street was flooded. I ambled on into my driveway, thinking I'd of been asleep at the wheel if I hadn't had to fight the wind.

Inside, I put the stove light on, had me a cocola and a peanut butter sandwich. Then I went to bed. I slept hard, dreaming, still feeling the wind and rain and the road, and didn't know if'n it was day or night when I heard the tree fall.

I know there was some unusual groaning before I heard the crack. The crack was big and sharp, like a snake of lightning right on top my bedroom, then there was a twisting and splintering and a whistling before the boom-crunching thud and the sound of branches crackling all about. I mean, I was

231

deep asleep but I shot up in bed and my window was broken and I could smell all the wet and could smell the sharp smell of fresh tree wood and sap and earth.

It didn't take me long to hop on outside and have a look-see.

It was still dark and the rain had come on again and I went on out—me just in my goddamn boxers—went out getting all fucking wet and going to the side of my house already knowing it was a fell tree, already knowing it was that tall pecan tree that'd done snapped and tumbled. I went out and the rain was picking up into a downpour again and there was some lightning and thunder and I could see it, saw where the pecan had broke near the base, right where ol' Cecilia Guffins had chopped at it for half a year. But it had broken kind'a backwards, it looked, it'd caved in on that dirty white bald side where she'd chipped away at it, caved and twisted and gone on down, a ribbon of wood still connecting trunk to stump. Only the worse thing was, the terrible thing was, it hadn't fallen on into her yard, on back where the bananas and magnolias was, nope, that pecan tree'd gone right on down into the backside of her house.

Her front door was locked solid so I raced on back where the tree'd crushed the house. I was all wet and the rain was just flushing down now and I had to skinny on under the fat trunk of the tree to get to the house. I got to a ripped part, the kitchen I figured, and tore away some loose siding where the wall was exposed, not thinking if there was any loose electric or if anything was due to collapse further, I kicked in some cracked two-by-fours and sheetrock, fitting my big body on through to the inside of her house, soggy pink insulation clinging to my bones.

Inside the lights was all out and the rain was blowing in all over. I knew where I was going this time and there was jacks

232

of lightning illuminating the damage as I made my way to her bedroom, not even calling her name.

And there she was.

Mrs. Guffins.

Cecilia, lying there, her bed knocked down and bent double, a whole thick black limb of that pecan tree smack dab on top of her. I slowed and walked up, crawled and scratched my way through the leaves and branches and tangled shadows of it all, up to her, and then the lightning flashed and I saw the blood in her mouth, saw blood coming out of her ear, saw her eyes was closed, her face as calm as in the daylight when I'd last seen it.

I took hold of her arm, her hand. I knew it weren't no good. I knew it.

"Ma'am."

I held her hand. I patted her white cheeks.

"Ma'am," I said.

"Cecilia."

"Ma'am."

I drew back and dropped her hand.

Her phone was working and I called nine one one. I told them what happened, gave them the address.

I hung up.

I went out her front door, to my own house.

I stood in the dark, dripping wet, my skin and shorts dripping rain water onto my filthy carpet.

I shook the water from my hair, stripped out of my boxers. I put on jeans and a dry shirt and shoes. I went back out into the rain, to Cecilia Guffins'.

I didn't go inside. I went to her little garage and got out that ax. It was near daylight but the rain was still coming down and there was still the big sparks of lightning and racks of thunder and I took that ax and put it to what remained of the

233

tree. I took that blade and whomped that pecan tree right where it'd done collapsed, where it still clung some to its base, chopping and chopping not halting for even a extra breath, my clothes getting all wet, my hair soaked, my face and arms just streaming with rain, I just swung and swung hard as I could, chipping and chopping until that tree was all disconnected from its stump and then I went and attacked that stump, whacking it, beating it, hurting it till I heard sirens on the main road.

The sirens woke me up and I flung the ax far as I could, over the tree and into the stand of magnolias.

I wasn't gonna take no ambulance ride this time. I wasn't gonna be around for this.

I went back into my house, grabbed my money and my keys. I went to the kitchen sink and grabbed my bottle of whiskey from underneath. The full bottle. I went out to my car, my clothes and hair and arms all waterlogged and achy and covered with woodchips, and I got going, the paramedic and police coming at me and cursing me for being in the way when we passed.

When I hit the main road I undid my bottle and took a long slash of George Dickle. This time I didn't bother to think of Crow or Wayne or Tam. I drank from the bottle and pointed my car for the beach.

I went right to Fob Langtree's fucking boat.

PART FOUR

Under Pensacola Skies

CHAPTER TWENTY-EIGHT

When I woke up I was still on the boat. I was lying down in some riggings, my face pointed to the sun which was dying out in the sky, leaving nothing in its place. Flies was zizzing about, alighting on me, trying to torture me some. But I didn't care. I couldn't get up and didn't much want to. The whiskey bottle was between my legs, empty, not even a lick in the corner. I knew because I tried it. I didn't have no hangover because I was still drunk—and I was gonna stay that way. The only thing that was hurting was my arms and my shoulders, aching and tight from swinging that goddamn ax. I didn't recall shit about the day, other than I'd seen Fob and he didn't feel like drinking and him telling me some about the storm and the party and a whole lotta crap that didn't count for nothing. I did recall about Cecilia Guffins. Wasn't too likely I was ever gonna forget that.

I sat up a bit and a couple of gulls went flying, screaming at me the whole way. It was evening but I didn't see no one. The bar was awful damn quiet: no music, no volleyball, no one vomiting off the porch rail.

Fuck.

Fuck, I needed a drink.

I tried once, twice, the third time I stood up, wobbly as a broke toy. I leaned myself towards the cabin door and fell the three steps to it. I didn't knock but just stumbled on in.

It was hot and quiet down inside. I wasn't seeing too clear and couldn't find the liquor, but I pulled out some beer from the ice box. I sat down on the floor, my butt and big legs wedged in the little galley, and I drank the beer and managed to light me a cigarette.

Night came on and there weren't any moon to speak of and I thought back to the morning. My mind went back to her house and how she looked and the way her arm dropped and then how goddamn loud them sirens was, how fucking terrible them sirens are. . . . I dropped my cigarette into the beer bottle and looked for Fob's whiskey again.

I found it.

Just goes to show what a man can do if'n he tries.

Just goes to show you.

I was sitting up deck, with the whiskey, when Fob come along.

"Well, if he ain't alive."

I grunted.

"Found you some dinner, I see."

I offered him up the bottle but he just smiled.

"Had enough last night. Whoo, that was some wingding."

"Sorry I missed it," I said.

"You ought to be, especially with Jimmy and all."

"What about Jimmy?"

"You know. . . . Don't you remember me telling you, or were you too drunk?"

"I was too drunk."

"Well, he's up there right now. Maybe you ought to get it from him."

I shrugged and looked up at the bar where there was a couple lights on, but no neons or any music.

"It ain't closed, is it?" I asked.

Fob laughed.

"You don't recall shit, do you? Yeah, it's closed. For today anyway. That hurricane ripped off the kitchen roof, rained on all the equipment and he lost some of the food. Nothing we could do but keep partying, at least until the wind slowed some."

"So Jimmy's pissed at me because his roof blew off? What'd he expect me to do, go fetch it and put it back on?"

Fob was getting a kick out of it all.

"No, Chester, that ain't why. But you go on up and you'll see, you'll see why."

I figured I just might do that.

And once I got up there and opened his office door and got a look at him sitting there under his desk lamp, doing paperwork, well, I sure as hell saw why. He had a shiner on him the size of a goose egg, only it was black red and some kind of blue they ain't never gonna think up a name for.

He looked up at me and weren't happy at all.

"This ought to be yours," he said and almost touched his bad eye.

"Who did it?"

"I don't fucking know. . . . And it doesn't matter. We had two big fights and I had to break them up because you, because your goddamn ass wasn't there."

"Well, shit," I said and took a step, caught my foot on a desk leg and almost fell.

Jimmy looked me over.

"You drunk?"

"Aim to be drunker," I said.

"You want a week off?"

237

"Didn't say that."

"Well, I'm giving you a week off. You could'a made a load of money last night, you could'a busted some chops, instead, you get a week off. Get as drunk as you want, but if you ain't half sober when you come back, well. . . ."

I didn't stick around to hear no more.

I went on back to the boat and Fob's whiskey.

He and I laid back on the deck. I slowed up on the whiskey some, only because I wanted to make it last. I even ate some crackers with some cheese shit on them. Fob stayed with me, sipping cocola from a glass. There was still a bit of wind, but nothing like before. Some clouds blew by, grey and thin as a mushed slice of white bread, leaving some stars twinkling if you looked hard enough.

I was okay, I reckoned. I was a hell of a lot better off than some others I could think of. Shit, if it weren't for the death of some old woman, I'd be feeling just fine: good and drunk, sitting on my pal's boat, nothing to do but smoke and stare at the sky. Maybe tomorrow night we'd rustle up some women.

Shit yes. I was back on the beach where I belonged, raring to rub my nose in it.

I was home on the range.

CHAPTER TWENTY-NINE

Turned out at least six people was killed from that storm. Two was up in Bay Minette, Alabama: tornado. Others was drowned or car crashed. Only one died in all of Florida, and that was Cecilia Guffins. There was a picture of the house on the front page of the newspaper.

I didn't go to her funeral, didn't even bother to find out when or where—or if—it was. I didn't need to say goodbye to her, that old lady. We was neighbors. I'd seen her when she was alive and I'd seen her dead. Maybe the police wanted to talk to me, because I called them on in. Then again I never gave my name. But I was staying on Fob's boat for a spell. Anyways, I never heard from no cops.

And I quit my job.

After my week off I just plumb didn't feel like working no more. The thinking of it didn't sit right with me. Fob was putting me up till he left and we was having a good ol' time. In fact, he was asking for me to come on along with him for a while, when he shoved off to putter on down the Intracoastal. But I wasn't set on that. Jimmy and I had no hard feelings when I quit. He asked if I was sure. I said I was. We shook hands and he bought me a beer. That was about the best I'd ever quit on anything.

It was easy not to work, to let Fob pay my way for a while. We had us some fun, hitting some of the spots I hadn't hit for near a year, hooking up with some tourist women for two nights, just drinking and jamming and hooting around with them in any way we pleased. Like riding a goddamn bicycle, it all come back to me. More fun than a fucking bike, too. Saw Tam that week, though it was Fob saw her first.

We was at some loud beach bar Fob drug me into, one with all them flashing lights and garbage music. I didn't even know it was there, or likely I'd missed it on purpose. Anyways, we was there, making the rounds and he says, "There's your friend." I turned to where he was pointing and there was Tam, up on the dance floor in a short black skirt and sleeveless shirt, looking just like any other stick of candy in them lights. I caught her eye and she stared me down, a hard stare with some mean in it. . . . Oh well, can't win them all. Fob and I left after one drink.

Things was a mite unsettled, but overall, I was having a good time. I never even got back to my own house until about two weeks later.

It seemed like a hell of a lot longer then them two weeks when I drove over the bridge into Gulf Breeze and then on to P-cola. It was sunny as shit and not so hot, a damn pleasant day considering it was the end of August. When I got to Warrington I got a little queasy or something, something sitting in my gut, squirreling around, as I came on up my road and to my house. On up to Mrs. Guffins' house.

Her house looked normal enough from the front, but you could tell there was something missing. And I didn't just mean where the back bedroom, the porch and part of the kitchen'd been tore off. I meant I could tell she weren't there, that no one was there. I could see it was a ghost house, even right in the middle of daylight.

I parked in my drive—my own home looking a mite ghosty itself—and I stood for a bit taking in the damage next door. Whoever done it had rolled that tree off the house and chainsawed the top and branches, but the most of it still was lying there, turned near lengthwise along the backyard. They'd done tacked up some blue and white plastic to where the wall was missing and on up over the tore roof. It looked to be holding okay.

I looked at the stump. It was all gnarled up with big ol' slats of wood taken out of it; what bark there was was pretty well skinned off and scarred up. That tree, that stump, didn't look alive no more. The wood was all grey and had already shriveled some. It looked like a old tree, dead for a hunnerd years as good as a day.

I went up to my door where my mail box was stuffed. There was also a couple handwritten notes stuck to it. I grabbed all my mail and them notes and went on inside.

I had to go around and open up some windows. The place was hot and smelled like a hole in the ground. I'd put all the letters and shit on the kitchen table, so I found a beer, made a sandwich with what weren't moldy, and sat down. I had a hankering to just file it all in the trash, like before, but sitting at the table where the sugar bowl was at and where the chair across from me was empty, well, I just couldn't do it.

I read the notes first. They was from Duck and Wayne. The first said they'd stopped by to see me after they heard about the tree and all. Then the one dated a few days later was just from Wayne, him saying that it was important I should call him or stop on over. He hadn't seen his girl for a spell and wondered if I had.

Well hell. I put them in my pocket and figured I'd worry about them some other time.

I went through my letters. There was some guy wanted to mow my lawn and spray chemicals on it, another one wanted to be my goddamn dry cleaner for the rest of my life and crap like that. Then there was the power bill and the last of my hospital payments and then there was some banks way out yonder in some other state that wanted me to apply for credit cards. Shit, me with a credit card? Be like giving a wild dog the night shift at a slaughterhouse. I didn't need that kind'a trouble.

I figured I'd go ahead and pay the bills. It felt like I ought'a: old Cecilia Guffins, the ghost of her still trying to keep me from ruin.

But as I was going back over it all, I saw I'd done missed one. It was a letter that'd got stuck to the back of one of them shiny advertisements. It was a letter postmarked from up north.

Connettycut.

It was from Marleen.

Hello, Chester,

I suppose you thought you'd never hear from me again. I guess I'm writing just to check in, sort of, and to let you in on what Crow and Della have been up to. I heard you all didn't see each other anymore. And Della sent me the newspaper clipping of what happened to our—your—neighbor, Mrs. Guffins. Sad. Must have been a bit scary and just think if that tree had decided to fall the other way. Then again, better not think about it.

Anyway, Della and Crow had a beautiful baby girl about a month ago. Seven pounds and some. Healthy and cute as a bug in the pictures they sent me. Did you know? I was hoping (if you haven't already) that you would go on over and congratulate them. Maybe bring a rattle or flowers or something. I know they'd appreciate it, especially Crow. Now, don't get all mad. I'm not trying to run your social life. God forbid. It's just a suggestion. I know they'd like to see you

— or at least, Crow would. (Ha ha.) I hope you'll do it and I hope you are okay.

As for me, I'm still adjusting. Life up here is a mite different and dealing with step-kids is not easy. But John and I are working on it and I figure it'll work out in the end. I'd be lying if I said I didn't miss Alabama or the beach. They do have some nice beaches not far from us, but it's not the same. And it was so damn cold this winter. Seems like I've been gone a lot longer than I have. I am planning to visit, probably in the fall, to see Della's little girl. Oh, her name is Dilsey.

That's about it. Like I said, I hope you're okay and you're working and not drinking too much. I reckon you are fine. Contact Crow and maybe he can tell you when I'll be down and maybe we can meet over there for a little while. I'll probably come by myself as John is always busy and the kids will be in school.

Love, Marleen

Hell.

I sat there for a while, not thinking, staring at the letter, staring at the sugar bowl on the table. Then I thought about Crow's kid, a little girl, but I couldn't really imagine it, couldn't make it real, and reckoned it didn't matter none. And then I thought about Marleen herself. And I couldn't figure if that mattered none either.

It was like everything with Wayne, Marleen and Crow's baby was just more things to put off. Things I'd get to when I got to.

I went back into my room and got me some clothes. I grabbed the tip money I'd stuffed in a shoe box in my closet

—my lousy life savings—putting most of it into my pocket. I'd been living on Fob's handouts. I already had some of my clothes because I never brought in my duffel, from when I ran from the hurricane. But it weren't much. I'd had to go to the laundromat a few times already. So I was glad to get some more of my shit.

And that was it.

I wasn't gonna stay any longer.

I'd pay my bills with cash before going back to the beach. Then I'd stay on Fob's boat, where I liked it.

Hell, I loved it.

I wasn't working. I was eating. I was drinking. I was even getting laid. Life was grand. It was just fucking grand.

CHAPTER THIRTY

I swear my days was about perfect. I mean, folks knew me, I had a reputation from working at One Leg Lafitte's and they wanted to be my pal. I was a right regular character in beachtown. Fob was too, but folks seemed to take to me better than him. Or maybe they was more scared. It didn't matter. I was on a roll. By the end of the week, the whiskey and women was coming full blast.

So I was drinking hard, wasn't eating any big meals and most the time I was walking down the road and back, with Fob, rather than drive my old car and get a drunk driving ticket. I kept my Super Bee parked at the Tom Thumb, where it had its own private oil slick, rather than leave it in Jimmy's lot and have him say something. The folks at the Tom Thumb was good sports. Fob knew every single one of them, every shift.

And as for Jimmy, we was okay. I hung out there almost as much as Fob did and he didn't say nothing. Brad slipped me drinks. Jack gave me food. And in return, hell, in return I was just me. I did break up a fight or two for Jimmy. Free of charge. So Jimmy was getting a deal out of my quitting. Damned right he was.

Labor Day weekend was coming up, the last big hurrah before the goddamn summer flubbered on out. Fob was gonna putter on off the week after—he had some business in P-cola first—and I was supposed to go with him. I reckon if'n I'd been sober for more than a day, I'd a thought better. But seeing as how I wasn't, I was leaning towards going. He promised me there was a doctor's ex-wife in Valaparasio who'd show me something I'd never seen before. Something to do with ping pong balls, canned tripe and a jar of mayonnaise. That right there was interest enough for me to tag along.

There's always something, ain't there.

So what if my mind was cloudy, my stomach achy and my shits runny? I was living the way I wanted to, everything in tip-top fucking-A shape. Goddamnit.

But even before the big blast of the weekend could get off the ground, I had a visit on Fob's boat. I didn't know what time of day it was, or what fucking day, but I knew who it was as soon as they woke me up from my nap.

It was Duck and Wayne.

I'd been sitting in the sun, shirtless, pantsless, just me and my boxers and the morning breeze. I'd drunk a little orange juice mixed with a spot of dark rum, bitters, vitamin C, E and a bunch of B's—a thing Fob drunk all the time and now had me drinking them, plus one of his prescription headache pills

245

he always had about. So I was sweet asleep on the top deck when I heard my name coming to me in that kind'a high, choppy voice.

I opened my eyes against the sun, seeing the both of them standing over me with their caps in their hands, them both saying my name.

At first I was gonna pay them no mind. Just flutter my eyelids and go back to sleep like they was some unwanted dream or another. But then, I reckon, I recalled how hospitable they was to me and I had no right not to be the same to them.

"Hey boys," I said, rubbing my bad eyes.

"Ahh, you awake."

"That I am. . . . I got your notes. . . . How'd you track me here?"

I shaded my eyes and looked up to the bar. The windows was half sun-struck, but I imagined ol' Jimmy was staring down from one of them.

"We asked management," Duck said, with a straight face.

Well, I hadn't seen them two in what seemed like a former life. I straightened myself up a bit, dragged my fingers through my burnt hair, and regular tried to act like I was full of my senses.

"Ya'll come to visit, or you had something on your mind?" I asked.

They took that pretty damn serious and discussed something between themselves and then Wayne told me he wanted to talk with me.

I fished out my cigarettes from the wad of clothes that was below me and I offered the pack to them. They both took one, which made me feel right, and I took one myself before we lit up on Duck's lighter. Then we smoked a bit before Duck wandered off and Wayne and I was left to stare at each other.

"So," he finally said, his head bent a bit, "do you know if Tam go to California, as she said? She has not been home in a week."

He looked at me then and I didn't want to look back.

"I reckon not," I said.

I had seen her, two nights ago, up in One Legs. She must'a knew I didn't work there no more. Hell, everyone knew. Beach gossip was short at the end of the summer.

"No?"

He had a hopeful look in his eyes that made it easier for me.

"I saw her last night. Didn't talk to her though, but I imagine she's staying with some friends on the beach, here."

"You didn't talk?"

"She ain't too keen on me, Wayne."

He shook his head like he knew what I meant.

"No. She's having a hard time. I don't know what to do. After I forbid her to go, to run off with that boy, she hardly stay home. She quit her job."

"She hated that job, Wayne."

He looked at me, like he was trying to figure just who's side I was on. It didn't bother me none. I was on my own side now, my own and lonely.

"You know, I cut off her money."

I tried to figure that, but for the shit of me I couldn't get what he meant.

"What? She got a trust fund or something?"

"No. We have a joint, what you call, a joint account. She put money in, I put money in, the same. I match it. Same name. But when I find out she going to San Diego with this boy, well, I cancel her name. I did that, Chester."

He seemed a mite proud of it.

"And how did you find out?" I asked.

247

"Find out?"

"How'd you know she was gonna run off to California?"

"Ohhh. Mizgriffins."

"Griffins?"

He nodded his head like I was supposed to understood.

"I'm sorry, Wayne, I don't get it," I said.

"Mizz-griffins."

"Mizgriffins?"

He nodded but saw I didn't know what the fuck.

"Your neighbor woman, Miz Griffins. She call me at work and tell me. She tell me you said for her to say."

He stood over me and grinned, like I was in on the whole goddamn deal. I got to my feet, lit a new cigarette and paced a bit.

Mrs. Guffins.

Old Cecilia Guffins had gone and called where I used to work, at the damn warehouse, and asked for the Oriental or Chinese or something and told the father what his young'un was up to. It was her who'd done told Wayne.

Shit.

And I started to laugh.

"Cecilia?" I said, still laughing.

Wayne acted like he was a gonna laugh with me.

"Yes. She call Marty, ask for father of girl in trouble. Asian, she say, like that. And then she tell me, but she say you tell her to call. You did?"

"Nope. Nope. But I guess it don't matter. That old lady, shit..."

Cecilia Guffins was to blame, sticking her nose where it don't belong, trying to direct other folks traffic, even right before she come up dead. And so Tam thought it was me, or maybe was told it was me. And it didn't matter much which way, because she was sure it was me and, come around to it, maybe it was. I was the one who'd done told Cecilia to begin with.

"What's so funny?" he asked when he'd got tired of trying to laugh with me.

"Not much," I said, "not much."

We stared at each other for a minute. I could see Duck up on the bar's porch, pretending to look at the bay.

"So you took her money away?" I asked.

He gave me a odd look.

"It was half and half. It was Tam's money, but I matched it. It was for school."

"But she's how old?"

"Will be twenty, this September."

"She been out of school for two, three years then, Wayne. And you still got a hand in her money?"

"I gave her half. What she put in, I put in. For school. For college."

"But she ain't in college."

He stood there on the boat, rocking gently with it, his hat back on his head. He stood there looking at me but not really looking.

"It is for university," he said.

"Shit, Wayne. Give her the money."

He shook his head.

"It's only money, buddy. She's on her own. Give it to her."

"I gave half," he said.

"And so did she."

"No," he said. "No."

"It's half hers. She worked for it too."

He sat down then, on the gunwale. I sat down too. It was hot. It must'a been afternoon, maybe a Saturday because they was off work. I didn't know, just like I didn't know what the fuck I was doing with Wayne . . . giving out know-it-all advice while half-drunk, I guess. But what the hell. I reckon I felt like Tam did, felt like maybe things was against me and the only deal anybody wanted to give was a raw one.

"No," he said and stood up, not looking at me. "I thank you for telling me what you know. And, I am glad she is not in San Diego. Thank you."

"No problem," I said and thought maybe I should shake his hand, but that made me think of Fob and how often he did that. "All right, Wayne. You and Duck, ya'll stop by again, okay?"

He nodded, then clambered out of the boat. He shuffled on up the dock, up the steps, and up to Duck. The two of them left without one look back.

And I was left standing there, sweating in my shorts, my hangover done shot. I did get to figuring that things was getting a little too curious and that I ought to just laugh.

But I didn't.

Because then I got to thinking I was right to tell Wayne to give Tam the money. I mean, if he give it to her, maybe she would go on to California. Or maybe not. Either damn way she'd be gone. She'd be off and out of his hair and he could just say to hell with it and it'd be over.

But I knew that weren't true. That it'd probably never be over between Wayne and Tam, never should be over. And who was I, who the fuck was I to be saying that kind of shit? I was a man with no kin, that's who. I was some idjit on a boat nursing his fifth hangover of the week who didn't have no parents and no kids or no wife left, or nothing much else to speak of. A man with no kin trying to tell others what to do with theirs. . . . Shit, I needed a night off. Twenty-four fucking hours of nothing but silence and sleep, sweet sleep.

That's what I needed.

And, soon as I got done feeling sorry for myself, that's exactly what I was gonna do.

CHAPTER THIRTY-ONE

I took the night off from drinking and the next morn I drove up to the Blackwater River. I rented me a all-day canoe and got out on the water with nothing but a bag of apples, boiled peanuts and a jar of sweet tea. And I drifted. I just let that slow current take me down, me staring up into the oaks and pines and patches of blue sky, me just slipping along with nothing on my mind but the bugs and garfish and the idea I was doing something good for myself.

I tried to relax and forget there was such a place as P-cola Beach, tried to forget about all the shit that'd brung me low. And then I thought some about Cecilia. And I missed her. I wanted that old woman to be alive. I wanted her to have some coffee with me and tell me where the hell I'd gone wrong. Tell me what I ought to do now.

I let my big feet drag in the cool water and thought of her calm eyes and her blue head, the wrinkles around her mouth. Heard her voice in my head then the silence, when she couldn't answer me, when her face was all scratched and there was blood in her ear and she was dead. And I about cried, there in the canoe on the Blackwater.

But she weren't around. Never would be. And I was just floating.

I brought the canoe to shore about suppertime. The folks I rented it from come on and picked it up and gave me a ride back to the start, where my car was. I had me a little andouille sausage and some headcheese I'd put in the cooler in my car, eating that and taking a look at the river some more, that water so late-summer slow it was about petrified. Petrified water. And that suited me just fine.

I went and stayed the night up there. I parked the car off a red dirt road, in under some pines and atop some palmettas, me trying to sleep while fighting the skeeters and the heat and listening to raccoons and things scramble around in the brush.

And even though I hardly slept and was hungry and had me some lousy dream about beer and boiled shrimp and a endless whiskey bottle, I still counted on it to be good for me. And the next morn, after breakfast in Milton, I drove on back to the beach figuring I was due for a change, that by going on up there under the trees and grieving for Cecilia I'd got a hold of something.

But it didn't take.

Because when I got to the strip and saw all the sun and water and near-naked women, I didn't go to Fob's boat and get my shit and go on back to my house in Warrington, like I'd done planned. Nope. I drove on over to Chan's and got me a blackened grouper sandwich and a load of fries all bloodied up with ketchup and had me a beer to drown it down. And then I had another beer and one more, putting the whole lot of it on my tab that I'd been running.

Then I went next door to the liquor store for a fresh pack of Camels, got me a single can of coldbeer to go, and went to the beach where I took off my shirt and shoes and went for a swim. I got out pretty deep and scrubbed my red scalp and tried to wash myself with the salt water. I stayed put there a while, floating once again, thinking some, nothing but sky and water and me, thinking if I was headed in the right direction. Was I going the right way or the wrong way? Up?

Down? Or any direction at all? Bobbing there with all that blue above and the blue below, I didn't have no answer. None at all. So I went back in to sit in the sand and stare at the girls, drying off, finishing my can of beer though it was warm-awful.

I put my dry shirt and shoes back on, lit a smoke, then went back and crossed right through the goddamn traffic, and headed on over to the Sundowner.

I liked the Sundowner. It was near the ugliest bar on the beach. It weren't hardly ever crowded. Richard was working and though he didn't have a hard-liquor license, he always kept his own jug-bottle of Pepe Lopez Tequila there, in his food freezer.

I sat down and let him know I was interested in doing a few along with my beers and he decided to join me. We had a grand ol' time, just drinking and shooting the shit and trying to figure out just when the summer was gonna play itself out. Me and Richard was pretty well gone, sitting there with the sun blasting in his screen windows, us drinking tequila and beer, a bunch of limes all cut up on a paper plate, us chawing on a stack of crab claws he'd boiled up in beer and hot sauce. That's what we was doing when the police come in.

There was two of them. One was a boney guy, had him a Adam's apple like he done swallowed a walnut and couldn't get it on down. The other was a woman. They both had their shirts buttoned up to their necks and had dark sunglasses on. Neither of them looked too happy, not near as happy as us anyways.

Richard right quick tried to swipe that big tequila jug off the bar top. All he managed to do was spill the damn thing. What was left of it flooded down the counter, drowning them lime pods like beetles in a rain.

The cops couldn't help but to notice, though it turned out Richard didn't have to worry none. They was looking for me.

The man come up to me while the woman stayed by the screendoor.

"Are you Mr. Chester Stubbs, sir?"

I didn't answer but just cocked my head at him.

"You live at three twelve Lusk, Warrington?"

It was then that I noticed they wasn't Beach police, but was regular P-cola cops.

"I reckon that's me," I said and I stood up, square, hoping to give him something to consider.

"Would you please come with us, sir," he said.

"I doubt it."

"Chester," Richard said.

The cop then looked over at him and then at the long puddle of tequila.

Richard gave me a pitiful stare.

"You gonna arrest me for being drunk? Inside a goddamn bar?" I asked.

"Take it outside, okay?" Richard said.

"I hope not, Mr. Stubbs. But I've got a court order. . . ."

"A court order?"

"Take it on out, Chester, please. . . ."

I took it on outside, for ol' Richard's sake.

I stood out front, ankle deep in sand spurs, the traffic slowing to a click, folks hoping to see what the police wanted with a big sonofabitch like me. The cop was asking me to get into the patrol car, trying to tell me what it was about, but I wasn't in the mood. I was a mite too drunk to give a damn.

"Mr. Stubbs, please, into the car," he was saying.

I was thinking about getting him to swallow that walnut in his throat—just one good punch ought to do it—but then I looked over at the woman. She was standing there, legs squared, her jaw stuck out, both hands gripping her nightstick. And it weren't even night yet. That's when I figured it to be a losing proposition. Just another losing proposition in a long string of them.

I got into the car.

They sat up front, I sat in back where there wasn't no door handles. They tried to talk to me and it wasn't until we was over the beach bridge that it sunk in that I wasn't in any trouble.

They'd been looking for me for about a week. Jimmy had told them I didn't work for him no more, but to try Fob. Fob, I reckon, had told them to try the bars, but I'd been up in the Blackwater for almost two days. And anyways, it all had to do with Cecilia Guffins, with me saying I was the one who'd found her and that I was the one who'd called nine one one.

"And the court order?" I managed to ask.

"You need to see her lawyer, Mr. Stubbs. He's the one that got the order, for us to bring you in to see him after we file your statement as to the night of Mrs. Guffins' death."

"You're taking me to see a lawyer?" I asked, nearly leaning up into their seats.

They both nodded.

They took my statement about her death, the woman writing it down. That was that. And now they was taking me to see Cecilia's goddamn lawyer.

CHAPTER THIRTY-TWO

The lawyer's name was Derrick Mal and he had him a little downtown office on the bad side of Seville Quarter. At least that's where the police let me out at and that was the name on the door they pointed to.

I figured it to be past five or six because downtown was pretty damn empty, all the responsible folks gone on home to their air conditioners and mortgages. But Derrick Mal, the lawyer, was still at work. Because when I went on in, the man was at a old metal desk in a one-room office. Not a big guy, he had his head bent down, showing me a bald spot while he was a scratching at a pad of paper. I got to about three yards from him before he looked up. He looked a mite familiar.

"Chester Stubbs?"

"You Mrs. Guffins' lawyer?" I asked.

He stood on up and stretched out his hand.

"Derrick Mal," he said.

I went ahead and shook the hand. He sat back down, stared at me for a bit then told me to have a seat.

I had a seat.

"I guess you don't know what this is about," he said.

"Not a fucking clue."

He looked at me for a little while.

"Mr. Stubbs, are you . . . have you been drinking?"

I smiled.

He cleared his throat and looked like he was deciding if'n he ought to go on through with whatever he was gonna go on through with.

256

"Well," him deciding to go ahead, "this is a matter of a will. Mrs. Guffins' estate."

Now I recognized him. I'd seen him over at Cecilia's once or twice, definitely the time she'd had her stroke.

"You call that a estate?" I said.

He kind'a rolled his eyeballs.

"You can call it what you like, Mr. Stubbs, because it's yours."

"How's that?"

"Mrs. Guffins' will. She left everything to you."

"Everything?"

"Well, the house and property, mainly. There was some life insurance, but most of that went to her plot and funeral and hospital debt and the cost of clearing the tree and covering the exposed part of the house. That leaves about five to six thousand, I think, after all accounts are settled."

"I don't get it," I said.

"She changed her will the day after she had the stroke, when she was in the hospital. She made you the recipient of her insurance as well. The house was paid off a long while ago and considering the State of Florida has no inheritance tax and the Fed. . . ."

"I still don't get it," I said, trying to stop his rambling.

But I was beginning to get it. It was starting to dawn on my dumb tequila-logged brain that ol' Cecilia Guffins had left me her whole fucking caboodle. What there was of it, anyways.

"I had a hard time tracking you down. If my brother-in-law wasn't on the force. . . . I was going to put your name in the newspaper legals, you know, people who have money and things coming to them but nobody can find. . . ."

"Hold on a goddamn minute. Don't Cecilia have some family? Don't she have a son somewheres? She's got a boy."

Derrick Mal shook his head.

"No. I've been her lawyer since, well since her husband died, but I've known her for a long time, way back. She never had family in the area, neither did her husband."

"I thought they was from Pensacola?"

He got to shake his head again.

"No. They were both from Georgia. Macon, I think. They came to Pensacola together and got married, after the war, World War Two."

He looked at me, but I didn't stop him and so he went on telling me.

"Mrs. Guffins was from a very Baptist family. Very. Jeffrey Guffins didn't believe in much of anything, I'd say. As I understand it, he was a wild seed in Macon. His family was pretty scattered. Her family essentially disowned her for marrying him."

"But the kid. Here in Pensacola. Her family'd want to see a grandkid and all, you'd reckon."

He looked around the little room for a bit then smiled at me.

"I don't know what Cecilia told you, Mr. Stubbs, but they never had a child. . . . It would have been impossible, considering Mr. Guffins' war wound."

Just when I thought I was sobering up, I was getting lost again.

"He was shot through the goddamn arm," I told the man. "Shot while trying to screw someone's little Dutch honey."

He shook his head some more, to where I thought maybe it was a gonna come loose and go skittling along the tile and I'd have to fetch it for him or something.

"No, no. He was shot a little lower, if you know what I mean. Where he wasn't able to procreate. Not to speak bad of the dead, but it's what made him such a son of a bitch, I believe."

I ran that around in my brain for a second or two.

"You mean he had his goddamn balls shot off?"

He got to nod his head this time. It looked a mite safer.

"So, you see, they couldn't have children."

"Well shit," I said. "But I know she told me..."

"They. . . ." he started then kind of stopped. Then he done started again. "They did have a child live with them, for a period. A boy."

"They adopted a kid?"

"No. They were foster parents. Or anyway, Cecilia was the foster parent. Mr. Guffins was more of a nightmare. The boy was twelve but he ran away when he was fourteen. He hadn't even lived there two full years when he ran away. Later he was put in another home and then eventually placed back with his natural mother."

"Ran off, huh?"

And then I felt awful bad for old Cecilia, knowing that she done lied to me because she wanted something she never did have, because she had her a broken heart over this kid. A kid she only looked after but less'n two years.

But the lawyer wasn't finished. He wanted to go on and tell the rest.

"But he turned out all right," he told me, looking down at his notepad while he talked. "Like I said, he was reunited with his mother, and a sister, in Pensacola, and he went on and got an education and did well, even if he did sell Mrs. Guffins a little short. And, like I said, it was Mr. Guffins that made him run. . . . So, in a way, Cecilia had a child, however brief."

He looked up at me then and then looked over at the wall where a window should'a been. And that's when it clicked, that's when I done figured it out.

"And you was that child," I said.

He looked back at me right quick. He took off his glasses and made to clean them on his white shirt.

"Maybe you're not as intoxicated as I thought," he said.

"No sir," I said, "I reckon I am. Sometimes things come to me that way, though. Sometimes they do."

I was gonna take a cab but didn't have enough money. So I waited for the bus to Gulf Breeze, figuring I could walk it to the beach from there. When it came I climbed on in, sitting down with a bunch of strangers, most of them with newspapers or books in front of their faces, the others just staring out the dirty windows as we headed for the Bay bridge. Everyone was quiet as hell. And all I could do was think of poor old Cecilia and also of that lawyer, Derrick Mal.

He told me that after the old man had died, he'd looked out for Cecilia the best he could. He had him a family himself, though, wife and three little kids, so he didn't have a lot of time. Cecilia'd told him about me and he was glad I was around for her, he said. And after that he went and showed me her will and told me about the costs and his fees and showing me all these numbers and shit I didn't give a damn about. Then he called up someone next door who come in and I signed some papers and Derrick Mal signed them and then this guy signed them too, notarizing it all.

And that was that.

We shook hands all around and they both wished me luck and I walked out into the empty downtown sunshine, me the owner of that ripped house and the big lot with its mess of magnolia's and banana plants and family of armadillas. And I had near five grand coming to me to boot.

Goddamned weird.

Things was getting awful damned weird.

I got off the bus right near the bridge. I went into a Seven-'Leven and got me a big lemonade, that I drunk right there in the store, and a tall-boy can of coldbeer for the walk across the bridge to P-cola Beach. I had had me a damn good afternoon-drunk going there, before it come undone, and when I got to the beach I was fixing to start me another.

Walking across the beach bridge, I didn't have to pay no toll. But I was thinking I was paying a toll of some other kind. I mean, there I was with all that sparkling water below me, the yeller sun just melting down, lending everything a brick red and orangy tang. And there I was with the whole white strip of the island just waiting for me, an island full of booze and women. A place I was right fond of. And here I'd just been given money and property in the blink of a eye. Yet, I felt nothing but sorry just the same.

And I wasn't feeling sorry for Cecilia Guffins or her lawyer no more, no, I was plumb plain feeling sorry for myself.

I drank from my can of beer in its little paper sack and tried to think what I was gonna do with that property. Because I didn't want it. It seemed to me that all it was gonna do was complicate things—a guy like me owning something I should never own—and I wanted to get rid of it.

Sure, I wanted to sell it. But who was gonna buy that mangy land with a house that was near ripped in half? And it was sitting right down the block from the main road with all its lousy traffic and junk shops and shit. Who was gonna give me a good price—any price—on something like that?

Maybe I just ought'a get rid of my own house too. I could go off with Fob for a spell, then come on back and move onto the beach. That's what. Then again, maybe I was the one who should go on out to California. Or maybe I ought to go all out, to some oddball spot like Iowa or North Dakota, someplace that ain't near the ocean, where they ain't never heard of no Redneck Riviera. Shit, I could go to Alaska if'n I wanted.

I walked off the bridge and headed on towards One Leg's and Fob's boat, it about dark night now, all the cars buzzing by me with their lights on. And I played with the idea of selling the property away, thinking about how much I'd get.

And as I was coming on close to the bar, walking past my car at the Tom Thumb, feeling mighty sober as I went towards the docks, I thunk of it.

I knew what to do.

I'd sell both properties, get me my seaman's papers outta the attic, or wherever they was, and shove off. Get me a job on one of them boats sailing for Singapore or Sweden or some such place clear across the planet.

Then I'd really be gone. Gone and lost with no Fobs or Tams or Marleens or Crows to think about ever again.

Shit. I could do that. I could.

I felt good enough that I backtracked it to the Tom Thumb, where Fob's pal Jan was working, and she let me buy beer on Fob's credit. A whole cold case of it. I was ready to celebrate now. I'd sell the goddamn house and land to some idgit or another, then me and Fob could take off. Or I could just give it all away, like it was give to me and I could take the five grand and sail off on some tramp boat. . . . I could do either-or. It was settled in my mind. At least for the night.

Now I could get good and goddamned drunk.

One Leg's was back in full swing. I made my way around all the drinkers and lights and noise in the volleyball pit, through the weeds and over to the docks which was empty. I lugged the suitcase of beer and myself onto Fob's boat and sat down there, ripping open the cardboard and drinking one.

It was a hot night, the air thick and snotty. You could hardly see the stars for the thickness of it all. I figured to drink a few and wash up, down below, before I went on out to find Fob. I wanted to let him know I was planning to come on with him when he left. I wanted to tell him about my crazy day. I wanted to spend the rest of the night drinking and smelling around for fun.

Sitting there, looking up at the antics of the bar, it hit me that it was September already, that it was a Friday and Labor Day weekend had begun.

The last weekend of summer. The last big blowout.

And for once, I was ready for it.

I got myself up and took the beer down into his itty-bitty cabin, the door unlocked like he was expecting me, though the door to his room was shut. I loaded what beers I could into his ice box, took off my shirt and was pumping water into the basin to wash with when I heard some strange noises.

The sounds was coming from his room.

I hushed up and cocked my ear. The noises was a mite familiar and I could hear ol' Fob talking in a whisper. It seemed pretty damn early for Fob to have gotten him a catch, but then I hadn't seen him in days and maybe he had him a semi-regular. Or maybe he'd got off to a good start on the day, like I had. Either way, I sat on down and listened for no better reason than I just didn't think not to.

And the more I listened the more I got me the idea that something was wrong. I mean, I could hear Fob saying this and that and talking his soft trash, but the woman was just kind'a moaning and rolling and saying—best I could tell—"no" and "don't care" and "no" some more and some mumbly nonsense. And she had a real young voice at that.

263

I was getting the impression that ol' Fob was up to something he oughtn't be.

I got my ear a little closer to his door. I even tried to open it a notch, but it was latched.

That didn't seem normal. Fob was a boy who liked to leave the door open when he did the tango. He was a show-off, kind'a kinky. But here he had this girl locked up.

I was curious enough to want a look-see.

I went topside into the ugly-hot night. I tried to be quiet and not rock the boat, but between Fob being busy and One Leg's blasting its music, I wasn't too worried about being found out. I kept my feet on the dock and hung on to the gunwale and tried to peer into his little port holes. He had his blue curtains closed, on the both of them. I stood back up. I knew I should just be off, on up to the bar and maybe sponge off'a whoever, but my curiosity was set on getting the best of me.

I clambered up on top of the cabin, where his bare mast was. The skylight was up there, just a plastic bubble tinted dark green. I got up there and sprawled out like a fool flounder. The hatch was open a crack and I got my fat fingers in there and creaked it up a bit, finally taking a good look on in.

It took me a while to see what I saw down there. But I saw his bed and him on it, naked as the day he was slapped, and there was a pair of pretty brown legs coming out from under him. He was still talking that easy talk but the girl was lying on her stomach—not that that'd ever stop Fob—but it looked she still had her some clothes on. And sure enough, when he rolled off to the side, she was there with a tank-top on and some little striped panties. A nice looking girl from what I could see of her.

But she didn't look too active. From my perch, she looked about passed out. Then Fob rolled her on over. He spun her over like she was a rag doll and commenced to remove her shirt. He was going to take off her pretty panties but she woke for that, pushing him off a bit, saying something. That's when I looked at her face. And it was a face I recognized.

Tam's face. Her legs. Her body.

I bolted upright, smacking the back of my skull against the masthead. Then I looked down again and saw him running his hands all over her warm skin.

It took but a second for my blood to boil. My skin heated up like a damn griddle.

I stuck my head back in there, far as I could, and I yelled.

"Damn you! You fucking cocksucking maggot you sonofabitch!"

Fob stiffened up and took a fast gander at the cabin door. He saw it was still bolted tight.

"Get your goddamn hands off her, you motherfucking dick. I'm gonna rip your goddamn insides out, Fob Langtree, you cunt-faced lizard!"

Then he looked up, seeing my burning face right there in the hatch above him. Tam hadn't even noticed a thing. But Fob sure did. He gave me a look with a giant smile, but it was a plastic smile, one pure with fear and surprise.

"Chester!" he finally coughed out.

"Fuck you Fob! I'm gonna beat your worthless brains out and tie your dick to the mast pole, you sonofabitch!"

He scrambled off the bed and outta my sight, but then I saw him pushing a big metal chest up against the door, blocking it tight. He even put a chair up there.

But that wasn't gonna stop me. Not with him in there with that girl.

I got a good hold on the skylight and yanked her up. The rusty metal arms of the hatch creaked and the plastic bubble splintered and then it all gave way. I broke the whole fucking thing off with a big thunder crack and held it there, aloft in

265

my hands, before tossing it down to clatter on the dock. Fob's face was hanging open like silly putty, his mouth but a bat cave, as I wedged myself in headfirst to come shooting on down into the cabin room.

Now he was locked inside with me.

Tam was trying to sit up a bit now, wondering what the fuck, still naked except for panties. I got myself upright, my head bent against the wood ceiling, my body all pumped up, feeling ten-times too big for the room. Fob stood across from me, his skin white and face sunburnt, him jittering like a itchy rodent, like a blind cricket ready to be stomped on.

And I went at him. He jumped but I caught a piece of him and he slammed against a bolted bookcase but didn't fall. Then he circled away from me, crawling across the bed where Tam was lying all dazed and confused and I reached over and grabbed Fob by the forearm and yanked him back at me. He rammed right into me and bounced off, me falling backwards to where I sat down on the floor. But I got back up and so did Fob.

"Chester. Goddamnit, Chester. You kill me and, and. . . . Don't you kill me, Chester Stubbs!"

He got back on the bed and jumped up, getting hold of where the skylight used to be, trying to skinny on out of the hole there. But I grabbed his legs. I got hold of his bony little insect legs and yanked him on down. I grabbed him and brought him to me and just plain squeezed the syrup out of him, him going like a goddamned jellyfish in my arms so that I let him fall to the floor. Where he then commenced to crawl. He crawled on over to the door and was trying to move the chest and chair and unlatch the damn thing, but I took the one step yonder, grabbed him, turned him over and got my knee right in his chest. Had him pinned like a fucking voodoo doll.

266

I had him exactly where he'd never ever want to be, had him down and stuck, a roach under my heel. But I was fixing to punch this roach square in the nose, louse up his whole fucking body. And he knew it. He couldn't but squirm and squeeze his eyes and slobber with painful expectation. And that's when I stopped.

I couldn't do it.

I had him by his slick black hair and had my big wrecking ball of a fist cocked right behind me, but I just couldn't. I couldn't snuff him out. I thought I wanted to, wanted to plow my knuckles into the shine of his face, but then I just couldn't, I couldn't want to.

Didn't want to.

So I stopped.

I let his hair go, his head clonking, and I got off him. My chest and arms and face just heaving and heaving, tide in and out, and he lie there with his face scrunched up and his eyes closed for a good long while.

I stood and hated him and heard Tam rustling about behind me, but I couldn't cripple the man. I couldn't bust him, though he sure as hell deserved it. I didn't want to bust folks no more. I didn't want to beat people up, no matter. No fucking matter.

And so I told him to leave.

I pushed him aside, moved the heavy chest for him, threw the chair, unlocked the door and opened it and told him to get out.

He sat up and rubbed himself.

"You can't kick me off my own boat," he told me.

"The hell I can't," I said.

"It's my fucking boat. You get out! You get the fuck out, Chester! I didn't do nothing. . . ."

"The hell I can't!"

Then I went and grabbed him, grabbed his naked ass and drug him out the door and up the little steps and out on deck and then I dumped him over the side.

He yelled and cussed the whole time, squawking till he hit the water, his mouth open wide enough to swallow the sea.

I didn't care if he could swim or not, but I watched as he sponged around and made it to the dock, climbed out dripping and screaming but heading for the steps just the same. I waved my arms in the air and he picked it up, him jogging down the planks and up the steps, his bare ass blubbering, on his way to tell Jimmy or call the police or whatever the fuck, I didn't care.

I watched him be gone, then went back to get Tam.

She looked to be asleep until she rolled around a bit and made some sounds. I managed to get her shirt back on and some baggy shorts I reckoned were hers. I tried to pick her up, but it was like trying to get a egg yolk into a spoon. Every time I had a hold of her she'd wake up enough to slip on back down into the silk sheets.

Maybe she thought it was still Fob that was wrestling with her. I figured it'd be best to wake her up some.

I went back to the galley and rummaged around, looking for coffee or smelling salts or even some cocaine, which I wouldn't put past Fob having on hand. But I already knew Fob wasn't a coffee drinker and all I found was one cocola and that jar of instant tea he'd bought that time.

So I mixed up some tea. I mixed it strong and ugly and took it on in to her.

But I couldn't get her to drink it. She did her slippery eel act every time I got her up, putting the glass to her lips.

So I threw it on her.

I took the whole works and splashed it right on that drunk face of hers. That got a reaction. She didn't exactly jump up and start yelling, but she opened her eyes and her hands went about to mopping her face. And while she was wiping herself with the sheets, I went back and mixed up another glass of tea.

When I came back in she was sitting up, looking woozy. I sat down next to her, put a arm around her, and got her to drink some of that tea.

"C'mon, Tam," I said. "You gotta do it. Drink it down and get up. We gotta get you on home. C'mon."

It worked some. She drank about half of it, come alive a bit, finally taking in just who I was and maybe even why I was with her.

But then she bust on out of my grip and staggered around the little room. She put her hand to her mouth and her eyes got wide. I looked at her, then reached over and opened up one of Fob's dresser drawers.

She threw-up right there, in on his clean shirts and socks and shit. She chucked it up good.

"Now can we get on out of here?" I asked.

She put her hand back to her mouth, looked at me near clean-eyed, and nodded her head.

I carried her to my car, the whole while thinking we'd be ambushed by Fob or an old boyfriend of hers or maybe even a new one. But we made it just fine.

I put her in the front seat and got in to drive. Her head was still lollygagging around and she wound up leaning against me as I backed up and pulled out to the road.

I got me a cigarette lit, smoking and hanging it out the window, driving with my right arm all stiff because she was leaning on my shoulder. We made it off the island. And then I heard her talking. She was talking right low and defeated-like but she knew where she was and, I hoped, why, and probably where we was headed.

"You wouldn't let me go," she said. "You told him, you're just like him, that's what you want, to run me. . . . I'd of been gone, I'd be out of this hole. . . ."

"You hush up," I said.

I wasn't gonna bother to say who told what to who, or that it was never me, or that–far as I was concerned–if she wanted to get the hell out of north Florida then she ought'a just go, money or not. All I wanted was for her to quit feeling sorry for herself and get on with it all, for her to get some understanding as to how goddamn young she was and how stupid she could be and how far she had to go to get halfway smart.

She rolled away from me and leaned against the other door. She fell quiet and I drove on a bit, and maybe she was asleep or maybe she wasn't, but I was gonna try and tell her a thing or two.

"Hush, girl and listen. Because you did an awful goddamn dumb thing tonight. And you was lucky I was there to save you from something worse, from something that'd probably stick with you for a long time. You listen to me because I'm gonna take you home to your Daddy and you treat him right. You tell that man you are a sorry daughter because he's the one that raised you, he fed you and housed you and taught you and he's the one that worries over you and he's the one you're putting to so much grief. And you're gonna need him, you'll need your Daddy for a long time a coming, so you listen to me. . . ."

I waited but she didn't say a thing as we clicked along the highway. I kept talking anyways. And now I didn't know how much of what I was saying was meant for Tam's education or how much it was for my own.

"You ain't got no problems, except yourself. That's what's going on here, you're your own enemy. And you are gonna have to change that if you ever want out of this hole or any hole. You got a long road and I don't care if you go back to work or go to California or go all the way to fucking Alaska, but you gotta let them that cares about you help. Understand? You got to listen to what folks is trying to say to you and learn. It's too tough to make it on your own, to be so stubborn you won't help yourself just to spite them that want's to help, just to spite life because it's bad now and then, always fighting what's good for you and giving in to what's wrong. . . . You're burning from the wrong end of the stick, Tam, the wrong goddamn end. Just like me."

She was still asleep, best I could tell, and though I wanted to say more, I was losing the train. I was hearing myself and couldn't figure if it made any sense or if I believed it myself, even right after I'd done said it. But then I knew I'd meant it and that it was true.

It was true about her. It was true about me.

Then I kept quiet and smoked and drove us on to Duck and Wayne's, to Tam's home.

I pulled on into her drive and shut the car off. She sat up then, not looking at me but straight out the windshield, at the dark house. I got out and went round to get her. I opened the door and she near fell out, right into my arms. It was then I noticed she didn't have no shoes. I hadn't thought of looking for any shoes on the boat. She'd been barefoot all this time. Don't know why that bothered me so.

I held her up for a while and she began to cough and her nose was running and she made her some sounds. I didn't know if she was gonna get sick again, but I held her. Then the porch light popped on.

Both Wayne and Duck come tripping down the steps in their pajamas. I looked up and could see Duck's wife in her robe, looking down on us. Maybe the boy was up there too. But the two brothers come on over with big expressions and Tam right off peeled away from me and went into her Daddy's arms and she began to cry.

She cried some and put her head in his neck and he picked her up and took her back, carrying her like a school-kid, on up the steps and through the screendoor and gone.

Duck and I watched them go. Then he turned to me.

"She's a mite drunk is all," I said. "She got sick."

He kept on looking at me.

"Maybe she had a scare, too," I said.

"A scare?"

"Sometimes I scare folks," I said. "Sometimes I scare myself."

He looked me over some more then looked in the car then looked back up at the house where we couldn't see nothing happening at all.

"Wayne still pissed at me?" I asked.

"Pissed?" he said.

"You know, for telling him to give her the money and let her go, you know."

"Oh," he said and took his time. "He was, was angry. But I think he angry at himself, you know."

"That so?"

"He think maybe you are right, Chester Stubbs. I believe Wayne will give her the money. She's a woman. She has to make her own way."

He nodded his head for a bit and looked at the ground. I was looking at the goddamn ground myself.

Duck put his hand on my arm.

"You come on up for a drink? Come on up and relax?"

"No," I said. "It's late. I reckon yall'd like to get back in bed. I know I want to. . . . I need to get home and get me some sleep."

Duck bowed and smiled at me.

I got in my car and pulled away from the house.

I drove back to the highway and headed for Pensacola.

But I was way too wired to sleep.

It'd been such a madhouse day–the maddest damn day in my life–that I reckoned I'd might as well make it madder. Because, just then, I'd done changed my mind about what to do with Cecilia Guffins property: I'd give it away. It was give to me and so I reckon I could just pass it on along to someone else.

And not only did I know who to give it to, I knew I had to do it now, no matter what time of the night it was. Otherwise I'd never get it done.

So, I headed back to Pensacola proper.

I was gonna see Crow.

CHAPTER THIRTY-THREE

This time I wasn't about to let any second thoughts stop me. I wanted to give that house and land to Crow. I wasn't sure how to wangle it–official-like–but I figured Derrick Mal would.

But that was all for later. Right now I knew I was gonna have my hands full just waking up Crow. . . . And talking him into taking old Cecilia Guffins' place.

I pulled out of traffic and down a street and then down Crow's street, where it was as quiet as it were dark. In Gulf Breeze I'd passed the Sun Trust Bank sign where it'd read 77 degrees hot and 12:36 late. But I still didn't care none. I was gonna get this over with.

I pulled into Crow's drive, parking behind some new car that he'd been working on. His house looked different to me, for a minute or so anyways. It'd been a awful long while since I'd been around.

I got out and walked right up to the front door. Some dog went to barking a ways down the block, probably smelling me if nothing else. I knocked. Waited. I knocked again. Louder.

I was standing there with a new cigarette in my mouth when I saw his face come from behind the door curtains. It didn't look none too happy.

He didn't turn on the porch light, but he did open the door about head-wide.

"What the hell you doing here? You're going to wake the baby."

"Come on out on the stoop," I said.

He looked to be ready to shut the door.

"C'mon out, Crow."

He didn't budge, but he didn't close the door either.

"Crow," I said. "I'm sorry."

He looked me over for a bit.

"You drunk?" he asked, talking in a whisper.

I was talking that way too.

"No, I ain't."

He come on out, standing in his barefeet, in his shorts and tee-shirt.

"What you want, Chester."

"Crow," I said, "I'm sorry."

"Tell me tomorrow," he said and made to go back inside.

"No, I. . . ."

"Shhh," he said. "Dilsey just started sleeping through the night, now. I'm bone tired. This is my first night of sleep in three months."

I smiled.

"And then I come around," I said.

He looked me in the eye. Almost smiled. It weren't a grin or nothing, and it weren't really a smile, but I took it as such.

"And then you come around," he said.

CHAPTER THIRTY-FOUR

Crow didn't take to it at all. That first night I done told him,
I don't think he even believed me. It took me about two and
a half weeks to convince him, me calling on him about every
other evening, me talking to Della too, and it being Della
who finally got him to come around and believe in it. Of
course, he wouldn't take the land from me. No sir. I tried and
tried but he said he had to pay for it. Only he didn't have the
fair price, what with his new baby and all, and him just making
supervisor pay for less'n a year by then. So he talked about
me being co-owner, but we both figured that wouldn't be the
smartest idea. But then we come up with the idea.

He'd rent it but I'd own the land.

Because he was gonna build himself a garage. His own
business.

So we had Derrick Mal draw up a contract where Crow
paid me month by month, no nothing fancy or expensive,
just something between the both of us. It weren't much of a
payment, but when you added it all up in the long run, it was
pret'near worth it. Then he got himself a Fed loan and a bank
loan and we got down to work.

And I mean we, because, though I owned the land, I was
gonna work for him. Help him build it. Help him fix the cars,
even if I only handed him wrenches and screwdrivers to start.
Learn something new.

And that weren't the only thing new, either. Because I went
and joined A.A. It was something I finally figured to be right.
Finally fingered it out. Was something I had to do. I mean,
after all that craziness and me starting a new career now, I

knew I had to quit drinking. And I knew I needed help. So when I got my telephone service back, I called and got invited to a regular meeting at a little building next to the Seamans Club in downtown Pensacola.

I went. I stood up. I said I was a alcoholic.

And the next night I went, who was there but Iris. She didn't look but half-surprised.

"I'm glad you came, Chester," she said.

"I reckon it's about time."

She gave me her number, told me to call if ever I was contemplating having me a whiskey or beer. If ever I was getting low and tingly from giving it up.

And I did get that way, but I called our group leader instead. I had the nerve to quit drinking, but not the nerve to call Iris. Like a schoolboy, I had a hankering for her but was too shy to even call her on the phone.

So I was drying up and getting down to work.

Crow had a guy draw up the blueprints and another guy come on in and clear out the land, taking a few trees that was in the way—but not that old pecan, I'd had it chopped myself, into fire wood—flattening the soil out where the garage was going in. He kept the house to use as a office, walling it off at the back. And he kept as much of them back-lot magnolias and bananas and palmettas as he could. The armadillas had done moved into the corner of my own yard—I saw them digging a burrow under that stack of pecan wood I'd put by my weedy fence. After that a guy come in and dug and poured the footings and the grease pits for the car bays. But from there, except for the electrical and the plumbing, we done the job pretty much by ourselves.

It was him and me mostly, working nights after he got off at the warehouse. On weekends we had some teenage kids help out, friends of Crow's, except for Duck's boy, Lon. He helped too. And all of us was there the day we poured the concrete slab. That was hard work, but we got it done, even with them oil pits in the way, Crow and I sweating like stuck pigs bull-floating and finishing the slab. And we got the studs up and then the siding, insulation and windows and we got the roof on, a shiny tin one, getting everything inspected and done official as we went. It got to looking like a right smart business for ol' Crow and his family. Fit right in with the way the neighborhood was heading and was a sight cleaner than my old house.

He already had him a sign made up: DUPREE'S GARAGE. I was damned pleased for him.

And one of the first things we put inside that building was that old wood stove, the one he'd had in his home garage. We got it on in and connected the chimney, sawing a hole in the new tin because he'd done forgot about it.

And it was a good thing he got it in, too. Because it was about the coldest November we'd had in a long spell.

That was when we were pret'near finished, at least with all the construction. He still had a boatload of tools and benches and other contraptions to get in there. He wasn't gonna quit his job till springtime, so he wouldn't open up till then. But it was all slapped up together by the end of November. And that's when Marleen decided to fly on in for her visit.

Because Crow was gonna throw a party.

It weren't the grand opening or nothing–like I said, that was gonna be in the spring–but he had a lot of stuff on order and he reckoned we could use a breather about then, maybe even till the first of the year. Anyways, he planned for the party outdoors, where it was expecting to be clear and near cold but awful damn nice just the same.

Marleen flew in on a Friday morning. The get-together was Saturday. She was gonna fly back to Connettycut early the morning after.

Crow and Della told me all that, but come Friday, I wasn't about to even talk to her.

I'd seen her, though. I saw her through my bedroom window in the evening, standing there with Della and the little baby, saw her out there talking and swatting at the last flies of the year, saw her there in her long pants and a jacket and I just couldn't bring myself to go on out and say hello. I just couldn't. I stood by the window, hiding and peeking, backing away every time she took a gander my way, my gut all squirreled up just by the sight of her.

I guess I'd wait for the party.

And then the thought of that only made my innards wind up tighter. Because I knew there'd be beer-drinking tomorrow. Maybe even a little whiskey. Being in A.A. all Fall, I figured I could handle it, but now I weren't sure.

Marleen and alcohol might be too much. Brought some old nightmares back into my brain.

So I made a phone call, this time to Iris.

"Chester. Hi. . . . What's up?"

"I hope it's all right, that I called and all." I was a shy kitten. "But you said. . . ."

"It's okay. You're not drinking, are you?"

"No. I ain't. But I'm going to a party tomorrow."

"Don't go," Iris said.

"Naw. I want to go, it's. . . ."

And just then I knew it weren't the party that got me to call, it was the seeing of Marleen again. That old sadness. And I didn't want any A.A. shop talk with Iris. I wanted to get beyond that with her.

She was quiet on the line, patient as photograph.

"I guess," I said, "I reckon I wanted to ask you out. Maybe."

She was still silent, but it was a different kind of silence. I could tell.

"You want to go on a date?" she said.

"Yeah, you know, I don't know. . . . Dinner somewheres, candles, violins, a bottle of mineral water."

She laughed.

"If I ever see you drinking mineral water, I'll slap you."

"Don't worry, I'd slap myself."

And then she said yes.

We set it up for next Saturday. Dinner. Not on the beach. Nothing fancy.

My gut had a new twist when I hung up the phone. A good feeling kind'a twist.

The next day I was still worried about seeing Marleen.

But she didn't come to the party right away.

It started about ten in the morning and had all kinds of food and a keg of beer that I ignored, though I could smell it. And we done set up a badminton net in my yard. A goddamn badminton game in my own yard? Shit, that's how I knew things'd done changed for sure. . . . There was a whole lot of Crow's pals, some I knew from the warehouse, and there was some of Della's family, kids and sisters and older folks, just a whole group of them like that. Wayne was there, and Duck with his wife, May, and Lon with a few of his friends who'd pitched in a couple weekends. Tam weren't there though. She was in San Diego.

Wayne had gone and given her the money.

I wandered around the people, drinking a cocola, eating some, trying to relax but feeling itchy just the same.

Finally I found me a safe spot on the sidewalk, away from the crowd, standing next to Wayne.

"So, how's Tam doing?" I asked, just because we had to talk about something or another. "She getting along with her professional volleyball player?"

"Not so good," he said.

We left it at that for a while, the both of us lighting up a smoke. Wayne'd told me he'd let Tam know that I wasn't the one who'd snitched on her. But neither of us knew if'n she believed it. Anyways, I never heard from her again.

"She's doing okay," he suddenly said. "She like California."

Then he went on and told me that she and the kid was already split and Tam was living alone, but that she liked living alone. He said she was working two jobs, at a video store and some beach shop there.

"But she think maybe she go to school. Next year," he said.

"Damn college?"

"Yes! Damn college!"

We kind'a traded glances for a minute.

"The only thing," Wayne said, "she want more money!"

And he got a laugh out of it.

So there it was, sometime past noon, me drinking my cola in the chilly air, still giggling with Wayne, when I felt a hand on my shoulder.

I turned around, my mouth full of nothing, and there Marleen was, smiling in the clear cold sunshine.

"Hey, Chester," she said.

I nodded and swallowed, though I was dry. And I couldn't get my mouth to say a damn thing.

"I heard you've been doing well," she said.

I nodded again, took a look around at everything and then looked back at her.

"It took me a long while to believe what Della told me, about you getting this place and then renting it to them. About you working. That's something. Really something."

I swallowed dry again, took a gulp of the cola, didn't know if she knew I was in A.A.

"Just something that worked out," I finally said.

She grinned.

"How long you been in town?" I asked, though I already did know.

"About two days, but I'm leaving tomorrow. I was visiting at the hospital and been staying out that way. . . ."

"You ain't staying at Crow's house?"

"No, Chester. They've got a baby. Family in town, too."

"Oh yeah," I said, feeling right dumb.

"Della did show me the shop last night. Sorry I didn't say hello to you."

"That's all right," I said. "I reckon I could'a looked for you."

We tried to talk some more but it didn't have no flow to it. Plus, there was all them other folks wandering around and coming up and saying howdy and all. I mean, I wanted to talk to her. If nothing else, I sure as hell wanted us to talk.

"You want to go for a drive?" I asked, after a spell.

"A drive?"

"A drive to the beach? The National Seashore?"

She gave me a close look, like she was suspicious.

"You said you missed the beach, in your letter. . . . But maybe you already been."

She cocked her head, looking away at the blue sky, and then she looked back at me.

"I do miss the beach," she said.

When we came to the Pensacola Beach bridge, I didn't turn. I went straight on ahead.

We hadn't said much yet and Marleen looked over at me, wondering.

"We'll take the Navarre Bridge, it's quicker," I said. "A sight prettier too."

I didn't want to tell her the truth, which was I just plain couldn't much stand to see Pensacola Beach. Not yet, anyways. I hadn't been back since the night I throwed Fob Langtree off of his boat and into the drink. I just wasn't ready, not even to drive through it.

We got out to Navarre, took the cheap toll bridge and then stopped at the Tom Thumb on the corner with the beach road. I got some gas for my car, bought a pack of cigarettes that I shoved in my pocket and got us each a cup of weak coffee that we drunk while I drove on into the white dunes of the National Seashore.

I parked in one of them asphalt lots, where there weren't another car in sight. It was awful damn quiet. There was a couple of kids with bikes goofing around on the back dunes, by the sound. Marleen and I walked up the boardwalk, over the front dunes, seeing the Gulf there. Then we kicked off our shoes, leaving them on the wood, walking barefoot even though the sand was a mite cold.

And the water was cold too. The waves was choppy and there was a steady breeze coming off the Gulf. We walked the packed sand, trying to keep our toes dry, shoving our hands in our pockets. We turned our faces from the stiff wind. The sky was damn blue, clear as shallow water.

We could see some people walking, wearing red coats, about a mile up the beach from us. Other than that, it was just Marleen and me out there.

We walked quiet for a while.

"You doing okay, up there, in New England?" I went and asked.

"Okay," she said. "I don't regret it, anyway."

We kept going, a big wind coming on us now and then.

"This is how cold the beaches feel," she said, "up there. Early summer at least. Spring, I should say."

"In Connettycut?"

She smiled when I said it.

"The sand still looks dirty to me up there, compared to here. And there's always people. Always more people."

"There ain't no place like this place," I said.

She nodded.

I shrugged. We was just talking. Spinning wheels. I wasn't even sure what I wanted to say to her.

"So. . . ." she said. "That was a shame what happened to Mrs. Guffins. Her husband, too. But you made the best of it. Della told me you helped that woman out some, Della and Crow told me and. . . ."

"Yeah, things came around okay," I said, stopping her.

"Anyway, Chester. I just want you to know that I'm proud of you. For what it's worth, I'm glad you did what you've done."

"Crow's gonna teach me how to work on cars, too."

"No?" she said, but she already knew.

"Yeah. I was thinking it'd be a shame living next door to a car shop and know nothing about it."

"You'll get the hang of it in no time."

I smiled.

"You seeing anybody, Chester?" she asked.

"Me? No."

"Nobody?"

I put my hand in my pocket, felt the pack of cigarettes there but didn't take them out.

"Well, I worked with this gal at One Leg's. I was thinking. . . . Hell. I got a date with her next week."

She made a little humming sound you could barely hear above the waves.

I changed the subject, remembering something.

"Hey, Marleen, I still got your boxes! You can't take them on the plane, but I'll mail them to you!"

She gave me a look, like I was joking, but I was serious. I'd mail them for sure.

The both of us laughed and then she turned around to walk back. I turned with her. The wind was better, heading back.

We fell to just walking again, the sea gulls coasting around and the sandpipers just clipping, staying about five feet ahead of us all the while. The waves was coming in regular and our feet'd got used to the cold sand. The beach was looking damn pretty again, the ocean a winter-blue with the sun spanking on it, looking like a big jewelry box.

And then Marleen stopped. She stopped in front of me and took both of my hands in hers. She stood there under me and looked up.

"Are you going to be okay, Chester Stubbs?"

I looked back at her best I could. I didn't answer, though.

"You still drinking so much?" she asked.

"Naw. I quit."

I still had me some dreams, about having a bottle of whiskey under the sink, but they was just dreams.

"That's good," she said, believing me, and dropped my hands.

We commenced to walking again.

"Seems like I was running on whiskey for a long while there," I told her.

"And what are you running on now?"

"I don't know. . . . I reckon I'm just plain running."

And then we went back over the dunes, getting our shoes, and back to the car. We wiped the sand from our feet before putting our shoes back on, seeing those kids on the bayside, now the both of them flying green kites way up yonder.

It was near four o'clock when we got back into the city. I dropped Marleen off at her motel, up by the airport. She said she'd call Crow to say goodbye. Then she hugged me and even gave me a little kiss. We said goodbye. I didn't expect no more.

I went on back to Crow's shop.

The sun was getting low and the party had pretty much died on out when I got back. Most of Della's kin was still around, though. I sat in the car, seeing a old lady chasing some teenagers away from the keg, them trying to milk it for half a glass of beer. I laughed.

"Keep on 'em, grandma."

I stayed in the car and thought about Marleen, then looked at my house and at the garage and ol' Mrs. Guffins' place, and it took my mind way back. I got to thinking that making a fool outta myself in Montgomery and me being around folks as nice as Crow and Duck and Wayne, that all of that was awful good for me in the long run. Fob, Tam. . . . Iris, too. All of that sure taught me some lessons I'd never of learned on my own. And Cecilia. What would'a happened if that old lady hadn't cared about me when I wasn't worth caring about?

I didn't want to think too much, so I got out and stood there and was gonna light a cigarette when Della come over with her child.

"Here, Chester," she said. "Hold Dilsey for a little while, I got to help my sister load up some of this food."

"Me?"

"Yes, you," she said and lifted the tiny thing right up to me.

"I can't hold a baby," I said.

"Go on," she said. "You can hold her. She won't break."

I looked at Della again and she put the baby right there in my arms.

"I'll be right back. Just kind'a support her head if she gets sleepy."

I didn't say nothing. I just held her tight with both big arms, her almost disappearing in my red skin and freckles. Just a little-bitty kid, she was. I felt like I was holding glass.

The kid got to kicking and fussing a little. I figured maybe she wanted to get down and try and walk or something. Hell, I didn't know when kid's was supposed to walk. So I got down low and took her hands and she got her feet down to the driveway. I held her and she bounced around a bit, kind'a happy maybe. Then I saw Crow inside the shop. He had one of the big overhead doors open and he was loading wood into that stove of his. Pecan wood.

I crouched down and put his baby girl on my knee, snug in the crook of my arm.

"There's your Daddy," I said, pointing at Crow as he was lighting the wood with some fluid. "There he is yonder."

That baby got relaxd in my arms, staring off towards the garage.

And I did the same.

Evening was coming in as I watched the first of the smoke curl up out of the stack, thick pecan smoke just floating and rising up and up, mixing with the low light.

So I sat there, holding that baby, thinking back again about Marleen and all, thinking back about too many things so that all I wanted to do was watch that smoke, just hold the baby and watch it come up outta the shed. A simple thing like smoke rising.

I watched it go. White trails rising up into the tangle of branches and waxy leaves. That old pecan smoke going up above us all, spreading out up there like some damn thing or another.

Smoke rising maybe like a feeling of hope, hope for about all of us under Pensacola skies.

Even me.